ZAGREB NOIR

EDITED BY IVAN SRŠEN

This collection is comprised of works of fiction. All names, characters, places, and incidents are the product of the authors' imaginations. Any resemblance to real events or persons, living or dead, is entirely coincidental.

Published by Akashic Books

Series concept by Tim McLoughlin and Johnny Temple
Zagreb map by Aaron Petrovich

The publication of this book is supported by a grant from the Ministry of Culture of the Republic of Croatia.

ISBN: 978-1-61775-308-4
Library of Congress Control Number: 2015934070

First printing

Akashic Books
Twitter: @AkashicBooks
Facebook: AkashicBooks
E-mail: info@akashicbooks.com
Website: www.akashicbooks.com

ALSO IN THE AKASHIC NOIR SERIES

BALTIMORE NOIR, edited by LAURA LIPPMAN
BARCELONA NOIR (SPAIN), edited by ADRIANA V. LÓPEZ & CARMEN OSPINA
BEIRUT NOIR (LEBANON), edited by IMAN HUMAYDAN
BELFAST NOIR (NORTHERN IRELAND), edited by ADRIAN McKINTY & STUART NEVILLE
BOSTON NOIR, edited by DENNIS LEHANE
BOSTON NOIR 2: THE CLASSICS, edited by DENNIS LEHANE, JAIME CLARKE & MARY COTTON
BRONX NOIR, edited by S.J. ROZAN
BROOKLYN NOIR, edited by TIM McLOUGHLIN
BROOKLYN NOIR 2: THE CLASSICS, edited by TIM McLOUGHLIN
BROOKLYN NOIR 3: NOTHING BUT THE TRUTH, edited by TIM McLOUGHLIN & THOMAS ADCOCK
BUFFALO NOIR, edited by ED PARK & BRIGID HUGHES
CAPE COD NOIR, edited by DAVID L. ULIN
CHICAGO NOIR, edited by NEAL POLLACK
CHICAGO NOIR: THE CLASSICS, edited by JOE MENO
COPENHAGEN NOIR (DENMARK), edited by BO TAO MICHAËLIS
DALLAS NOIR, edited by DAVID HALE SMITH
D.C. NOIR, edited by GEORGE PELECANOS
D.C. NOIR 2: THE CLASSICS, edited by GEORGE PELECANOS
DELHI NOIR (INDIA), edited by HIRSH SAWHNEY
DETROIT NOIR, edited by E.J. OLSEN & JOHN C. HOCKING
DUBLIN NOIR (IRELAND), edited by KEN BRUEN
HAITI NOIR, edited by EDWIDGE DANTICAT
HAITI NOIR 2: THE CLASSICS, edited by EDWIDGE DANTICAT
HAVANA NOIR (CUBA), edited by ACHY OBEJAS
HELSINKI NOIR (FINLAND), edited by JAMES THOMPSON
INDIAN COUNTRY NOIR, edited by SARAH CORTEZ & LIZ MARTÍNEZ
ISTANBUL NOIR (TURKEY), edited by MUSTAFA ZIYALAN & AMY SPANGLER
KANSAS CITY NOIR, edited by STEVE PAUL
KINGSTON NOIR (JAMAICA), edited by COLIN CHANNER
LAS VEGAS NOIR, edited by JARRET KEENE & TODD JAMES PIERCE
LONDON NOIR (ENGLAND), edited by CATHI UNSWORTH
LONE STAR NOIR, edited by BOBBY BYRD & JOHNNY BYRD
LONG ISLAND NOIR, edited by KAYLIE JONES
LOS ANGELES NOIR, edited by DENISE HAMILTON
LOS ANGELES NOIR 2: THE CLASSICS, edited by DENISE HAMILTON
MANHATTAN NOIR, edited by LAWRENCE BLOCK
MANHATTAN NOIR 2: THE CLASSICS, edited by LAWRENCE BLOCK
MANILA NOIR (PHILIPPINES), edited by JESSICA HAGEDORN
MARSEILLE NOIR (FRANCE), edited by CÉDRIC FABRE
MEMPHIS NOIR, edited by LAUREEN CANTWELL & LEONARD GILL
MEXICO CITY NOIR (MEXICO), edited by PACO I. TAIBO II
MIAMI NOIR, edited by LES STANDIFORD
MOSCOW NOIR (RUSSIA), edited by NATALIA SMIRNOVA & JULIA GOUMEN
MUMBAI NOIR (INDIA), edited by ALTAF TYREWALA
NEW JERSEY NOIR, edited by JOYCE CAROL OATES
NEW ORLEANS NOIR, edited by JULIE SMITH

ORANGE COUNTY NOIR, edited by GARY PHILLIPS
PARIS NOIR (FRANCE), edited by AURÉLIEN MASSON
PHILADELPHIA NOIR, edited by CARLIN ROMANO
PHOENIX NOIR, edited by PATRICK MILLIKIN
PITTSBURGH NOIR, edited by KATHLEEN GEORGE
PORTLAND NOIR, edited by KEVIN SAMPSELL
PRISON NOIR, edited by JOYCE CAROL OATES
PROVIDENCE NOIR, edited by ANN HOOD
QUEENS NOIR, edited by ROBERT KNIGHTLY
RICHMOND NOIR, edited by ANDREW BLOSSOM, BRIAN CASTLEBERRY & TOM DE HAVEN
ROME NOIR (ITALY), edited by CHIARA STANGALINO & MAXIM JAKUBOWSKI
SAN DIEGO NOIR, edited by MARYELIZABETH HART
SAN FRANCISCO NOIR, edited by PETER MARAVELIS
SAN FRANCISCO NOIR 2: THE CLASSICS, edited by PETER MARAVELIS
SEATTLE NOIR, edited by CURT COLBERT
SINGAPORE NOIR, edited by CHERYL LU-LIEN TAN
STATEN ISLAND NOIR, edited by PATRICIA SMITH
STOCKHOLM NOIR (SWEDEN), edited by NATHAN LARSON & CARL-MICHAEL EDENBORG
ST. PETERSBURG NOIR (RUSSIA), edited by NATALIA SMIRNOVA & JULIA GOUMEN
TEHRAN NOIR (IRAN), edited by SALAR ABDOH
TEL AVIV NOIR (ISRAEL), edited by ETGAR KERET & ASSAF GAVRON
TORONTO NOIR (CANADA), edited by JANINE ARMIN & NATHANIEL G. MOORE
TRINIDAD NOIR (TRINIDAD & TOBAGO), edited by LISA ALLEN-AGOSTINI & JEANNE MASON
TWIN CITIES NOIR, edited by JULIE SCHAPER & STEVEN HORWITZ
USA NOIR, edited by JOHNNY TEMPLE
VENICE NOIR (ITALY), edited by MAXIM JAKUBOWSKI
WALL STREET NOIR, edited by PETER SPIEGELMAN

FORTHCOMING

ACCRA NOIR (GHANA), edited by MERI NANA-AMA DANQUAH
ADDIS ABABA NOIR (ETHIOPIA), edited by MAAZA MENGISTE
ATLANTA NOIR, edited by TAYARI JONES
BAGHDAD NOIR (IRAQ), edited by SAMUEL SHIMON
BOGOTÁ NOIR (COLOMBIA), edited by ANDREA MONTEJO
BRUSSELS NOIR (BELGIUM), edited by MICHEL DUFRANNE
BUENOS AIRES NOIR (ARGENTINA), edited by ERNESTO MALLO
JERUSALEM NOIR, edited by DROR MISHANI
LAGOS NOIR (NIGERIA), edited by CHRIS ABANI
MARRAKECH NOIR (MOROCCO), edited by YASSIN ADNAN
MISSISSIPPI NOIR, edited by TOM FRANKLIN
MONTREAL NOIR (CANADA), edited by JOHN McFETRIDGE & JACQUES FILIPPI
NEW ORLEANS NOIR: THE CLASSICS, edited by JULIE SMITH
OAKLAND NOIR, edited by JERRY THOMPSON & EDDIE MULLER
RIO NOIR (BRAZIL), edited by TONY BELLOTTO
SAN JUAN NOIR (PUERTO RICO), edited by MAYRA SANTOS-FEBRES
SÃO PAULO NOIR (BRAZIL), edited by TONY BELLOTTO
ST. LOUIS NOIR, edited by SCOTT PHILLIPS
TRINIDAD NOIR: THE CLASSICS (TRINIDAD & TOBAGO), edited by EARL LOVELACE & ROBERT ANTONI

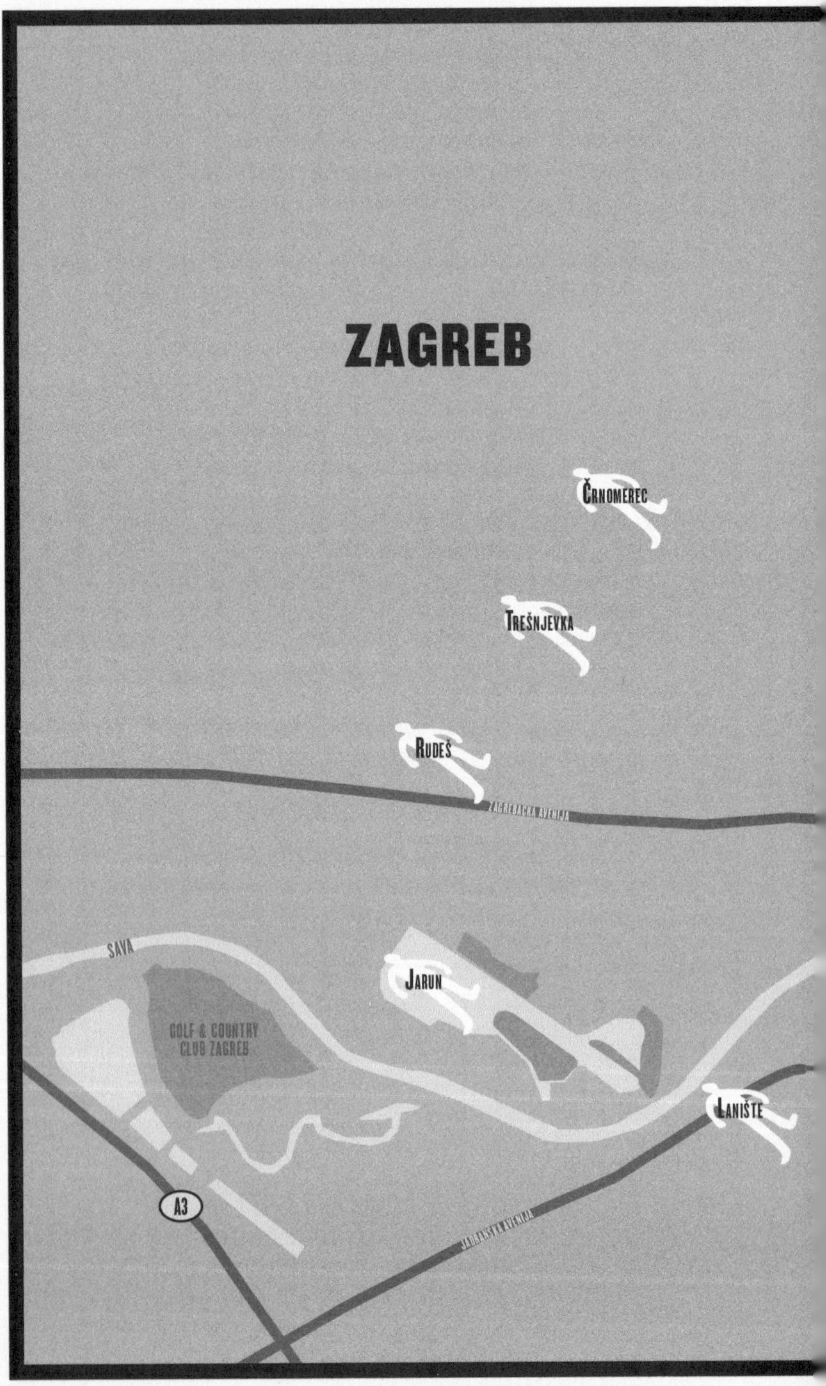

ZAGREB

Črnomerec

Trešnjevka

Rudeš

ZAGREBACKA AVENIJA

SAVA

Jarun

GOLF & COUNTRY
CLUB ZAGREB

Lanište

A3

JADRANSKA AVENIJA

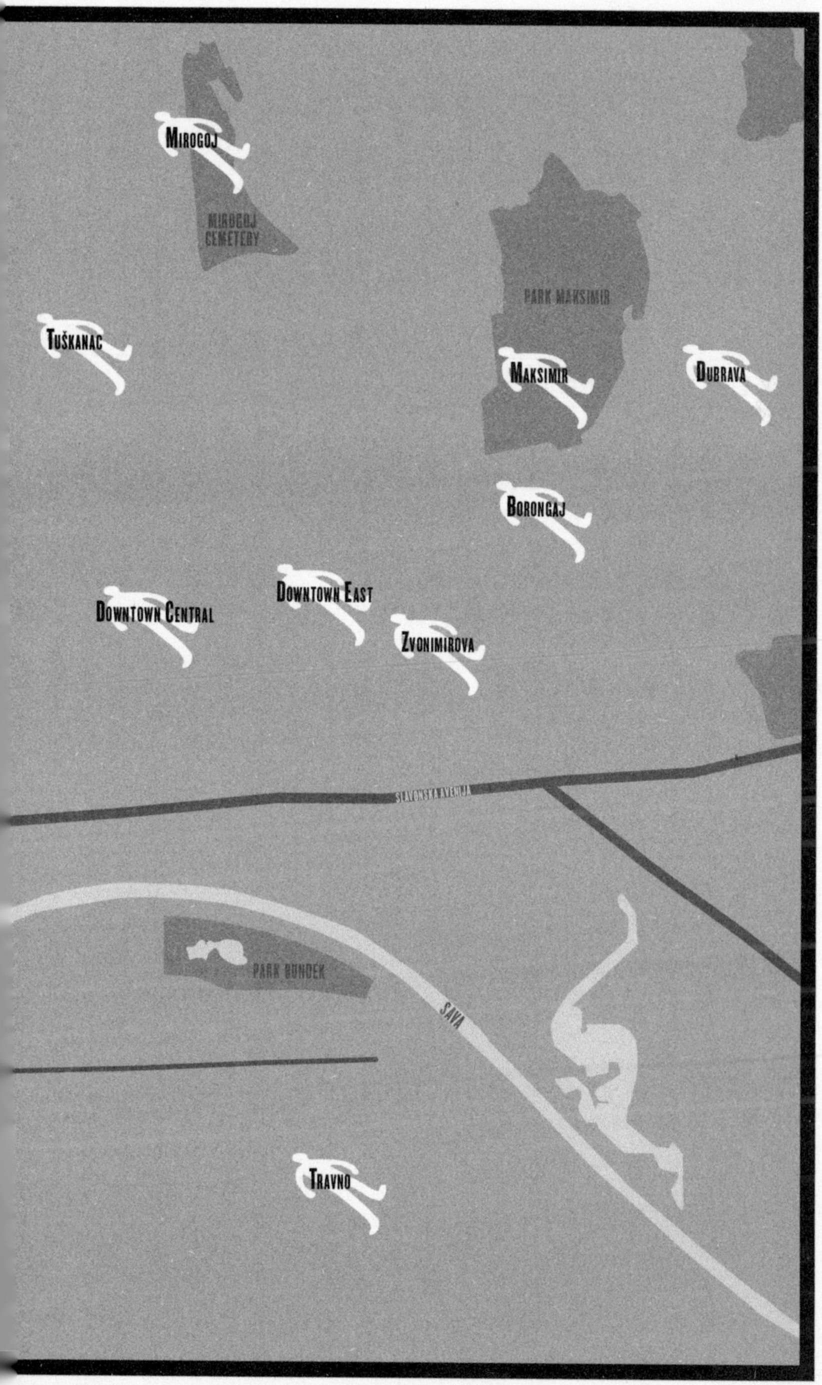

Mirogoj
MIROGOJ CEMETERY
PARK MAKSIMIR
Tuškanac
Maksimir
Dubrava
Borongaj
Downtown East
Downtown Central
Zvonimirova
SLAVONSKA AVENIJA
PARK BUNDEK
SAVA
Travno

Table of Contents

11 *Introduction*

PART I: A PERFECT OUTING

21 **Darko Macan** — Travno
A Girl in the Garage

41 **Josip Novakovich** — Maksimir
Crossbar

51 **Ivan Vidić** — Jarun
The Old Man from the Mountain

70 **Ružica Gašperov** — Downtown Central
The Gates of Hell

PART II: KNOCKING ON THE NEIGHBOR'S DOOR

87 **Mima Simić** — Dubrava
Horse Killer

102 **Robert Perisic** — Črnomerec
It All Happened So Fast

119 **Pero Kvesić** — Tuškanac
Night Vision

146 **Nada Gašić** — Zvonimirova
Numbers 1–3

PART III: DOWNTOWN FREAKS

163 **Zoran Pilić** — Downtown East
Wraiths

183 **Andrea Žigić-Dolenec** — Borongaj
Slices of Night

196 **Darko Milošić** — Mirogoj
Headlessness

PART IV: ON THE LOOSE

213 **Nora Verde** — Lanište
She-Warrior

233 **Ivan Sršen** — Rudeš
Wiener Schnitzel

254 **Neven Ušumović** — Trešnjevka
Happiness on a Leash

268 **About the Contributors**

INTRODUCTION

Surviving to Tell the Story

Translated by Ellen Elias-Bursac

I was maybe ten years old when my grandmother took me and my cousin to the movies one afternoon. This was in the second half of the 1980s, a romantic time from today's perspective, especially in the Croatia, or rather the Yugoslavia, of the day. Yugoslavia—comprising six republics with equal standing—fell to pieces in a bloody war that began in 1991. But a few years before, no one would have believed this communist state would ever cease to exist, begun as it was in the most tenacious anti-fascist armed movement in Europe during World War II, led by Marshal Tito. The socialist institutions had been functioning for nearly fifty years, workers and peasants had been given access to education, there were low levels of unemployment, and most families could afford a small, domestically produced car. Again, from today's perspective, this sounds like a middle-class dream.

To conjure for you what kind of society this was: during the forty-five years of the socialist system in Zagreb there was only *one* bank robbery! The perpetrator, never apprehended (as I recall from the stories of my childhood), acquired a magical aura—he strolled right into a branch of the most powerful Croatian bank in the middle of the day on the main Zagreb square, emptied the safe, armed with a Yugoslav-made pistol, and disappeared forever—children and, I must say, adults leaned toward fairy-tale explanations: if you were able to elude the Yugoslav police you must be a master with supernatural or, at the very least, illusionist powers. The man somehow made himself invisible—first to the passersby on the street, and then to the powerful secret service who collared most other criminals within twenty-four hours maximum, and only needed a few more days to bring the person to justice. Today, bank robberies in Zagreb are news that seldom capture any attention unless someone is seriously injured.

From time to time during the 1980s, films would find their way to Yugoslavia from the West, with a few years' delay, so it is now impossible for me to pin down exactly which year it was and how old I would have been, but that doesn't matter. What matters is that I remember almost everything: the cracked pavement on the city streets, the thousands of wads of chewing gum stuck to the sidewalk, and the hundreds of cigarette butts littering the tracks at the tram stops. The traffic cops wore silly white belts over their gray-blue shirts, the cheap restaurants served beans and sausage or fried fish that smelled foul, and through libraries wafted the fragrance of bygone times, because at that point they still hadn't introduced air conditioners or air fresheners. Movie theaters were also places that stank a little, but there wasn't a child who disliked them for that; everyone was eager to gaze at the big screen. Another plus for the youngest filmgoers during the socialist period was that there were no age limits in effect. Any child could see any film showing in any movie theater. They can do the same, theoretically, today, but back then there wasn't even a thought given as to whether something might be appropriate for children. And that was the very best aspect of the system.

And so it was that our elderly grandmother, who had survived World War II and always kept an eye out for the nearest place into which she might duck in the event of a sudden bomb attack, was able to take me and my cousin, the little rug rats that we were, to see *Angel Heart* by Alan Parker starring Mickey

Rourke and Lisa Bonet. This was a movie that a ten-year-old boy should definitely not have been watching. But I did, thanks to my grandmother who was always reading detective stories and had liked the tagline on the poster, *Harry Angel has been hired to search for the truth . . . pray he doesn't find it.*

The movie shows all sorts of violence, sex, blood, racism, magic, and Satanism; in the end the devil himself appears, and, hats off to film director Parker, Satan (played by Robert de Niro) does not come across as trivial.

As we left the movie theater my cousin and I nodded just once to each other—we knew the film had aged us and everything had changed; suddenly I could see how, decades earlier, tanks had rumbled over the cracked pavement, I saw how people around me, grimacing, were spitting those wads of chewing gum onto the ground, and the cigarette butts at the tram stop were discarded by workers with wracking smokers' coughs that signaled slow, painful deaths.

This Zagreb which suddenly laid itself out before me was the grimy little provincial town that Miroslav Krleža, the great twentieth-century Croatian writer, portrayed in most of his books. A town which was relatively well connected to the rest of central Europe—the drive to Budapest isn't long, one is in Vienna even sooner, it's just a little farther to Munich, and you get to Trieste and Venice in no time. Because of its location, Zagreb was already at a key intersection in the Middle Ages; in the eighteenth century it took its place as the definitive capital of Croatia, within the Hungarian Kingdom, part of the Austrian Empire. This distinction as the capital has meant that money has poured into the Zagreb city coffers over the last three hundred years. In the late nineteenth century the city was transformed into an appealing middle-European city with charming architecture, typical of lesser well-tended towns throughout the region.

An important dimension of Zagreb life is also its transience and inconstancy. It has never managed to hold on to anyone who wasn't forced to stay there. In the literature you won't find a single foreigner in love with Zagreb, because to be in love with Zagreb is more or less the same as falling for a single mother who has nine children—theoretically possible, but even the most generous groom would have to realize he would be giving much more than he'd get, and for most people this is simply off-putting. Those born in the city (you are free to imagine them as the nine children) are inured to the unscrupulous winner-takes-all gambit, the emotional blackmail that tramples everything in its path, knowing no one wants this place. It is unwanted because of the burdens it brings, its potency, its brazenness, its naked greed, its stink—in short, its love of life. In Zagreb, as became clear to me when I was stepping out of the movie theater, there is a meeting of a continental optimism and a Mediterranean relativism, and this is why the city has never found its peace. Its restlessness has enthralled me, and for years I have tried to delve into the wellspring of the vitality that gives the people who live here their boundless cynicism, arrogance, and ambition.

There are, in its restlessness, certain elusive qualities, a slippery charge that young people are best at recognizing, those who have nothing to lose, who are ignorant enough of the fragility of their existence that they are prepared to risk even their lives. An example of this was when Zagreb high school students stood up to the fascist government when it seized control of the government in 1941 after Nazi Germany occupied the Kingdom of Yugoslavia. The new government imposed racial laws and members of all undesirable ethnic groups were dispatched to killing fields and concentration camps. All high school students were summoned to Maksimir Stadium, one of the pivotal locations in several of the stories in this book, and at the end of the "sports exercises" held on one half of the pitch, all Jews and Serbs were ordered to step over onto the other half. After the summoned students began to obey the command and step over, several Croats stepped over with them and soon all the high school students joined in and crossed over to the other half of the pitch. This was a symbolic gesture of defiance to a division the fascists had thought would be easy to impose. They were wrong.

However, young people are seldom asked for their opinion, and it is even more rare that their opinion is taken into account. That day, the day we watched the movie, it became clear to me that I didn't have much time left to get to know my city better. I hopped on my bicycle and within a month I had traversed all of Zagreb from one end to the other. This freedom I had as a young boy is yet more proof of how different life in that long-ago age under the iron socialist hand was, more peaceful in a way. My parents were not at all worried about me being out wandering for hours to the farthest corners of the city, such as the elite residential quarters on the lower slopes of the Sljeme hills that loom over Zagreb to the north, neighborhoods that had been built by bankers before World War II. I enjoyed riding through Trešnjevka in the spring when fruit trees bloomed in all the little gardens in front of the modest family shacks. And when the trees were in full leaf and green grass grew lushly around the open sewers, even the factory neighborhoods like Žitnjak and Dubrava did not seem out-of-bounds or repellent. The Sezession center of the city acquired a romantic sheen during the spring rains and it was fun spraying the passersby when I raced through the puddles on the uneven streets.

All this was irretrievably lost in the years of the war that soon followed and now I feel that, by watching *Angel Heart* with Mickey Rourke roaming through postwar New York, I was looking into Zagreb's future, a future that was far from rosy; indeed it was gray, embittered, enriched with all a postwar period brings—war profiteers, major and small-time criminals in the new authorities, unnatural surpluses and shortages, convoluted morals—with a sweep that pulls no one along with it; its sole constant, an unquenchable desire for life.

The story collection here before you will guide you through several different perspectives on the city; each of them exposes Zagreb's neuralgic points: Robert Perisic, Mima Simić, and Pero Kvesić take us directly or indirectly into the war years of the nineties and the air of uncertainty and fear that ruled over fragile human lives, while Nada Gašić's story reminds us of the multiple layers of trauma embedded in a city that has purged itself of its *unsuitable* inhabitants several times during the last century.

The beginning of the book offers incredible angles and fascinating views of locations that inspire both great ambitions and tragic endings, both of which Zagreb's inhabitants have borne remarkably well. It opens with a tale by Darko Macan that provides an ideal urban legend for the sleepless nights of thousands of men and women in Zagreb who prefer not to stick their noses into someone else's business. Ivan Vidić has sketched a plan for the renewal of a Yugoslavia in the realm of the Balkan underworld, and Josip Novakovich has transformed hooligan violence into a fateful perpetuum mobile at the Zagreb soccer stadium; while in Ružica Gašperov's story, anyone who has fled from a situation because of societal censure will be able to recognize herself.

Several of the stories remind us that among us there are others, people we abhor, people Zagreb has never accepted, who live right next door and abhor us in equal measure. Zoran Pilić explores the character of an anonymous city loner; Darko Milošić speaks out about the social stratification of on-duty freaks, and Andrea Žigić-Dolenec plays with violence as a leitmotif for contemporary Zagreb life.

At the end of the book surface the veiled frustrations of "creeping fascism," as Naomi Wolf, supported by the ever-present naming system, terms the phenomenon of the upsurge of intolerance in society. Nora Verde thrusts us into a nighttime action by a young Zagreb activist, while Neven Ušumović reveals how a slow-moving retiree can preserve his pride even after all the reinterpretations of the history through which he has lived.

The authors of *Zagreb Noir* peer deep under the skin of this old city on the banks of the Sava River, some of them checking it out from above, at a safe distance yet with the precision of a surveyor. Some of them look it right in the eye, facing off in round after round of an exhausting boxing match. All of them have succeeded in creating a convincing and amazing gallery of characters, people we avoid because they move through the city at night, stick to the side streets, congregate in garages, cheap bars, hospitals, and are up to their elbows in suspicious activity.

Come on in, neighbor, for just one glass . . .

Ivan Sršen
Zagreb, Croatia
September 2015

PART I

A Perfect Outing

A GIRL IN THE GARAGE

BY DARKO MACAN
Travno

Translated by the author and Tatjana Jambrišak

The rumor that there was a girl in the garage underneath the She-Mammoth—arguably the biggest building in the Balkans at the time it was built—started a week before Christmas. A married couple was storing their kid's presents in their garage unit when they heard odd noises from next door. A moment earlier the wife had told the husband they should sell the unit, since they hardly ever used it.

"Once or twice a year," she said. "We store apples when my family sends them and we hide presents at Christmas. We should sell it."

"The market isn't right," said the husband, who really liked the idea of having a garage, his own space, no matter how empty.

"Hush! Did you hear that?"

"Hear what?"

She was listening close to the concrete wall between their place and the unknown neighbor's unit. "I think I heard a noise," she said.

"That was me talking," he attempted a joke. It sounded more bitter than he intended.

"Hush!" she said again, listening at the metal door painted a tired shade of dark green. "I think there's someone inside."

"Probably a dog," he said.

"Why would anyone keep a dog in a garage?" she frowned.

Perhaps somebody really wanted a dog but had a wife who wouldn't allow pets inside, thought the husband but said nothing. "What do you think it is, then?" he asked instead.

"I don't know," she said, "but it's definitely something alive. Come, listen!"

Hesitantly, he approached and listened at the door with her. There was indeed an occassional scratching noise behind the dark green door.

"Perhaps it's a cat," he said. "Somebody locked a cat in there by mistake."

"I don't think it's a cat," she said.

"A rat, then. Too much food stored in here and the rats found out. No, wait . . . perhaps it's a pig!"

"A pig?"

"A suckling," the husband said. "A Christmas dinner." His mouth watered at the idea of the succulent, crispy flesh of a freshly roasted piglet.

"Don't be ridiculous," she said. "Who'd do such a thing?"

"Okay, why don't you just tell me what you think is in there," he sighed.

"A girl."

"A girl?"

"Slave trade, you know. It happens. It's called *human trafficking* now and it's real," said the wife, who had recently seen a poster at the library. An emaciated model, carefully made up to look as if crying, had been watching her pitifully from the poster, apparently chained to the wall in some godforsaken basement. Or in a garage, why not in a garage?

"A suckling is a ridiculuos idea but a girl isn't?" The husband shook his head. "I'm glad you set me straight."

"I'll knock."

"Oh no you won't!" he said. There are some things you just do not do. You do not knock on another person's garage door any more than you take a look at his penis. It is simply not done.

She knocked.

The silence answered. After a number of long seconds, some more scratching came. Then silence.

"It's a girl," the wife said. The model on the poster reminded her so much of her younger, pretty self.

"No, it's not," he said. "Otherwise we would hear something more. I don't know, muffled screams or something. C'mon, think, if someone locked you in there, what would you do? Just scratch a little or raise all kinds of hell to attract attention?"

"Maybe she's really, really scared," the wife said. "Maybe she feels really, really trapped."

"Well, if it's a suckling, it's fucked and it knows it. C'mon, let's go already, it's cold down here."

The wife conceded to his voice of reason and went, but the image of a beautiful girl in the garage would not leave her. She thought about calling the police or the number from the library poster but feared sounding ridiculous. So she turned the whole thing into an amusing anecdote for her friends and acquaintances, thrilling anyone who would listen to how she believed there was a girl in the garage. But there was none, right? There could be none, right? Just a rat or a piglet for somebody's Christmas table.

The anecdote idled around the She-Mammoth—five thousand people living in the building on top of each other—retold in the dull moments of waiting for an elevator or in line at the supermarket on the terrace level. It would have died a quiet death if not for Domagoj Delić, a fifty-year-old veteran whose war nobody cared about anymore, whose only family was the sister living a hundred miles away and who had too much time on his hands. Domagoj Delić decided to rescue the girl from the garage.

But *which* unit? By the time the story reached Domagoj there was no way of telling where it had originated from nor where in the ground-level maze lay that terrible dungeon. All Domagoj had to go by was the dark green color of the garage unit's door, which was not much since that was the original paint on all doors in the She-Mammoth's underbelly. So Domagoj resolved to search the corridors until he found the girl, strengthening his resolve by dressing in his old military camouflage outfit and fighting the cold with a small brandy bottle in each of his breast pockets.

He walked the corridors for a full day, rarely meeting anyone, not greeting anyone. He listened at every dark green door but heard nothing. On the second day, Domagoj Delić systematically knocked on and then listened at all the doors—two hundred and fifty or so of them—regardless of color. On the third day he slept late, spent the afternoon drinking and thinking in the park, then stalked the corridors until dawn. On the fourth day, December 23, he met Emil Kosovac.

Emil Kosovac was thirty-six or—as he often thought of himself—three years older than Christ. The comparison was apt since Emil felt he would have been better off if he had croaked three years earlier while things were still going his way: he'd had a mother, a halfway decent job, and a girlfriend. In the meantime his girlfriend had left him, he had lost his job and was working part-time as a warehouse monkey for minimum wage, and his mother had died after a two-year bout with cancer, leaving him nothing but a shitload of old yet worthless pieces of furniture that he had to move out of her flat by Christmas.

I should've called the junkies and let them take the whole fucking lot, Emil thought, while tying the last antiquated piece, a two-color wardrobe, on top of his twenty-year-old Nissan Primera. By "junkies" he meant the recovered addicts who collected and repaired old furniture. In the end, Emil did not call them for he did not want anyone else to make a buck off his junk, if a buck was to be made at all. This he doubted more and more as he was making slow progress through the pre-Christmas traffic, the wardrobe on the Nissan's roof. Emil hoped for a string of green lights, no overzealous cops, and enough space in his garage to fit this last piece of crap.

There was space but just barely. It took Emil an additional hour to rearrange the furniture so that the unit's door, when lifted, would fit neatly over the wardrobe. All that work and for what? he wondered. He would not be able to give away the junk, let alone sell it. Why then? Memories? Were such memories good enough to be worth all this hard work, these long cold hours? Emil stretched his aching back and cursed, within a single thought, his rotten luck, his dead mother, lazy-ass junkies, the bitch who had left him, and his whole fucking life that was perfectly mirrored by this roomful of crap lit by a bare, winking lightbulb.

"Who do you have in there?" Domagoj Delić stepped out of the dark. Most light fixtures in the She-Mammoth's garage were long broken, leaving the job to the shy daylight, gone by four in the afternoon.

"What?"

"That's not what I'm asking," Domagoj said. "I said *who*."

"What do you mean by *who,* you fuckin' moron?" said Emil. The fatigue started to seep into his limbs. All he wanted was to close the door, forget the whole furniture business, find a place to park his car, take some aspirin, and sleep until his morning shift. He did not call for this drunken idiot and he felt not at all charitable.

"You've got. A girl. In there," Domagoj said, smugly triumphant.

"You are out of your mind," Emil snorted, and turned to switch off the light.

"That's why you. Have. All the furniture." Domagoj tried to push himself by. "Lemme see!"

"Oh, fuck off!" Emil's outstretched arms hit Domagoj's chest. Domagoj toppled easily and was now paddling on the ground like an overturned turtle.

"You have no right!" Domagoj was yelling after Emil, who closed the door and was now backing the Nissan slowly through the narrow passageway, all four signals flashing red. "No right to. Do that. To the poor girl!"

Emil found a parking spot nearby, across the road from the elementary school. Domagoj was chasing after him the whole time, shouting at the top of his voice that Emil had no right to keep the girl in the garage. A few idle passersby stopped to watch the show. Emil knew there was nothing he could do but get out of there as quickly as possible. He locked the car and stuck his fists—the right one balled over his keys—deep in the front pockets of his jeans so as to avoid the temptation to deck the drunkard. After a few steps, he realized that he was stooping like a guilty person, so he made a conscious effort to walk upright.

"Good people, look at him!" Domagoj was bellowing. "He is a criminal! The worst kind! He keeps a girl in his garage! A hungry girl! In the cold!"

Some of the passersby had heard that rumor before so they tried to make out Emil's face, to see if he was someone they recognized. One woman snapped a photo on her cell phone: perhaps she could sell the picture to a tabloid for a hundred kuna or more? The cell phone was not very good so the picture turned out too dark. Still, perhaps it would be a conversation piece? A girl in the garage, imagine if it were true!

Everybody got a good look but nobody tried to stop Emil—why get involved? Domagoj followed him to Emil's foyer, hollering accusations the whole way. Emil unlocked the foyer door—its metal frame was dark green too, but with a much fresher coat of paint than the garage doors—and thought he had left his problem on the other side of the wired glass, with the drunkard. Perhaps it would have been so, if not for Leda.

Leda was seventeen, a short, thin, blond angel with a carefully practiced bitchface, a jacket too short, and shoes too tall. She hung around the She-Mammoth's terrace level with a plainer friend looking for boys to mooch a drink or two from and then dis.

"You think he's for real?" asked Leda's curly friend.

"Naah," said Leda. "Didya look at him?"

"I know, right?" said the friend. "No way, huh?"

"Uh-huh," said Leda, but her eyes said something else. Her life was boring, everybody she knew was boring, Christmas was the most boring time of the year, but this . . . somehow, this was interesting.

Leda missed Emil going to work the following morning—it was way too early for her to get up—but she sat perched on the She-Mammoth's dark green railings, waiting for him to return home. A kind old busybody warned her about the danger to the kidneys from sitting on the cold metal and Leda thanked her sweetly but remained on the spot. Around noon she ran to a café to pee and then came back to her watchtower. She spotted Emil shortly before three p.m., quickly clapped her hands, and moved to the staircase he would most certainly use to get to the terrace.

"Hey," she said when he reached the top of the stairs.

He glanced at her, puzzled. For a moment he thought she was someone he knew, but when this turned out to be false, his confusion grew. Why would a strange girl greet him on a shitty Christmas Eve afternoon? A strange, quite pretty girl. "Hi," he said; it came out as a strangled cough.

Emil waited for the girl to say something but Leda kept giving him nothing but a pout and an eyelash stare. He soon concluded that he had imagined the greeting and headed over to the supermarket to buy cigarettes and a few groceries he would need over the next couple of days. Leda chuckled and ran after Emil with a quick, poodle-like, tiptoe gait.

In the supermarket, Leda cut the cashier's line to stand right behind Emil. An older bearded gentleman grumbled about it but she waved a candy bar at him to show she was only buying one item and melted his resistance with a chipmunk smile. Then she leaned forward and startled Emil by brushing her cheek against the sleeve of his worn-out leather jacket.

"Is it true?" she stage-whispered. He looked at her with bewilderment bordering on fear.

"What?" he asked.

"About the girl," she replied.

"No," he said, looking around uncomfortably. Nobody was paying any attention to the two of them except for the bearded gentlemen who was idly mindfondling Leda's perky buttocks. "God, no."

"Too bad," sighed Leda. "I wanted to see her."

That surprised Emil and he gave the girl another good look. Really, really pretty. Maybe even the prettiness that lasted, although you could never be sure about that. A bit on the short side which was not a bad thing: if taller, she would have been totally unattainable. *As if she's attainable now!* Emil ridiculed his own train of thought. And yet she was talking to him, that's . . . that's something, at least. He glanced at her: she pretended not to look at him while suggestively sliding her lips over the unwrapped candy bar. *The little minx*, approved Emil.

It was his turn at the cash register. He paid and was packing his few items in a plastic bag when Leda showed the empty candy wrapper to the cashier and proclaimed that she had forgotten her money. "I'm so sorry," she said to the cashier while looking at Emil. "I don't know what to do."

Now everybody was staring at Emil: Leda, the cashier, the bearded gentleman, and all the harried customers behind him. Emil was looking at Leda, at her smirk, at the wisp of hair that carefully half-hid her eye.

"It's okay," he said. "I'll pay."

Leda slipped out of the supermarket while Emil was getting his change and for a moment he thought the whole elaborate game was about getting a free candy bar. But she was waiting for him outside. It was barely past three p.m. but the huge mass of the mammoth building was already blocking the light of the setting sun and the streetlights would not go on for another hour. Leda was a dark, elfin figure awaiting Emil in their own private twilight.

"Hey," she said and giggled.

"Hi," he said.

"Will you show her to me?"

"There's no one to show."

"But there was, right?"

Emil thought about this. Leda was waiting for his answer with bated breath and it had been a long time since a girl, especially a girl this beautiful, had expected anything from him with such intensity. It was impossible to say no to a beautiful girl, reasoned Emil. "Yes," he said.

She beamed. "Show it to me!"

"What?"

"The garage."

"Okay."

They went down a flight of stairs and into the somber underground. Neither of them spoke a word. Leda was humming the chorus of some awful pop song that she ironically adored and Emil was basking in her presence. There was no one else down there, as usual.

Emil lifted his unit's door, turned the bulb on, and let Leda squeeze in. Then he pulled the door back down, not admitting even to himself what he was hoping for.

"*Niiice*," Leda said, looking at the furniture. Emil could not tell whether she was being sarcastic or not. "I thought, y'know, there'd be bare walls and stuff. Chains. This is kinda comfy."

"Well . . ." Emil was thinking hard what to say, "you don't want to, um, damage the merchandise."

"Merchandise!" Leda laughed. She, too, had seen the poster in the library window and wanted to be that good looking when she grew up. She believed she was getting there. "What did you feed her?"

"Bread," Emil said. "Water."

"Classy!"

"She wasn't here long." With every sentence the girl in the garage became more real to him.

Leda sat on the couch, pushing down with her palms and her little ass to test the springs. She looked up at Emil, first at his crotch and then at his face. Emil was licking his lips. Leda said, "Did you ever, y'know, test out the merchandise?"

Emil dropped the plastic shopping bag on his mother's old scratched dresser and first knelt, then sat on the couch. His fingers went and touched Leda's hair. She did not seem to mind; if anything, her eyes mocked his guarded approach. "Yes," he said.

"What did you do to her? Y'know, in the end?"

Emil cupped her sweet face with his palms and was lost in the moment but not enough not to know that everything depended on his next answer. What did he do to the girl in the garage? Did he sell her? Let her go? Those were not the answers the young body in his hands was quivering for.

"I killed her," he whispered. Her shiver and her kiss told him he had guessed right.

They fucked fast and hard on the old couch in the garage on Christmas Eve. The girl was eager and definitely not a virgin, and Emil was very glad that six months ago he had remembered to put a condom in his wallet.

While they were still lying on top of each other, in the few minutes before the December cold penetrated the warmth of their embrace, Leda asked: "How did she die?"

"Ugly." Emil paused to think up an answer that sounded true. "I couldn't bear to watch her die so I tied her to that chair," with his chin he indicated the low off-white armchair, "and put a plastic bag over her head." He was quite enjoying the frisson his tale produced in Leda. He stroked her pale arms with his large, rough palms.

"Was she beautiful?"

"Very," Emil nodded, and kissed her. She sighed like a kitten, then wriggled from under him and picked up her jeans from the floor.

"Gotta go," she said. "Mom'll kill me if I don't help her with dinner."

Emil wanted to ask her if he would see her again but was not sure whether merciless killers do such things. "Okay," he said, feeling empty.

"See ya!" Leda chirped, pushing the garage door three feet up, then ducking under and disappearing.

Emil sighed and reached for the shopping bag. He tossed out everything to find the cigarettes, opened the pack, and lit one with the lighter he had fished out of his jacket pocket. The warmth of the cigarette smoke reminded him how icy it was in the garage so he started to slowly dress himself. His mind's eye was full of the girl he had just fucked, the girl whose name and phone number he had forgotten to ask for. *Girls are good*, he thought. *Sex is fucking great, man, even fucking Christmas doesn't suck so much if you add some sweet fornication to it.*

He squashed the cigarette butt against the wall. Who knew that this garage, this fucking furniture, would do him such a solid? Who knew, indeed? He pulled the door up. The single bulb strained to light a few yards of the garage floor and in the process revealed the lumbering, unstable mass of Domagoj Delić.

"Oh fuck," Emil groaned. "You again?"

Domagoj was high on booze and himself. He had figured there was no better time for the slaver to show up than the evening when all the decent people would be celebrating, and he was right. He pointed an accusing finger at Emil—well, almost at him—and said, "I saw her. I. Saw. Her."

"The fuck you talkin' about?"

"The girl," Domagoj grinned. He had not felt this good since he and the boys had been at the frontline, more than twenty years earlier, drinking hard, roasting pigs, and fighting the Serbs. This guy seemed like he could be a Serb too. Domagoj poked the guy's chest with his cruddy forefinger. "I saw. The girl. Coming. Outta here."

Emil slapped Domagoj's hand away. "Are you a moron or are you a *fuckin'* moron? If she came out, then she was no prisoner, right?"

Domagoj waved his finger left to right. Shook his head too. "That's what you. Want me. To think," he said. "That's why. You've let. Her go."

"The fuck?"

Domagoj poked him again. "You got scared," he said. He tried to stand tall and look menacing but a grin kept slipping out, betraying how much he was enjoying himself. "Of me."

"Yeah, right," said Emil, and turned his back to Domagoj in order to collect his stuff and then get out of there. He was in too good of a mood to waste it on this cave-dwelling imbecile.

Domagoj grabbed him in chokehold but not a very strong one, so after a moment of panic, Emil managed to elbow the drunken vet in the ribs and free himself. However, Domagoj was not going to quit: he stumbled forward, his arms flailing, his mouth spouting obscenities. Emil was not a very good fighter but this was not a hard fight. He managed to step aside and grab Domagoj's greasy hair with both hands. Domagoj yelped and Emil spun him around twice before throwing him against the wall.

"Had enough, you moron?" Emil panted. "Had fucking enough?"

"Fuck you, you fucking Serb," Domagoj croaked. "Fuck your fucking mother, you motherfucker!"

"Leave my mother out of this!" Emil yelled, and kneed Domagoj in the gut. Twice. The drunkard started to puke. *Great,* Emil thought, *just fucking great.* The spectacle was making him sick too, so he turned away, and within a second Domagoj was on his back again.

This time Emil made short work of the fight. He shook Domagoj off, grabbed him by the throat, and slammed his head five or six times against the cupboard in the garage. When Domagoj lost consciousness, Emil dropped him in the off-white armchair, and fumbled another cigarette from the pack with shaking hands.

What to do with this moron, he wondered. And why the fuck couldn't something nice ever happen without a pile of stinking manure following the very next moment? Emil watched the cigarette smoke billow around the bulb. Then he glanced at

Domagoj. The guy looked pale. Maybe dead. Emil felt his back turn to goose bumps so he went over to the armchair to check. Domagoj was breathing shallow but undeniable breaths.

The fucker, Emil thought. The cigarette was helping him think. The fucker has to be dealt with, scared to the point that he would never ever think of bothering Emil again. Scared fucking shitless.

Emil crushed the cigarette against the side of the dresser and started looking through the drawers. In one of them, he was sure, he had some duct tape—he'd taped the drawers tight so they would not open during transport. He finally found it and taped Domagoj's arms and legs to the armchair. He looked over his work and then, as an afterthought, put a piece of duct tape over Domagoj's mouth too. There was no one in the She-Mammoth's underbelly but it couldn't hurt to eliminate any noise.

Emil lit up another cigarette and waited for the veteran to wake up. He got bored with it after a minute so he pressed the cigarette against Domagoj's earlobe. Domagoj came to with a start and the duct tape killed his scream in a satisfying way. Emil watched him unsuccessfully try to wiggle himself free and was pleased. Good thing the fucker had puked already, Emil thought, lest he choked on his own vomit. After all, Emil did not want him dead, just scared.

And Domagoj was scared. Bound and burned, his alcohol courage gone, he was trembling and his cloudy eyes were begging for mercy. A tear escaped from his right eye and perished on his unshaven cheeks.

Emil was enjoying himself. Not a bad Christmas Eve, after all. First the girl and now this unexpected victory over another man. He could imagine no better day.

Emil reached behind him and picked up the red and green plastic bag he'd gotten at the supermarket. He flapped it in front of Domagoj's eyes. "See this?" he said. "You pissed off one Serb too many, you fucking moron. Now you're gonna pay."

Domagoj's eyes widened in terror. He started to shake violently, straining his limbs against the duct tape, but the tape held. So did the armchair. They used to make furniture strong in his mother's day, Emil thought, ugly but strong.

Emil spread the bag open and pulled it over Domagoj's head. The plastic started to move in and out in the rhythm of the veteran's panicky breathing. "Are you sorry now?" Emil asked, making a show of reaching for the duct tape, measuring a length that he would wrap around Domagoj's neck, and tearing the piece off with his teeth. "I bet you're sorry now. I bet it'd never cross your mind to bother honest folk again as long as you live, if only I'd—"

Domagoj spasmed forcefully. And again. His head hit the armchair's headrest. The plastic bag stopped moving.

"The fuck?" Emil said.

Domagoj was sitting perfectly still, his back somewhat arched. For a moment Emil suspected a trick, but the moment did not last long. He reached out to pinch the vet's arm but could not bring himself to do it. He felt a sudden need for air, for lots and lots of fresh winter air. The air in the garage was dead.

He went out, sat on one of the chess table benches, and stared at the little church, recently built and quite unimpressive compared to the She-Mammoth. A few people went in, a few came out. There would be more of them for the midnight Mass, he thought. He was thinking of the church so he would not think of the garage. He smoked one cigarette after another.

Perhaps he should have given the old guy CPR? That might have saved him. There were no guarantees in such matters, and anyway, Emil felt slightly repulsed by the thought of touching mouths with another guy, especially an old drunk who had recently vomited. And he would have to get him out of the armchair first and what if the CPR was successful—what would the old guy do next? Not fight, probably . . . but tell? And what would Emil do then? It was probably better this way. And even if this were not true, it was too late now. How long could a brain survive without oxygen: half an hour, ten minutes? Emil wished he knew. He wished he did not feel as if his own brain was critically starved for oxygen.

Emil sat on the bench until he had finished his pack, then crumpled it up and threw it to the ground. He knew he had to go back. He did not want to, but he could hardly leave the old guy in there. Perhaps it was cold enough now and he would not decompose right away, but sooner or later . . .

In a way, it was funny to see the dead guy in a camouflage jacket and pants with a plastic bag over his head sitting in his mother's off-white armchair, among all the other furniture. He looked like just another thing, a pile of dirty clothes. His hands had turned the gray color of clay to fit in better.

Emil sighed and fished through the dead guy's pockets until he produced a wallet and found where he lived. He also learned his name. "I'll be right back," Emil said, and went up to buzz the dead guy's apartment on the intercom. He buzzed it three times at five-minute intervals, the last time holding the buzzer until he counted to a hundred. No one answered. Either the old guy had lived alone or everyone else had taken off somewhere for Christmas, which was equally fine.

Emil went to the supermarket, now reasonably empty, and bought two more packs of cigarettes, then returned to the garage.

He used his house key to cut the duct tape and hoped that nobody would notice the glue residue on Domagoj's cuffs, nor the missing hair on his wrists and chin. He unrolled his mother's old carpet and laid Domagoj on it. The dead guy smelled faintly of shit. Luckily, his pants were tucked, military style, into his boots so not much seeped out. Emil rolled up Domagoj in the carpet and then rolled the whole thing out of the garage. He switched off the light and closed the door.

Emil hoisted the bundle over his shoulder, grateful for the workout the warehouse job gave him. Slowly, he headed toward the exit. On the way he passed a husband taking an armload of carefully wrapped presents out of the garage. Emil nodded at him, but the guy did not seem to notice.

Hefting the corpse up a flight of stairs, across the terrace, unlocking the foyer door, getting into the elevator, and stepping out onto the dead guy's floor—Emil did all these things as if in a dream. Nobody paid any attention to another guy carrying another load.

Emil lowered the carpet in front of Domagoj's door and looked around. There were two other apartments on the floor, one silent, one with dining sounds coming out of it. Emil stretched his back then fished for the keys, unlocked Domagoj's door, and dragged the corpse in.

No wife, no family—that much was clear from the first glance at the clutter. Emil told himself not to get distracted and pulled Domagoj into what seemed to be the living room. He thought he would switch carpets and make it easy on himself but the dead guy did not have a carpet at all. "You can have my mother's," whispered Emil as he unrolled the carpet, trying to judge whether Domagoj was prostrate naturally enough. He could not tell.

Emil forced himself to take the bag from Domagoj's head and stuffed it in his pocket. He left the keys in the ashtray on a small table by the door. It occured to him to wipe the doorknob although he figured he was fucked if anyone cared to investigate. He went home.

* * *

By Christmas morning Emil had smoked both the packs he'd bought. He tried to eat but couldn't. Couldn't sleep either. He went out and watched the people go in and out of the church. He bummed a couple of cigarettes from passersby but did not really feel like smoking. He stared at what he thought was Domagoj's window. In the evening he went home, found some hard liquor in the cupboard, and drank himself to sleep.

On Boxing Day he went to work, came home, managed to eat something, shat, drank a little, went to sleep.

Domagoj's body was not found until Thursday and nobody, it seemed, suspected foul play. Emil was there, just back from work, when the metal coffin was being carried to the black hearse. "What happened?" he asked.

"A veteran died," somebody replied. "A suicide, probably, you know how that goes."

Emil nodded. He spotted Leda in the crowd and waved at her. She did not wave back, the corpse interested her more.

A short, pale youth with a shaved head and wearing an olive-and-orange flight jacket was waiting for Emil at the terrace. "You Emil?" he asked.

"Who're you?" Emil frowned. He felt good about the corpse being found, bad about Leda.

"I'm Neno," the kid said. "We heard you keep a girl in your garage."

"We? Who the fuck is *we*?"

"I'm asking the fucking questions here, okay? You answer, okay?" Neno was spitting a little. "Do you have a girl in the garage?"

"No, I do not." Emil lit a cigarette.

"We hear you do. And I'm here to tell you that you better not, because that's our business. The girls are."

"The girls in garages?"

"You fucking with me? You better not be fucking with me!"

"I'd rather be fucking a girl but I don't have one," Emil said. "In the garage or anywhere else."

"Mind showing me?"

Emil thought of doing just that, but then he remembered the duct tape and the shit stain on the armchair. God, why had he not cleaned that already? "Yes, I mind," he said.

"Why?" Neno was staring at him slit-eyed, trying to look tough but appearing myopic.

Emil sucked on his cigarette and thought hard about what to say. The inspiration struck. "'Cause I have a guy in there," he said.

"A guy?" Neno frowned. "Why?"

"Why do you think?"

"You fucking him?"

"Not personally, no. But there are lots of faggots who pay for a nice piece of ass. Hell, the ass doesn't even have to be that nice, if you know what I mean."

"Jesus, that's disgusting!"

"Wanna try him?" Emil was starting to have fun.

"Me? Christ, no! Who do you think I am?"

"I dunno. You tell me."

"A guy . . . Jesus!" Neno was feeling increasingly uncomfortable.

"So I guess guys aren't your business? Just girls?"

"Just girls," Neno quickly replied.

"I guess your business and my business don't overlap, do they?"

"I guess," Neno said, then spat on the terrace. "You're in some disgusting business, man."

"Just trying to make a buck," smiled Emil. "Lemme know if you wanna get in on it."

Neno left, trying to shake the images nesting under his shaved scalp.

Emil smiled and went home. *I really should clean up the garage*, he thought, but then shrugged. Nobody would investigate another dead vet. The autopsy would show a coronary, some distant cousin would be happy to inherit a flat in Zagreb, and nobody would spare the vet even as much thought as Emil already had.

He decided not to bother. He opened the window to air out his apartment and stood there enjoying the winter chill, the cigarette warmth, and the hot memories of the evening when he had a girl in the garage.

CROSSBAR

BY JOSIP NOVAKOVICH

Maksimir

This event happened a few years back, in 2017, the year when Serbia and Turkey became members of the European Union, shortly before the EU dissolved. Dinamo Zagreb was trailing 1:2 against Crvena Zvezda Belgrade in a semifinal UEFA cup match in Maksimir. Maksimir is a strange name—meaning "greatest peace"—but it isn't famous for peace. The Yugoslav war of 1991 started at the stadium as a soccer war, when these two clubs played and the Yugoslav police attacked the Croatian fans, injuring about a hundred.

In Maksimir, as a ten-year-old, I had seen my first first division match three decades before, also between Dinamo and Zvezda. My brother Zdravko brought me to the game. Being a Hajduk fan, I didn't care who won; for some reason, Zdravko was a rabid Zvezda fan, and I rooted with him, and rejoiced when Džajić scored the winning goal, with a fantastically curved lob that licked the crossbar and fell just below the line into the goal. We walked out of the stadium in a procession of Zvezda fans. Somebody handed us Zvezda flags (they were red and white, strangely enough, Croatian colors)—for all I know it could have been Arkan, who was an active hooligan at that time before becoming a war lord—and we marched down Maksimirska toward Republike Square, at the head of the procession. The flag was heavy, my brother was screaming, "Zvezda! Zvezda!" and I mouthed the words after him, the way I did when we sang national hymns and other things I had no reason to believe in.

On the sidewalks, Dinamo fans had whistled and sworn in such a colorful vocabulary that I was startled, but not nearly as much as when a rock hit me in my rib cage, on the left side. It was big, probably a cobblestone picked up between the tram tracks. It took my breath away, so much that I failed to utter a sound. I would have screamed out in pain if I'd had the breath to do it with. The flag fell out of my hands. Although I never swore, after gulping some air, I said to my brother, "Fuck this!" and ran to the sidewalk, where a fat man slapped me, knocking me down on the pavement. Since then, I'd detested both clubs, Dinamo and Zvezda, but a lot of years had passed, and my addiction to soccer had not subsided, and so here I was, right behind the goal, shrieking for Dinamo for no reason other than it was a Croatian club. I must say that I am not particularly nationalistic, except when it comes to soccer, and then I tremble for the national team.

Rooting for Croatia was hardly a rewarding experience. The national team would usually play well and sometimes be ranked as high as third in the world by FIFA and go far just enough to crush you with some unfortunate miss or defeat—such as against Turkey in the European elimination stage, when during celebration for having won 1–0, and imagining that the game was over as it was in its third minute of overtime, they failed to defend and Turkey scored; and then the Croatian guys missed a couple of shots in the shootout, losing the game. The coach, Bilic, may have been to blame, because instead of a psychologist to prepare the players for the shootout, he had invited a priest to pray with the team.

Anyhow, back to 2017. The match in Belgrade had ended 3–3, so 2–2 would advance Dinamo into the finals as goals scored away were still valued more than those at home. There were only ten minutes left and Dinamo was still trailing. Davidović, Zvezda's halfback, deflected a ball with his hand. The Dutch referee should have blown a whistle for a penalty shot in Dinamo's favor, but he didn't. Is it possible that he didn't see the handball, and that the assistant referees hadn't either, while the whole stadium had? The fans were shrieking and throwing crackers and for a few minutes the match was suspended, and after a deliberation, the referees decided to let the game resume, which was a big mistake.

Big guys around me kept jumping up and down so that the cement stands shook. I knew it was safe as it was not the first time they had been jumping up and down en masse, and it would not collapse the way the stadium in Milan had years ago, killing dozens. I have no idea how these guys grew up to be like human bears—most of them in the range of six-two to six-six and weighing between 250 and 350 pounds. And it looked unseemly that such huge guys would be so passionate about what short and stringy players did in the grass with a ball. But passion is inscrutable, and to tell you the truth, I was one of those guys, jumping up and down and shrieking. It's hard for me to explain how I got into this. Ordinarily I was a civilized denizen of Zagreb, an architect with a taste for macchiato and single malts, and at the beginning of the match I was still a civilized human, but now, by the end, I had taken off my shirt and was hollering for blood and retribution with my tribesmen.

The game became frenetic. See, I am cultured enough to use words like that (and I am even writing this whole thing in the damned English language, not all that patriotic of me) when I am away from the stadium, but in it I am a Roman barbarian wanting to see gladiators kick balls around like they are chopped-off heads. Dinamo exerted fantastic pressure, shooting at the goal almost twice a minute, and then there was a great chance as

Marić advanced rapidly to the goal. Then he was felled by Branislav Ivanović, who slid into his shins from behind. Ivanović is a fine player—Chelsea captain until recently—and I am sure he intended to get the ball rather than the player, but rules are rules. As long as you touch the ball first, anything goes, but if you get the foot or the shin of the player before the ball, it's a grave foul. At that speed it's impossible to always be accurate.

Anyhow, it was a clear penalty, and strangely enough, the stingy Dutch referee did whistle and point to the penalty spot. Marić—the new star player for Dinamo, best scorer in the UEFA championship in 2015–16, who had sunk Bayern—got the honor to shoot. The rules had been changed since 2015, so that instead of eleven meters now it was twelve meters to the goal. Eleven meters had given too much advantage to the kicker. That one meter didn't equalize the playing field between the two but it made it less predictable, giving the goalie somewhat more time to react. But still, a good shot like Marić should make it more than 90 percent of the time. However, in a crucial situation like this one, the anxiety of the penalty kicker has to be great, and certainly it must have been for Marić.

I knew that Marić probably hated the Serbian players. Marić was born in 1992 in a Croatian village near Bugojno in Bosnia, and both of his parents disappeared at the beginning of the war, never to be heard from again. He was raised by his grandmother as a refugee in Austria, and for him eliminating Zvezda must have been a dream . . . a form of revenge. I am not sure he thought in such nationalistic and simplistic terms, but in the stadium, he probably did. He certainly wanted to score more than anyone else. He was a bony guy with sharp cheekbones and a long hooked nose, kind of hawklike.

At the whistle, Marić ran, took a full swing at the ball, and the ball flew straight and hit the inside of the crossbar in the right corner; the metal resounded and the ball bounced onto the line and back up to the crossbar. The Zvezda goalie, instead of catching the ball at this point, kicked it out and it hit Marić's chest. Marić had another chance: he shot and yet again hit the crossbar and the ball flew far out, where Ivanović cleared it, sending it far away into the Dinamo stands. Now, you had to admire Marić's shots, even though they didn't go in. I think there should be a different scoring system, whereby each hit on the crossbar counts as half a point. Not that it would have helped the outcome of this game; it was lost. The crowd was in a wounded state, bloodthirsty, screaming, throwing crackers. The place was a stinging smoke screen, anything could happen at this point . . . and it did. Many of us jumped over the fence, and right in front of me, I saw a man with a machete. Another one grabbed the referee, a Dutchman by the august name of Rembrandt, and pushed him on the ground onto his knees, and the man with the machete brought it down, beheading the referee. Somehow it looked normal, at first . . . easy. The head fell and rolled and ended up sideways in the grass, stopped by the nose.

After thinking about what had just happened, I shrank back in horror. The Serbian team was gone, to safety I imagined, and because of the prediction of potential violence, there weren't many Serbian fans (the buses from Serbia were not allowed to come to the game), so these were Croatian hooligans. The Croatian police, some fifty of them, ran down and surrounded the murder scene.

I followed another group of hooligans who somehow got ahold of a few Dinamo players and beat them systematically. Somebody knocked Marić down, and several people kicked him, shouting insults, "Scumbag! They bribed you, didn't they? Fucking whore, faggot . . ." One of them said, "I have a better idea, let's take him to the zoo!"

I was still furious and drunk . . . I think I had a whole bottle of Hennessy during the game, and instead of sobering up upon seeing the beheading, I went along with the hooligans. Hell, I was one of them. I must admit, I even gave Marić a kick, somewhere in the kidney area, and I was one of the guys carrying him to the zoo. There were five of us, like pallbearers. It's strange that in triumph, we carried our coaches like that and tossed them in the air, and in loss, we carried the culprit pretty much the same way.

The zoo had modernized recently. It used to have barred cages, but now, with being members of the EU, the zoo had to become more humane—the tigers got a bigger cage, an acre of land with trees to sharpen their claws on, with a little pond to drink water from and bathe in; they were new Siberian tigers, Putin's present to Croatia. Putin had just retired to Croatia, having bought the island of Ugljan.

Anyway, we tried to toss Marić over the fence into the cage, but the fence was too tall and the guy fell out of our hands onto the pavement. He shrieked in pain. "Oh shut up, you should have kicked that ball a little lower. Why go so high with it, freaky ass?"

"Let's take him to the grizzlies," someone proposed. So we picked him up and carried Marić to the grizzly cage. These magnificent creatures were a political present too, from Obama, delivered by John Kerry, the secretary of state, when he visited a couple years ago. Croatia had proven to be a faithful peon of NATO, starting with smuggling arms for the Syrian rebels and sending peacekeepers into Egypt. There'd been a long tradition of presents in the form of animals. Indira Gandhi had given the former Yugoslavian leader, Tito, elephants; Mao Tse-tung gave us panda bears; and now we had grizzlies as well, named Bill and Hillary. Anyway, these guys were massive, male probably 800 pounds, female 450—even bigger than the Siberian tigers.

We had to climb the fence to throw him into the cage and he landed on a rocky little island. Bill and Hillary jumped to the island and sniffed Marić. We shouted, "Tear him up! Eat him!" but the bears merely sniffed him all over for a while, and then licked his face. They did not bite him. Marić didn't move, sprawled and loose like a rag doll. Bill roared and lunged at us, but the fence was ten yards removed over a chasm, so he fell into it, then climbed out and growled at us. He jumped again and managed to reach the fence and climb it. Once over, he knocked down one guy and snapped his neck. I ran. He bit my right calf and tore a huge chunk out of it. I pissed in terror and ran out of the zoo and into the streets; a cab driver who was right near the zoo entrance gave me a ride to the Rebro hospital. I bled richly and groaned until they cut off the circulation to my leg and gave me shots to stop the bleeding, and morphine to dull the pain. At first it had hurt less than I imagined it should—the shock is a natural painkiller—and that's how I had managed to run for my life.

I passed out at the hospital from the loss of blood combined with the dose of morphine. When I woke up, I was in horrifying pain; my nerves were severed too. I stayed in the hospital for days. The surgeons patched me up, and without my calf muscles, it was clear I would have a permanent limp. At least I had the rest of my life. I wondered how Marić was doing so I looked it up online.

Marić had a broken spine, a concussion, broken ribs, and a ruptured kidney. He was in critical condition at the Rebro hospital. Thank God we didn't kill him. I swore I would never watch another soccer game if I could help it, and I would never root again for any team. In any event, Croatia, both individual teams and the national team, was now banned from international competition for four years. If I hadn't been there, the same thing would have happened—there were enough hooligans. Maybe I shouldn't feel terribly guilty, but of course I should.

When Marić recovered enough to go around in a wheelchair, and when I recovered enough, I volunteered to take him places and we became fast friends. I took him to Gradska kavana every morning for macchiato. Because of the damage to his spinal cord, he'll never be able to walk again unless there's some medical breakthrough.

And what do we talk about? Anything but soccer. For a whole year I couldn't bring myself to tell him that I was one of the thugs. But one day, we were relaxing and were both in a particularly fabulous mood. I'd just told him a new Mujo and Haso joke.

"What would I do without you?" said Marić.

"I don't know. Maybe play soccer?" I said.

"Let's go to the zoo," he suggested. "I want to say hi to Bill and Hillary. You know, she saved my life by licking me and nursing me. I think I was clinically dead. I saw my dad and mom in heaven, and we ate baklava together. I think there's life after death."

We took a cab. On the right side was the Dinamo stadium. He turned away from it.

I helped him get out of the cab with his electric wheelchair, and we went past the Siberian tigers, to the bears. I had no reason to be glad to see them, but Marić shouted, "Hello, my friends!"

Both bears stood on their hind legs and made strange noises, something between a growl and a roar, but a couple of octaves higher, the way they would talk to a cub.

"Beautiful, aren't they?" he said. "See, they remember me. Next time I'm going to bring them some trout."

"You aren't supposed to feed them."

"I can do what I want. You'll help me get here, right?"

"Of course."

"What would I do without you?"

"You know, Bill ate my right calf. I am not that eager to feed him. I already did."

"I know. I've read the articles."

"You knew all along? How? That's crazy. Why would you talk to me then?"

"I saw the pictures, security camera pictures, and I could tell that one of the silhouettes was you. And then there were articles about the bear, how he killed two hooligans and tore up your leg."

"And you don't blame me?"

"Of course I blame you, you ass, but I understand. You were a fucking hooligan. Anyway, you weren't the ringleader."

"Generous interpretation."

"Not generous. Let me show you something." He leaned over, opened his jacket, and I could see he was carrying an Uzi. "Guess what that is for?"

"Security?"

"No. I am waiting for the other two. You are okay. You suffered, and I got to know you. Bill avenged me, and you weren't the ringleader. But when I see those motherfuckers, off they go."

"Wow!"

"It's *vow*, not *wow*. So when can you come back to feed Bill and Hill with me?"

"I'm not sure. Seeing that gun makes me lose my appetite."

And as I stared at him, looking kind of like Stephen Hawking in his wheelchair with thick glasses, a proper black jacket, and a red tie, I imagined I was seeing him for the last time. But am I stuck with him now? If I quit seeing him, will he put me on the list of people to shoot? With thoughts like these, we couldn't be friends anymore.

"Adios, my friend!" I said, and turned my back to him, my hard-sole leather shoes crunching the sharp gravel, every little stone imprinting itself into the skin of my feet as I started to walk away. An uneasy feeling sent goose bumps up my back, as though a bullet would pass through me at any second.

THE OLD MAN FROM THE MOUNTAIN

BY IVAN VIDIĆ

Jarun

Translated by Stephen M. Dickey

I

Zaza danced with her arms raised, tossing her long black hair in all directions as she sang. She stood on an elevated narrow stage, only a step away from her loyal audience, who repeated her every word and imitated her every move. Between songs the throng screamed with excitement. She was tall and buxom, with piercing eyes, full lips, and an unreal tan. The girls copied her. The men were wild about her, and all it took was one look at her to drive them crazy. Except for her high heels, she barely wore a shred of clothing.

II

The old man from the mountain's coming down to town
Look out, look out!
No one's happy, no one but me,
No one's happy, no one but me,
I'm waiting for my man.
My Old Man, my man,
My man, my Old Man,
'Cause he's the one's gonna give it to me . . .

III

No drinking or fighting, it said on the wall. *No throwing bottles, ashtrays, or other hard objects at the performers*, it said. *No grabbing or groping the singers. Absolutely no firecrackers, flares, M-80s, or other fireworks. No knives or firearms under any circumstances.*

Prohibitions, nothing but prohibitions.

And I violated the most important one.

I shouldn't have said it. I shouldn't have said it out loud, but I did. It only took a moment. It took me less than a minute to say it, and that was followed by a few minutes of laughter, surprise, and comments. Yes, I boinked Zaza, the singer. Not Zaz, that boring French girl, but Zaza, our girl, the one who sings the folk songs. *Ooh, get out, lucky devil, what a looker, what a piece . . . ! But how?!* After the concert I went into her changing room and congratulated her. I said I worked for the Old Man; otherwise they wouldn't have let me in. We talked, smoked some of my terrific hash, and it just happened. And that was it. That was literally everything I told those people I thought were my friends. I made it up to show off. It only took a minute, people, no more. One accursed minute that would determine my life, or what was left of it, which might be very, very short. I might die any moment, and all because of a lie, a little lie that I told just to amuse some guys. Besides, I'd smoked a lot of hash. I was high—I couldn't be held so accountable, right? That should be a mitigating circumstance. Because sober I'd never say something so stupid, tell such a horrible lie that it might get me killed. Now they are coming, and "the sound of harpists and musicians and flute players and trumpeters will not be heard in you any longer."

IV

I shouldn't have gone home. That was the last thing I should have done. What a stupid thing to do—it was the first place they were going to look for me. I turned out the lights in the apartment and kept out of sight. I was in the hall when I heard footsteps and the sliver of light under the door was broken by the shadows of their legs. So, they were already there in front of the door. Now they would ring the bell.

They didn't ring. Instead they started pounding wildly. But their beating on the door couldn't drown out the beating of my heart, which had started pounding like crazy in my chest. It made my whole body shake. I knew that I had very little time before they would burst in. A bad door, a cheap one, can be forced open with one well-placed kick. And didn't my parents tell me when I moved into the apartment to replace it with a security door? At least it would have been able to take a little more. But who cares what old folks who are paranoid about thieves say? I realized as I listened to the pounding that they were right.

I had a few seconds to find somewhere to hide. It didn't make any sense to lock myself in a room—the kitchen or bathroom. I couldn't jump from the sixth floor.

A moment before they burst in, I slipped into the closet in the hallway. I knew they would fly right by me, the idiots. There were four of them: Tafilj, Rico, Hoxa, and a fourth one who I didn't recognize. I tiptoed out of the closet behind their backs and slipped out of the apartment. I didn't start running until I was on the stairs. I flew out of the building, got into my car, and raced down Maksimirska Street.

V

He sat at a large desk and listened to me. He was calm and full of dignity, with the poise of a king. He spoke softly and looked me straight in the eye.

"You insulted the Old Man. What else did you expect?"

"But how did he find out about all this? And why? It was only a stupid joke I told some friends."

"He hears everything."

"I need to find a way to tell him that nothing happened."

"Did nothing really happen?"

"Nothing."

"Not even what you said?"

"I said it was a joke."

"A joke?"

"A white lie."

"Just a white one?"

"It happened."

I closed my eyes and hoped someone would get me out of there. But there was no chance of that happening. All that was left to do was watch everything I said and stick to my story no matter what.

"I was joking. It's just that at the time I didn't realize how inappropriate it was. That was because of the hash."

"As you've heard, the Old Man doesn't even forgive a joke."

That was true. According to the stories the Old Man was dead serious, vain, and so unbelievably touchy that he didn't forgive anyone for anything.

No one knew of any of those who the Old Man pointed his finger at escaping their fate. They were condemned to run their entire lives, with his assassins on their heels, who would follow them to the end of the world, forever, if need be. That was why I needed to get my words just right.

"I completely regret what I did."

"Why did you even go into the Raspašoj?"

"Because Zaza was singing there. I wanted to see her concert. I was just looking to have a good time. I didn't have any bad thoughts or intentions. I respect the Old Man; everybody knows that. I was just acting like an idiot; it was a mistake. It was a very bad joke. I wouldn't ever do anything to offend his girlfriend."

"Zaza isn't the Old Man's girlfriend. He owns her."

I shrugged my shoulders. "I'd like to know if the Old Man can forgive me."

"During the day you sell his stuff, at night you hang out at folk music clubs, hit on other men's wives, all full of yourself. You think you've got God by the balls. Tell me, why should the Old Man spare you?"

VI

I wondered that as I raced out of my apartment on Maksimirska Street and headed for Jarun, to the Raspašoj, a folk music club I liked and where I was a welcome guest. Most of my friends prefer Košmar or Rusvaj, but I don't know, those clubs are a little too wild for my taste.

I never thought I was such a bad soul, regardless of the work I did. And now I didn't think I deserved what was happening to me. I like telling stories, making things up, maybe because of the hash I smoke every day, maybe that's just the way I am. Although I worked for the Old Man's people, I wasn't one of them. I like to dream and let my mind roam; I like to walk the streets of this city and look up at the sky, enjoy the flight of a flock of pigeons and swallows, and let my spirit take in their freedom.

I'd never seen the Old Man before, but he was everywhere. I once heard a fable about his predecessor, some Old Man from the Mountain of old, from whom he got his name, and who created a paradise and populated it with murderers. That was in the north of Persia. The Old Man shut himself up in inaccessible gorges whose entrances and approaches were protected by impregnable fortresses. Inside them he arranged the land to look like a garden of abundance. In gleaming castles painted with birds and animals, brave young men cavorted with beautiful young women. All around them pipes poured out water, mead, and wine. And everyone thought it was paradise. But whoever wanted to enter it had to agree to serve the Old Man and become a murderer. These men were called *hassassins*, from the hashish that they enjoyed. And they killed all the Old Man's enemies and anyone who didn't obey him.

But at that time I didn't care about fables. I didn't care about very much, and I didn't know much about this world at all. I only enjoyed life. And hash. I adore it; it casts a miraculous and intoxicating light on all things; it creates new scenes and landscapes from old ones, and makes familiar paths unfamiliar.

So, was I then the Old Man's servant? No, I wasn't. He and his men traveled the world with swords. I was only a dealer, and I liked to fly in my dreams.

But it was a fairly dangerous job. The market here was divided, and there was continual conflict. The Old Man had the heroin and hash, along with his other activities that I knew nothing about. Since chemical techniques had appeared and since the kids had started swallowing tons of pills and smoking tons of grass, it had become difficult to get real hash. But I had it. And I had all kinds of other things—money, girls, and good cars—and now, because of some tactless words, I was losing it all.

VII

Zaza had agreed to five concerts in Zagreb and tonight was the last one. When the intermission came, I asked the bouncers to take me to her. I said that it was something personal, a matter of life and death; not even that would have worked if her personal bodyguard hadn't recognized me. He lifted the thick barrier rope and led me into a passage next to the stage. I went behind him into the changing room.

"What were you doing telling everyone about that?! Are you crazy?!" she screamed into my face as soon as I entered the changing room.

"The Old Man is after me. I have good reason to believe that he's issued my death sentence."

"Yes, you do. But what do I care about you? You don't deserve any better. And why me? I thought you liked me, that you cared about me. What did I do to make you want to destroy me?"

I told her about the circumstances of my little joke, which had spawned something terrible. Zaza listened to me in silence.

"The Old Man will kill me too," she said when I finished.

"Why?"

"If he won't forgive a man, he'll forgive a woman less. He'll just kill you and then he'll be even with you. What he's preparing for me is much worse."

"What's that?"

"Who knows? He's come in his private jet. I haven't seen him yet and I have no intention of doing so. How can I explain to him that I didn't do anything with you?"

"And that kiss?"

Zaza slapped me. "You fool. You killed me with that kiss."

Her bodyguard ran in without knocking. He was her trusted man and didn't work for the Old Man.

"They're coming. Quick!"

As Tafilj, Rico, and the others approached, pushing their way through the crowd, Zaza's loyal bodyguard led us out through a back exit out of the club.

"Run, run!" the man said. "I'll try to hold them off for a bit."

We ran into the darkness. I thought it would be best for us to somehow get to my car, but it was parked out in front of the club. Zaza pulled me in the opposite direction and we ran for the lake. We stumbled, staggered, getting stuck as our feet sunk into the loose gravel.

"Over there!" Zaza shouted, and pointed toward the lake in the darkness.

"What's that?"

"A boat!"

I didn't see it at first; it was barely visible. It was tied three or four meters out from the shore, bobbing in the water. We stepped into the lake and got into the boat. I untied it just as we heard shouts behind us in the distance.

"Row! Row, you slob!" Zaza shouted as they drew closer.

I had no choice. I grabbed the oars and started rowing as hard as I could. We managed to get away from the shore before they got close to it. I rowed like crazy. An hour later we were walking in the mud and reeds on the other side of the lake. We spent a good part of the night hiding in the brush and running from any light we saw.

VIII

We found ourselves in a luxurious suite atop a hotel, with a beautiful view of Zagreb. A flock of ducks flew past the rectangle of the window. My life would soon pass by like that as well.

He looked me straight in the eye and I could hardly take it. The Old Man was standing in front of me, gray-haired, slim, and handsome, in an expensive suit with a large gold name-bracelet around his wrist. He looked more like a well-groomed fifty-year-old than someone who was said to be at least seventy. He was the complete opposite of what I probably looked like. But that was hardly important now. Much more important for my survival was another kind of impression that I would make.

"How did you reach those feminists?"

"That was Zaza's idea. She made that decision for both of us.

She told them she was threatened with abuse and murder. They took me in at her insistence. She figured we had some chance against the Old Man if we went public with the whole story."

"And did you go public with anything?"

"We didn't. If they do anything today, it's because they were frightened by the break-in into their safe house."

"They won't." The Old Man had evidently threatened them. "And you? Do you always hide behind women? Don't you have any shame?"

"Zaza insisted. At first they didn't want to take me in."

"How did you even think of that . . . safe house of theirs?"

"Zaza planned everything out earlier that day and got their phone number."

"And you just surrendered to her leadership?"

"I had no choice."

"And what exactly did she say when she was asking them for help?"

"I don't know what she said."

He took out a piece of paper and looked at it for a few moments. "She told them you were being chased by mafia heroin dealers and hit men who never give up."

"I didn't know about that."

"That's exactly what she said about the Old Man and his people."

"I'm sorry."

"It was stupid of you to run. And she's even stupider than you."

IX

When we got there, the feminist activists put us up in their safe house, somewhere in Lower Dubrava. It wasn't easy. At first they didn't want to take us in at all. They had a negative opinion of

Zaza and everything she represented. They downright despised me.

Zaza broke into tears.

"I won't survive. I can't survive. I'm the Old Man's property."

That was the key word that stung them like a wasp. That was crucial for their decision, and eventually they let us stay with them.

The house was a spacious two-story building, the ground floor of which was occupied by the offices of their association and the Cake and Cookies Bakery—a project the association set up to employ some of the women who came to them; it was run by two Slavonian women who made various pastries. Upstairs, on the second and third floors, there were abused women who had found refuge because they had either fled their homes or had been left without roofs over their heads. Some had children with them. Most of the women had sought safety from dangerous, abusive husbands.

The activists were unhappy at our arrival from the first moment. Some speculated that we were runaway lovers and thought that we had no business seeking refuge in the house. Zaza tried to explain to the women running the place what kind of danger we were facing. Not all of them could truly grasp the situation, and they didn't understand that the Old Man from the Mountain wasn't just another enraged husband. An argument or two even broke out. In any case, our arrival was a disturbance for all those in the house.

After a long conversation attended by an attorney, Zaza and I were allowed to stay for a short time. They gave us a room together. The first day Zaza didn't want to say a single word to me. She crawled into the bed and cried until evening. And then, as we ate dinner, something snapped in her. Our food had been brought to our room because the feminists didn't want us to be with the women and children in the dining room. We began to talk a little bit and considered our options until we turned in. We knew they were limited, most likely zero. Eventually we turned out the light, and a difficult, sleepless night began for us.

X

Since I had never seen the Old Man from the Mountain before, I had imagined him to be completely different. Hardly anyone had seen him. They said that he hid in various Balkan gorges. They said that he slept in a different location every night. They said that he never parted from his bodyguard of assassins, and that wherever he went an invisible army of sick, lame beggars accompanied him. Some said that no one guarded him, that he was his own best protection. Then they said that he'd been dead for years, if not centuries. And others said that he didn't even exist.

"And so, did you and Zaza end up together?"

"Oh no, Zaza can't stand me, she can't stand the sight of me. She thinks I've destroyed her life with my indiscretion."

"You have."

"Can't someone be forgiven for a blunder?"

"It depends on how bad it is."

"A drunken lie."

"A dirty, low lie, no blunder. A lie that has deprived the Old Man from the Mountain of respect, and deprived the man and woman responsible for this of their lives."

"But she didn't do anything at all."

"She did: she ran away and acted badly later. That's what got her into trouble."

"Can't it be made right somehow?"

"That's a good question."

XI

On the third day of our stay in the safe house, the activists held a meeting. Another argument broke out. We heard everything because they had brought us into an adjoining room and left the door open. We could see them sitting around the table, serious and worried. They evidently wanted us to hear everything, including what they thought about us.

Nevertheless, they kept their composure to a degree and started following their agenda. First the representative of the obese women, someone named Vera, got into it with Marta, the one who was protecting us, about the cakes and pastries, demanding that the bakery leave the house and move somewhere else.

"That's out of the question. The bakery is one of our key projects and we receive considerable financial support for it."

"But those two Slavonian girls don't have to always be shoving those cakes under our noses and tempting us."

"But that's how they try to show their appreciation. If we refuse them, we'll insult them."

"Those of us on the committee of weighty women have decided that they have to go. The members of the committee alone have gained more than fifteen kilograms since the Slavonians have been here."

"Well, show some restraint. Nobody's forcing you to eat so many sweets."

"You're fattening us up on purpose," another one interjected.

"Control yourselves, you're not little children."

"This doesn't concern you, because you don't eat sweets. We can't control ourselves," Vera responded.

The chairwoman looked her up and down scornfully. Marta was one of the eco-feminists. In the house we heard them calling her "Lettuce Head" behind her back.

"Calm down, everyone. We'll tell the women from the bakery not to bring so many cakes and cookies to the offices. From now on that stuff will be in the dining room. Are you happy now?"

"No. The bakery is on its feet; its sales have finally picked up and it's time for it to go independent. At the annual meeting I will request that the budget for next year include financial support for a seamstress shop for portly people. We want that to be our next project, and that's our final word."

"We'll talk about that when the time comes."

Fat Vera, not at all satisfied with the answers she'd received from Marta, withdrew indignantly. The next woman to talk was a gaunt blonde with hair hanging over her brow.

"What are we gonna do with the Serbian singer and her mafioso?"

At the mention of us, all those present started saying basically the same thing: "We don't want them here! They should go! Now! Everyone in the house is uncomfortable because of them."

"Hold on, everyone, please," the chairwoman said, trying to quiet them down somehow.

"That Zaza represents everything we struggle against in this life, not to mention the criminal they're running from," the gaunt woman said. "They have no place here among us."

Marta tried to explain some things to them concerning the Old Man and his business. She spun a story greater and more dangerous than the old Persian tale. But those at the meeting were not impressed.

"We don't care. Who is this Old Man anyway, and what's his line of work?!"

"Drugs, human trafficking, funneling Muslim terrorists into Europe. People say all kinds of things, but no one really knows."

"Is he some Arab? An Iranian?"

"No. But he's a very dangerous and mysterious guy," Marta explained, not without some admiration. "You hear all kinds of things. Nothing reliable, because journalists don't dare write about him. As of late something strange is happening around him. People say he's trying to unite all the Balkan criminal gangs into a single, invincible one. He's something like a Tito of crime."

"Serbian folk singers and mafia!" the blonde exclaimed sarcastically. "That's the only thing that can bring us together!"

The others stayed silent, quietly fretting. Even Vera had become nervous and kept glancing down at her watch.

"They'll stay here until we arrange legal protection for them, and if something happens we'll inform the media about their situation. Up to now we haven't gone public about it, the matter is too sensitive."

"What's been done so far?"

"We informed the police. And they are seriously concerned about the guys who are after them."

That wasn't easy to listen to, not for Zaza or myself. Zaza lowered her head. Ashamed and turned into culprits, we couldn't even look one another in the eye.

And then, at exactly three o'clock, the Old Man's squad burst into the room with their weapons drawn. The assassins and the activists looked at one another for a moment without a word, and then the activists jumped up and there was screaming and yelling. A real battle began. At first the assassins didn't handle themselves well, and the feminists, to their credit, fought like real men. Hoxa and another man immediately grabbed hold of me and Zaza, while Rico and Tafilj started wrestling with the women. The blonde bit Tafilj, and the chairwoman took some pepper spray out of her purse and started spraying the intruders. Then two more women grabbed pepper spray. Vera and her colleague threw themselves on Hoxa and knocked him down. Her colleague grabbed him by the legs and Vera stepped around Hoxa, raised her skirt, and sat down on his face with all her weight.

"Oh God! Uh-huh! Yes! Yes!" the fat woman shouted, wriggling her behind on Hoxa's face.

The battle was short and bitter. People bit and hit at everything. In less than a minute the whole room was full of a cloud of pepper spray. In that chaos we broke free for a moment. We tried to run, but all I saw was Rico grabbing Zaza and knocking her down on the floor. And then someone got me from behind; I felt a sharp pain and lost consciousness.

XII

I woke up in a wooden trunk—awakened by both the noise of it hitting things and my being jostled around in it. At first I thought that they were lowering me into a grave in a coffin, and that they were going to bury me alive. Then they opened the trunk, untied my hands, and took a blindfold off my eyes. I had to get used to the light—and everything was shining all around me.

Was this paradise? No, more likely it was a luxury hotel room. A little later I found out where I was. Definitely not in a grave. Rather, I was in the royal suite in the Opera Hotel, one of the most luxurious and expensive places in the city, which offered a magnificent view of Zagreb—one I would probably never have an opportunity to see again. Neither would I get to go back down to its streets. Nor walk and breathe.

Zaza wasn't in the room.

The room was full of the Old Man's assassins who were tending to their wounds from the battle with the feminists. They had been roughed up, but had done their job. The Old Man had evidently forbidden them from shooting, which was probably part of his deal with the fat woman. I remembered her being tense, nervous, how she kept looking at her watch. We'd been given away; I don't see how they could have found us so quickly otherwise. Of course, it could have been any of them, even Marta. It no longer mattered anymore.

Everything around me looked kind of like a hospital. Tafilj's leg was being bandaged; it was all swollen with bites. Others put wet towels on their faces, trying to recover from the pepper spray. Only Hoxa was sitting in an armchair, somehow sullen and absent. The whole time he licked his lips as if he had something sweet in his mouth.

"After they attacked us, we should have killed them all."

"And just look at him," someone said, and pointed at Hoxa. "Poor thing, he's gone crazy."

Hoxa seemed quite all right to me, just a little out of it.

"And you? What are you looking at? You gave us a bit of work!"

I lowered my head.

A half hour later I was summoned before the Old Man.

XIII

I sensed that the questioning was coming to an end. Our fate would soon be decided.

"So, you say that nothing happened between you and Zaza?"

"Nothing at all."

"If I ask her, will I get the same answer?"

"You should."

"Of course. She wouldn't be acting in her own interest. Only, I don't know why the Old Man should believe either of you."

"Okay, what do I have to do so the Old Man will believe me?"

"That's what I want to know." He gestured with his hand for me to leave. He called Hoxa over and they spoke briefly. He intended to question his assassins and finally Zaza, so they led me out of the room.

The Old Man held council with his men for a long time before they called us back in. I couldn't know what his men had said, or the eyewitnesses that they had brought before him and who had bad-mouthed me from the beginning, and least of all what the beautiful Zaza told him. It was on account of her that I was in the worst trouble of my life. In other circumstances she'd probably have offered him my head on a platter to save her own. I wouldn't blame her; many would have done that, probably most. But now, in order to protect herself she had to protect me. We would live or die together.

On the other hand, a fair amount was also at stake for the Old Man. Our case might have consequences for his organization, for the success of his various business ventures, especially since we'd been abducted in front of numerous witnesses. I doubted whether someone whose existence was shrouded in such a veil of mystery would want that kind of publicity. Especially now, when there was more and more talk about the Old Man fashioning some terrible plan for a great unification.

XIV

The old man from the mountain's coming down to town,
Look out, look out . . .

He put a pistol to my temple. It seemed this was it. Now it was a little too late to become a believer and pray. I closed my eyes and waited.

Boom! And everything would be over.

That was that. *The sound of harpists . . .*

And then there was only a click.

Maybe that was all you heard in your head. But—I kept on thinking. That meant I was alive.

I let twenty or thirty seconds pass and only then did I open my eyes. The Old Man was at the window looking outside, with his back to me.

"I'm sparing your life," he said, "because you didn't do anything. A joke doesn't bother me, the Old Man from the Mountain likes more than anyone to hear a good joke about himself. But yours wasn't any good. And you told an ugly lie, and so you can never work for me again. Too bad. I trusted you and was intending to invite you to an important meeting in a small town, as a delegate, where we're going to talk about important matters—about business, the future, and the great unification. I forgive you for that too. But you remain excommunicated; you won't participate in the making of history. Because the Old Man doesn't forgive lies—so go away. Get lost before I change my mind."

XV

And that's how I was cast out of paradise.

They let me out of the hotel and I strolled down the street once again free. I have no idea what I'll do with my life, but I think everything will be easy from now on. I'm not going back to my old business. I assume I'll never see Zaza again.

I have no plans to go back to the Raspašoj, or to Košmar or Rusvaj. I no longer have friends there.

I'll never attend that meeting, and I don't want to, not even if it's held in Jajce. It doesn't concern me.

Right now I don't know what I'm going to do, but I'm not lost. From down here, on this sidewalk, everything seems easy to me again. What will be will be. Maybe I'll leave Zagreb for a while and travel. I love this city, and I'm sure I'll come back to it.

Though others prepare for trips with lots of stuff, I plan on carrying my provisions in my heart.

A flock of wild ducks.

A flock of swallows.

And one more flock of pigeons.

I'll release them along the way, when it's necessary: the wild ducks and swallows in endless expanses. The pigeons I'll release so I can follow them as I wander through cities, so I won't get lost again. I'll follow the birds.

THE GATES OF HELL

BY RUŽICA GAŠPEROV

Downtown Central

Translated by Will Firth

I have to find out the truth before my cirrhosis deals its final blow. I've been a coward, hiding behind the excuse that the past is over and done with. I've lived for forty years trying to avoid the issue, but now there's nothing more to lose.

The tram stops at Jelačić Square. I get out. The rain has just stopped and the sidewalk is wet. I turn around and look at the main square, a stone's throw from where I spent the most beautiful and most ugly days of my worthless life. Everything has changed, but then again, in a way, everything is still the same.

Here are the buildings I used to look onto from my little subtenant's room on the nights I stayed up studying, when the world was waiting for one young economics student to become its academic citizen. Yes, that's how it was, up until *that* day.

I light a cigarette and draw the smoke deep into my lungs. The doctor ordered me to stop smoking. He banned a lot of other things too, but I don't want to give up my vices in the few months I have left. The smoke burns my throat. I let out a wheezing cough. I throw the cigarette onto the wet sidewalk. It hisses and goes out.

I cross the tram tracks. The statue and the fountain weren't here back then. Two obese women go into the City Coffeehouse. They'll indulge themselves in a moment of rest, a way of breaking up the day between boss and husband, work and home, hammer and anvil. I walk past them. Once I used to ask myself if people could see my monstrosity, but those days have long passed. I left them here four decades ago.

I enter the cathedral. The hushed semidarkness calms my thoughts. I try to pray, but prayer doesn't help. Nothing helps anymore.

"Jesus be praised," the priest greets me quietly.

"Jesus be praised," I reply.

"Would you like to confess?" he inquires with a smirk.

"I guess I would if I knew what to confess. But it's too late now, at any rate," I say, and head down the long aisle toward the exit.

The day has darkened. The colors are ever drabber. A soft rain drizzles down. I walk up to the marketplace. Here I used to do everyday shopping for Elza. Madam Elza. I called her *Madam* but what went on between us was far from dignified and ladylike.

She stood at the door of my room in her silk housedress, a belt tied lightly around her waist. She lifted her arms and took the little comb out of her hair. Her peroxide-blond curls spilled over her shoulders like rubbery tentacles. She came slowly toward the bed and sat down next to me.

"It must be hard being so far from your family," she said.

"I'm used to it."

"I know very well what it's like to be alone," she sighed.

"I study a lot. Time flies," I replied politely, like a good girl.

She caressed my shoulder. I enjoyed that touch after months of separation from all those I loved and who loved me. I didn't move away even when her hand slid down my back and stopped at my waist. She pulled me toward her and I leaned my head on her shoulder. She kissed my hair. I felt safe, and when she began to caress my face, a wave of warmth passed through me. She felt me tremble. She gently took me by the chin and turned my face toward hers. Her lips gently brushed my forehead, and then they glided with little kisses down the ridge of my nose. I shamelessly tore off my clothes, kissed her like I'd never kissed anyone before, let alone afterward, and encouraged her to give me pleasures I didn't know even existed.

"Martin," she said to her husband that evening, "perhaps it would be a good idea for me to cook for our student. I get bored sitting around all day, and making a little more money never hurts."

My mother was happy, my father grumbled a little about the money, and I was spared the horrors of eating at the student cafeteria.

The market is dark and empty. I walk between the stalls. No idea what brought me here. I raise the collar of my coat to try and keep the rain off. Three men stand in the shelter of the eaves. Maybe this isn't the time and place to be going up to people, but I've got nothing to lose anyway. Except this miserable life that's in free fall.

"Do you have a light?" I ask, pulling out a cigarette.

One of them puts his bottle down on the stall and wordlessly produces a lighter.

"I used to live near here, you know," I try again to elicit a response. "Just off the square." I gesture with my cigarette in the direction. "It was a long time ago. I studied here."

"I told ya, bud, this rain ain't gonna stop," one of the men says to the others.

"Nope."

"I'm from Šibenik. It's still summer down on the coast," I try one more time, although it's clear they don't want my company.

"I oughta be off," one of them says, then finishes his beer and puts the bottle in his coat pocket.

I go down the broad, dark stairs toward the square. The chestnut vendor takes a little shovelful of chestnuts out of the fire and wraps them in a sooty cloth. The smell of roasted chestnuts on a fall evening reminds me of Elza.

We sat at the kitchen table eating chestnuts. The weak lightbulb cast a dreary light. Martin's snoring came from the bedroom.

"I can't go on like this. We have to get rid of him," Elza said.

"But . . . but . . . why?"

"I love you. I can't imagine life without you."

"I thought I was just a bit of fun for you," I said, trying to keep some distance.

"Just a bit of fun? I love you more than I've ever loved anyone!" She burst into tears and threw herself into my arms.

That night my insomnia began. I lay in the dark thinking. I mulled over various scenarios, turning them this way and that, and I didn't like any of them. Not in the least. What if Elza wrote to my parents? What did she mean when she said we had to "get rid of" her husband?

I found studying harder and harder, and I came to detest our morning sessions in bed. I tried to avoid Elza. Stealing out of the apartment before she got up, I would spend the days at school and the nights in pubs. I was running low on sleep. I sold some of my textbooks, withdrew into the darkest corner, and drank. Only alcohol would allow me to not push Elza away when she crept into my bed at night.

I hand the vendor a bill and take a paper bag of chestnuts. I walk slowly over the square, eating even more slowly. I'll delay the inevitable for a little while. Only delay it, not avoid it. Elza is waiting for me at the end of it all. That's why I've come back to Zagreb.

The storekeepers are pulling down the shutters and padlocking their stores. The working day is over for many, and the night has begun. The river of people ebbs and flows; some leave for home, others go out looking for a good time. I join the latter. I long for a stiff drink to soothe my mind. Pills don't help anymore if I don't wash them down with something. It's crowded on Cvjetni Square. I find myself a table, with difficulty, and order a double cognac.

Martin used to go away on business from time to time. On those few days, I wouldn't come back sober. I needed more and more alcohol to cope with Elza's touch. The more disgusted I was, the more demanding she became.

"Darling, you know I love you. Why are you so cold toward me?"

I collapsed in the middle of a lecture. There followed first aid, a neurologist, a psychologist, a psychiatrist, and three months in a psychiatric ward. Diagnosis: schizophrenia. Medication and the return to Madam Elza. I recovered under her watchful eye for two weeks, and then she was back in my bed.

I sat at the open window trying to understand what I was reading. The summer heat was at its height. The city groaned in the grip of a heat wave, and people went into hiding or left for somewhere cooler. Elza came into my room. She stood behind me without a word and began to massage my shoulders. I don't know if it was because of the pills or if time had lessened my disgust, but we soon found ourselves writhing on the sheets.

"You're back to your old self again," she told me, gently fondling my breast.

"Something's burning," I said, sniffing the air.

"Jesus Christ!" She sprang up and opened the door.

A cloud of black smoke drifted into the room; the corridor behind it was black. Elza charged into the darkness. I was afraid to run after her, so I lay on the bed and waited. I heard the kitchen window being opened. Elza coughed, and I stayed lying there, trying to fathom what I was going to do with my life. Finally the smoke began to disperse.

The kitchen was ruined, the walls of the apartment were fire-blackened, and I got to see for the first time what Martin's rage looked like.

"Chin-wagging with the neighbors again, I suppose? And our meal? Oh, just let it burn!" Martin shouted.

"That's not true. I was at home."

"How did the damn food turn into a fire then?"

"I put some oil on to heat up and left it for a minute—"

"A minute? I know what a *minute* of yours is like when you go see damn Katica."

"I didn't go to see Katica," Elza said softly.

"Then you were seeing some other chatterbox. And the house? Oh, just let it burn. *Martin will pay for everything. Martin always pays for everything.* Madam strolls the building all day, and Martin works till he drops dead." His cheeks glowed red and he thumped the table with his fist.

"I was in the apartment."

"In the apartment, huh?! What were you doing that was so important that you didn't notice the fire?"

"I was in the bathroom."

"The apartment is burning, and Madam takes a nice bath." Martin reinforced his statement by banging both fists on the table.

"I wasn't in the bath."

"No?"

"No, I was washing that new red underskirt—the one you like so much," Elza said, trying flirtation.

"Washing? You spent three hours washing an underskirt?" he growled, without matching his words with a blow of his fist this time. The thought of the red underskirt had taken the edge off his fury. "And where was missy here, may I ask?" he sneered, turning toward me.

"I was . . . I was sleeping."

"Brilliant!"

The crowd gets denser. Two young women sit down at my table. I signal the waiter, and he brings me another cognac. I take two pills out of my purse and swallow them together with the booze. The meeting with Elza requires several cognacs and several pills. If there will be a meeting at all. I don't know if she's still alive. If she's dead, I will die too, without sorting out the last forty years of my life. I'll die without knowing if I'm a murderer or not.

Martin was away on a business trip. Elza threw off her silk and knelt with one leg on the bed, and all the pictures of soppy embraces came back to me: rouged lips shimmered before my eyes; I heard her husky smoker's voice. And then it simply happened—I jumped up from the bed and started hitting her.

"Get away from me, you repulsive creature!" I yelled, and my hands pounded her all by themselves.

She threw herself on the bed and curled up into a ball. I continued to hit her wherever I could. Later I often replayed that scene in my head. She didn't say a word or let out a single sound. She just lay there like a fetus, protecting her head with her hands, and waiting.

In the morning I felt ashamed and was afraid to leave my

room. What if she reported me to the police? Perhaps she had called Martin? Or the psychiatric hospital?

"Breakfast is on the table. I'm going out," she said from the door. She was buttoned up to the throat, and dark glasses covered most of her face.

That evening I saw what a monster I'd become. One eye was swollen and bloodshot. One lip cut. Her neck—purple. I didn't remember throttling her, and I didn't even want to think about the bruises she must have had all over her body.

"What will you tell Martin?"

"That I fell."

"Just like that? You fell?"

"I fell."

The young women at my table are talking about exams. I listen to them halfheartedly and occasionally sink into memories. One more cognac ought to remedy the situation. I wave to the waiter. Just this one more and I'll head off for Elza's apartment. The pills have begun to take effect and I'm ready to face the memories of that night.

The heat became more bearable as September wore on. Martin was heading out on a business trip, and I was studying like crazy and not understanding much. My head was in a terrible muddle. The medication slowed me down and made me sleepy. Elza was becoming almost aggressive.

As soon as Martin left with his suitcase, she came in and sat on my bed. "Admit it! You're in love with some man."

"I'm not in love with anyone. Can't you see I'm studying?"

"Why are you always trying to avoid me then? Don't you know I cry every night, waiting for you to come home? You're everything to me. Am I asking too much? Just a little attention." She was practically begging now.

I didn't like that tone. I found it disgusting, just like everything else about her. "It's over. I'm leaving soon."

"Don't do that to me, please!" she screamed, and threw herself at my feet. "I'd die without you."

"You'll find a new subtenant. Maybe you'll have more luck with her."

"You're my everything . . . everything," she cried, rubbing her head against my knees.

Something in Elza's devastation turned me on. A tremble ran through my body that I didn't recognize at first, and then it began to go down and down until it stopped in my groin. I didn't want her. Her carnality was repulsive. Her layers of fat and flab made me feel sick. I felt disgusted at myself too. It was because of her that I no longer knew what I wanted. Now I'd make her pay for everything.

I grabbed her by the hair and jerked her face toward me. Tears had soaked her makeup and made it run toward her chin. I stood up and dragged her to the bed. She didn't resist when I kissed her savagely, putting all my fury into that bestial kiss. I threw her onto the crumpled sheets. I was ready now, readier than I had ever been.

The springs of the iron bed squeaked as I ground myself against her. Everything around me was red, sweaty, and smelled of musk. That's how the jasmine smelled in our courtyard. That's how old Matej's goat stank. That's what pleasure looked like—the only pleasure I could still achieve. That's what revenge looked like.

"I love you! I love you, darling!" Elza moaned.

"Shut up, you bitch!" I yelled, and slapped her.

"I love you, I love you, I love you! I know you'll never leave me. We're made for each other," she crooned, one of her lips now bloody.

Suddenly Martin's icy voice came from the door: "I'm gonna kill you! I'm gonna kill you both, you perverted animals!"

"No!" Elza shrieked, covering her flabby breasts with the sheet. "It's not what you think."

I jumped up and tried to grab my dress off the floor. Martin headed toward me.

"Fuckin' dyke, you're gonna burn in hell!" he hissed through clenched teeth, and then raised his fist.

I took a step back and tried to dash past him in the narrow room, but I got caught on a chair leg and stumbled. The chair fell in his path for an instant—long enough for me to lunge at him. He howled like a wild thing as my nails left a bloody trail across his face. Then I pushed him and started hitting. I was young and strong, and fear doubled my strength. He staggered and fell to the floor. I didn't see him hit anything on the way down, but he didn't get up. A fine stream of blood trickled from his head. The puddle on the floor became bigger as I frantically gathered up my clothes. Elza cried loudly as I whipped on my dress.

"Stop blubbering, stupid cow!"

"You've killed him! He's dead!" she shouted through her tears.

"It's your fault, you slut!" I yelled in panic, trying to cast off the blame while pulling on my jean jacket over my creased dress. I slipped shoes on my bare feet, snatched my purse and some coins from the table, and rushed out of the apartment.

I drink one final cognac, pay, and leave. I feel a twinge in my stomach. The diner at the train station is still open. I go in and walk down the stairs, and my hunger leaves me. The air is heavy. It reminds me of that day the apartment caught fire. Everything stinks of burnt oil. A few older folks are sitting at the tables and eating in silence. A young couple at a table in the corner are laughing uncontrollably and drawing something on a piece of paper.

"This is how they should look," the woman says, and chortles again.

"Shouldn't they be a bit freakier?"

"No, this is just great."

I sit down at the table next to theirs. I have to hear some laughter. The waitress comes and recites the menu although everything can be read off the tablecloth. I order Zagreb schnitzel and a beer. The wood-paneled walls make me feel like I'm suffocating. The little signs on them add an edge of queasiness. I drink the beer but leave the meat untouched. I pay and leave.

The clock on the main square shows nine. The right time for a visit. Forty years later. My hand in my pocket squeezes the switchblade and I think: *Should I make Elza pay for what she did to me?* I've been living with the conscience of a murderer for so long that it wouldn't be hard for me to pass judgment on her too. I cross the square and walk along Jurišić Street.

I rushed out of the apartment, ran along Jurišić Street, crossed the square, and turned down Praška Street. My lungs hurt and my head drummed. I tried to remember how much money I had in my purse. Would it be enough for a ticket to Šibenik? What would I do when I got there? Where could I hide? The police would find me. Elza would tell them everything. Or maybe she wouldn't? Did she love me so much that she'd take the blame herself?

I ran through Zrinjevac Park. The shade tempered my fear. It was quiet, perhaps too quiet. No one to be seen anywhere. If the police were on my trail, they'd immediately notice a woman running. I left the sidewalk and walked quickly over the lawn and through the dying ornamental bushes, went around the pavilion, and continued on to the railroad station. A train was leaving at eleven.

Once home, I told my father I'd passed all my exams and had a month's vacation. He believed me, and I spent days feverishly leafing through all the papers looking for news of a fatality on Jurišić Street. I wrote to Elza, but a reply never came.

I arrive in front of the building where all the highs and horrors of my youth took place—experiences I kept reliving again and again, year after year, feeling there would be no end to it, until my diagnosis came and limited my shameful life to several weeks, or months at best. The realization that everything will soon be over has brought me here to this building.

In place of the old five-story building with its massive wooden door that was locked with its rusty handle at ten in the evening, there now stands a seven-story, steel-and-glass edifice, threatening and cold, with a large opening instead of the former vestibule.

I go in and stand at the doorman's booth which is protected by thick greenish glass. A young man sits reading a book under the neon light. He looks up, brings his mouth to the microphone, and says in a metallic voice through the speaker: "Good evening. How can I help you?"

I ask him if Elza and Martin Heigl still live at this address, hoping that the tenants are perhaps still the same even if the building's exterior has changed.

"I'm sorry, madam, there are only commercial tenants here," he says mechanically, and picks up his book from the desk again.

"But where are the old tenants? Do you know where they moved to? And when was this built?" I bombard him, as a sense of panic starts to creep over me. It seems all my plans of the last few days have been futile.

The doorman puts his book down on the desk again, reluctantly gets up, and comes out of the booth. He stands next to me in that passageway that leads to the rear courtyard, where there were once wooden sheds, and now a nicely paved parking lot. He tells me about a fire that destroyed much of the building forty years ago, and also about an old lady who often drops in at the beginning of his night shift, recounts the past with sadness in her voice, and talks with even more sadness about her bleak life in a high-rise building on the city's outskirts.

"What's her name?" I ask.

"Katica. She's the one who told me about the fire. But you know, that all happened long before I was born," he says with a smile.

"Has she mentioned Elza? Or Martin? You don't have Katica's address by chance, do you?" I desperately ask.

"Madam, honestly, I don't know anything about Katica either. For me, she's just a crazy old lady who comes here, stands where you're standing now, and talks to herself."

"What else does she talk about?"

"Oh, nonsense. She talks nonsense, so I don't make any effort to listen."

"But surely you picked up something?"

"Well, yes, she's constantly going on about the fire, and about her friend whose apartment she heard an argument in, and about some student, and then about the fire again. She cries a little for that friend who died in the fire. And then she's gone. That's all I know."

"How did the fire start?" My voice is beginning to tremble.

"I'm not sure. In any case, it was after a nasty fight the couple who died in the fire had. The old lady claims it was arson and suspects her friend's husband. I find it all a bit far-fetched, but I don't want to start arguing with her. You know what old ladies are like—they're just waiting to leech onto someone."

"Did the whole building burn down?"

"No, but it was so dilapidated that the council decided to demolish it and rebuild. And the new building fits in just fine among the older ones, don't you think?"

"Yes, I guess so," I say, feeling a shudder come over me, and then I realize I might be able to persuade him to show me around. "Could you perhaps let me see some of the building from the inside? I'm an architect, and this is a fascinating example for me. I'm currently working on the interpolation of a building in the old town of Šibenik."

"I'm not actually allowed to, but there's nothing to steal anyway. The offices are all locked," he tells me abruptly, as if he's just made one of life's difficult decisions.

I follow him into the building. From somewhere in the distance there comes the humming of vacuum cleaners.

"Let's take the elevator to the fifth floor. The cleaning ladies have finished up there. It would be best if they didn't see us," he says almost apologetically as we get into the elevator.

Aluminum banisters and glass. As we're rising, my stomach cramps up, and my head tries to sort out everything he's told me. The elevator comes to a halt with a metallic *clack* and we get out. The landing has been enlarged and the entrances of the four apartments are gone. In their place I see a wood and iron desk and a corridor stretching off to the left and right. Neon lights reflect off the smooth imitation-stone flooring.

I turn right and go past a row of closed glass doors. Behind them is darkness. My heels tap in time with my heart. My palms are sweaty and I clench my fists spasmodically. I feel my fingernails digging into my palms as I try to work out where my room used to be. Perhaps where that wooden door is ajar—the only one in this silent realm of glass, neon, and metal.

"Why is that door open?" I ask the doorman.

"That's the lumber room. We call the door the Gates of Hell because, however you shut and lock it, it always opens again by itself. Something's probably wrong with the lock, but since it's not an essential room no one's ever had it repaired."

I look into the dark streak grinning at me from behind the slightly open door. I sense this was my student room where Elza used to visit me whenever Martin was away. Yes, this is it. I am drawn to the door. Elza and Martin's fight with slapping and crying echoes in my head. I hear someone shouting, "Call the fire department!" and the doorman yelling after me: "Madam, you can't go in there!"

I step in through the noise. The door sucks me in. I close my eyes for a moment, and when I open them again I see Elza's round face right above mine. I'm lying in bed, lit up in the morning sun. Elza kisses me tenderly.

"I love you too, Elza," I whisper.

PART II

Knocking on the Neighbor's Door

HORSE KILLER

BY MIMA SIMIĆ
Dubrava

Translated by Ellen Elias-Bursac

Behind the well-worn counter of the hotel's front desk and the beehive of key cubbies, there is a small office. The furniture—a green-surfaced particleboard desk, a classroom chair that survived the eighties, a rickety cupboard spilling loose-leaf binders, and a hotel safe with a combination lock. The walls are yellow with smoke and decades of breathing. There are no pictures on the walls, only a little window looking out on the hotel's neon sign. The only item at the hotel that keeps pace with the times—the fixed surveillance camera aimed at the safe at a diagonal tilt from the room's upper corner. It records this frame twenty-four-seven; the videos are stored on the camera's memory card, and every forty-eight hours the new material overrides the old. At least that's how it has been for the last few months, since I've been living here and working off my room fee by sitting at the front desk, repairing this and that around the hotel, changing faucet washers and shower heads, fuses and lightbulbs, fishing costume jewelry out of the drains, tidying the rooms, and distributing the threadbare bed linens and coarse pink sheets of toilet paper that are only manufactured for the nameless hotels on the edge of town. A surveillance camera and a safe? In hotels like this, all a person is likely to find in the safe is the owner's farewell letter or a roll of three-ply toilet paper. This hotel is so unremarkable (no contract and negotiations, no prying neighbors) that it's better living here than renting an apartment. A hotel with a black hole where the stars should be, with one of those cheap neon signs that either burns out regularly or shines with gaps, spelling *HOT* or *HOE*, and promising the nonexistent tourists a wild fling and take-home syphilis. It has no restaurant, no kiosk, not even a café—for years you can nonexist here, below the radar, off the grid. It must be thanks to the long-suffering tenants that the hotel limps along as it does, against all reason. In fact, it seems to be living its life quite solidly; like a benign growth with a very resilient system of recharging.

Just as during the war, sometimes there is no running water and hot water is a rarity. The water pressure in the pipes is best in the dead of night when the sinks and toilets everywhere are dormant. But people quickly realize there's no point in waiting. In stale dreams and under a brown synthetic blanket, one's body comes to a simmer countless times before dawn. And there's no ventilation to cool the room or at least cocoon the sleeper with its hum. The thin walls leave the sleeper enveloped in sounds, like those paper partitions in the one-story houses in Japanese movies behind which neither body nor voice can hide. You put your ear to the front desk, as to a train track, and you know what's up at the hotel. You know even more if you don't sleep. Who has escaped a spouse, children, family, debt collectors, or the police. Who steals, who begs, who sleeps around, who gives the beatings and who gets them, who stares all day long at the ceiling, at the wall, at the warped parquet floor, and forgets to breathe. Who snores, who paces, who talks, who cries out in their sleep. When you don't sleep, the foot on the gas pedal gets heavy, traffic lights change a little slower, and the signals leap out at you just a second too late, but life is clearer and louder than at any IMAX movie. And it stinks, insufferably.

Midnight passed hours ago, and no longer can the voices be heard through the walls or the water in the pipes. In the small room behind the front desk the air is thick and stale so I breathe thriftily like a diver. For a moment I hold my breath and think I am in tomblike silence. But tomblike silence is not the absence of sound. It is a fabric of peripheral sounds at a frequency beyond the range of the human ear. Wormwood crackling in the oak of a coffin lowered into a concrete chamber. Grubs squirming in rotting flesh. A cobweb undulating in the nooks of a grave, mold surging. These sounds do exist somewhere, someone hears them. There is no absolute silence, not in these black holes nor in the five-star ones. All it takes is putting an ear to them.

I push the chair noiselessly over to the safe, place it squarely in the frame. I sit and look up at the dark protruding eye of the camera. And then down again at my hands. There was no water last night, despite the apocalyptic flood still raging outside, or maybe because of it. My hands stay in my pockets; edging my fingernails is a crust of blood and in the circular furrows on my fingertips, the pixie dust of gunpowder. From my pocket I finally take the revolver, shift it from hand-to-hand; it's army issue and sits well in my palm. It has survived the Foreign Legion, wars—both intercontinental and local—urban and rural confrontations, hand-to-hand; and over picket fences, break-ins into full houses and empty flats, holdups of bookmakers and gas stations. The grip is grooved. Scars from wars, or notches. It has the heft of a loaded gun, but when I cock it and pull the trigger, it comes up empty. As if after a protracted, serious illness, it has nothing left to retch. No fire or pain, just sound. I look up at the camera again, check to see the red light pulsing, pull a breath up from the depth of my diaphragm, and for the first time in the story, I speak.

The plan was drawn up long ago; all that was needed was

the flick of the flag in the air, the signal. And that, as it happened, came from above. For several weeks, more frenzied than ever, the media had been warning of impending climate change, cyclones of hot air to the north and the shrinking of the polar ice cap. Screaming headlines, white-hot weather maps, professional analyses, and caricatures in which the sun, deep in the polar realms, rests between the sweaty buttocks of glaciers. And this time it was really happening. In record-breaking heat, the permafrost crackled and gasses that had been trapped there for centuries flashed and snapped like fireworks. Boundless curtains of dust blazed on all sides and hundreds of meters up in the air they swirled again into clouds. Dense and toothed. Launched by winds and pressures, monitored closely by satellites, they inched southward in fleets. Along the way they sucked in the skeletons of birds, airplane debris, meteor dust, until finally, dingy and greasy from the journey, they ran aground on the city skyscrapers, blackening a stretch of sky from the massive shopping complex in the west all the way to the army hospital in the eastern part of town. They sizzled with electricity, spewing sparks. And, overnight, the climatic circuit panel blew its winter fuse and summer plugged in.

It hit on a Sunday morning like an eighteen-wheeler, its hot breath sweeping people from the street, battering windows and doors. Bears at the zoo reeled on the verge of cardiac arrest around the empty wading pools, their biological clocks shot. Bees collided, befuddled, and pelted people and houses like living hail. The Sava shivered in its riverbed and the window panes on the office buildings vibrated even when there was no wind. Within a few days, amidst the crisis of emergency interventions and grimmer and grimmer forecasts, hope spilled over into panic and people rushed to the gas stations, filled their tanks and cans, stuffed photographs into plastic bags. The traffic jams on the roads leaving the city grew wider and longer, more anxious, and at night there were cascades of light coursing out of town. No one had expected the end of the world quite so soon, but people adapted quickly, they were resourceful. Big and small businessmen left, one by one and in groups, in small cars and in large cars. Their own, borrowed, stolen. Family homes with front yards that had been cultivated for years were abandoned, and along the way the yards of others were invaded. People jumped to aid their neighbors in distress, proffered helping hands, and stabbed each other with knives and screwdrivers. The shelves and display cases in the grocery stores were emptied. Just in case, signs were posted announcing inventory, collective vacations, a speedy return. They shut down restaurants, striptease bars, night clubs, and cafés—all but one. The one to which the Horse had been coming every day for months.

Right from his first day there he found his spot. A booth in the shadows from which he could survey the entire place, all the tables, the doors to both restrooms, and the bar. His own little piece of dark from which he scanned the waitresses and the guests. When he wasn't there, the booth stood empty, on indefinite reserve. Why they dubbed Pero Vidović the Horse, I don't know. Maybe because he looked like one: widespread eyes, broad nostrils, a long deadpan face, long powerful legs. Where I'm from, people used to say a person is stupid as a horse, but I'm from Dalmatia while he's from Bosanska Posavina and who knows how smart the horses are there and what properties the local people ascribe to them. Maybe his father was the one who gave him the nickname in childhood out of faux tenderness, for putting up with his beatings. Or it was his best friend, or his brother, as they raced each other down a dusty street, never guessing he would later choose a path such a noble animal has never yet trod.

All the tram lines lead there. By day this is where they turn around and at night, their terminus. When the state of emergency was declared it became the tram dump. On the last tram, displaying the *Out of Service* sign instead of a destination, the driver and I ride alone to the Dubrava terminus. The blue awning of Voljeni Vukovar puffs noisily in the wind, brown, wicker chairs stacked one on top of the other shiver, bound with steel bands to the iron railing. So they won't blow away or be carried off by someone on the run. A gust of wind opens the door. Inside the air is stale and warm. The silence seems temporary, like an awkward lull in a conversation or a gap in a radio broadcast.

I go up to the bar, mellow, as if this is the most normal of days. The waitress is not expecting any more customers. Surprised, she halts midstep, forgetting to say hello. I sit at the bar and her surprise quickly melts into indifference. She asks what I'll have. I order a whiskey, or anything with the equivalent alcohol content. Some treat their insomnia with it, but mine, deeper than the Arctic Ocean, drinks it readily like rainwater. As if we're at a firing range, the waitress lines them up and I take them down. Exhaustion is flight. Exhaustion frees. The feeling is correct, accurate, and truthful. From a distant corner of the bar a gaze slices into me. I do not have to turn, I know Pero the Horse is there.

In elementary school, with a name like that, he must have been sitting at the back of the class with his friends teasing him, maybe even the teacher. Maybe she was the one who gave it to him for his efforts in, say, math. The Horse would have to stay after class as punishment and write out countless fractions on the board, snorting with helplessness and pawing at the linoleum with his school slippers. That is what Pero the Horse would have been like in elementary school. As commander at the Donja Mahala camp, however, Pero the Horse is a much more fucked-up character.

I turn to the side and block his view with my elbow. With the damp bottom of my glass I press one more Olympic circle onto the headline of the newspaper in front of me, blurring the big print and bloated, pixelated profile into a leaden blob. The paper is from last week, but the news is fresh. Raped, murdered, buried, who knows in what order. The body, it says, was washed out of a shallow grave in the Sljeme hills by a freshet of rapidly melting snow. This is followed by a catalog of injuries and speculation about the tools used to inflict them. Pliers, handcuffs, a razor, a bottle, cables, a rifle butt. The identity of the woman is still unknown. There is a search on for the perpetrator, or there will be once all this is over.

Pero Vidović a.k.a. the Horse first sat with me and my mother at Jelačić Square in Zagreb in the midnineties; the war had only just ended for us down on the coast. As if we were celebrating, we sat on the sunny terrace of a café and ate cream pie in the shade of the tail of the Jelačić statue of a horse. We were laughing (there is at least one photograph that shows this), he had this accent that made everything sillier, even when it wasn't funny at all. As we parted he pressed my hand firmly. He may have even given me money, I can't remember anymore. Mother laughed and waved, she was in love, for real, for the first time ever—she had met Pero's brother in the war. She was a doctor at the front, he a commander or a deputy commander—anyway, something important, high up, and powerful. There was love galore.

Through the misted-up front window of the bar, the awning is now barely visible. Dark blue, it merges with the gray air dense with droplets of water that seem, after days of anticipation, about to explode. And sure enough, like an orchestra of rocket launchers, the sky bellows, cracks open wide, and with the grunts of a sumo wrestler the rain sluices down onto the pavement, the ground, the treetops, and the broad Voljeni Vukovar awning. Leaves and plastic bottles swirl on all sides across the empty multilane road. There used to be summer storms like this in Zadar. Everything would cascade down onto the ground for fifteen minutes, all the demons would slosh down their buckets. That was the right moment to leap into the sea. Water is the best cure for water, and saltwater heals all wounds.

The second time we sat with Pero the Horse and drank and ate and laughed was in the late 1990s at the seaside. The Horse was spending the summer in Kožino near Zadar with his mistress. His wife was in Posavina, in Orašje, with the kids. The Horse and his mistress (whose name and nickname I cannot recall for the life of me, but I do know she was Miss Slavonia and Baranya and in the moonlight in the shadow cast by the Venetian blinds she looked like Kim Basinger in *9 1/2 Weeks*) had rented an apartment in Kožina on the cheap from Mother's friends Emila and Zlatko, a comfortably retired middle-aged couple. Otherwise frugal to a fault, they always welcomed Mother with unfeigned glee. Emila would bring out a platter with store-bought prosciutto and cheese, and Zlatko would produce his most recent blood and urine test results and the shivery printouts from his EKG. With passion they would pore over his physical and psychological symptoms, the side effects of the medications, prescribed and otherwise, and with horror and thrill would soak up Mother's diagnoses and advice. So Mother's friends could always summer there at a discount, even if Emila and Zlatko did not approve of their lifestyle.

That summer the sun was closer than ever to Kožina. My brother and I rowed out in an inflatable rubber boat, far from conversation and all shelter, on that vast sea mirror that infinitely multiplied the sun's rays which bounced off us. Having long since lost touch with the sea, my skin blossomed instantly with blisters. Pero the Horse lounged in the shade in fatigues, unshaven and bare to the waist, smoked, and laughed. He said I should put yogurt on it, but Emila and Zlatko only had processed cheese which was already sweating profusely in the sun and was no longer good for anything. It was Sunday and the nearest grocery store was kilometers away, but Pero the Horse said, "I'll go." He came back an hour later with a liter of fruit juice, melting chocolate, and two cups of yogurt. We sat in the garden, on the carpet of dry pine needles smelling of healing herbs. He scooped the yogurt from the cups and carefully slathered it over my shoulders and back. Tenderly. He didn't spill a drop. The fried skin soaked in the yogurt with the desperation of someone drowning and after a time my body finally relaxed. Maybe I would even sleep. While the sun smoldered over the horizon, the Horse once more laughed from the bottom of his throat, patted me on the thigh, and said, "There, there. There are plenty of worse things in life."

After everyone had gone to bed, the Horse and Zlatko stayed out late that night, sitting on the veranda drinking wine. The Horse talked about fighting in Corsica, in Rwanda, in Ghana, in Chad. He showed Zlatko his medal for valor which he had earned before he was twenty. Zlatko, who knew more about disease than most doctors and more about the sea than most sailors, was speechless for the first time ever. He too had dreamed as a boy of the Legion, the cruel and exalted choreography of boot camp, the powerful, bare landscapes, the salty deserts, the boys from all sides of the world joined by a superhuman bond, a brotherhood that, born in jousting, hand-to-hand, sprouts like an oasis in an adrenaline downpour.

Beyond the steamed-up Voljeni Vukovar windowpane a fleet of stranded buses blinks in panic. The waitress buzzes once more between me and him, her hair pulled back, her face taut from exhaustion. Just as I am about to order another round I see the Horse get up and come over to pay. I watch him live and near for the first time in fifteen years. The time has added nothing to him except a few gray hairs and wrinkles and some new scars. I glance back at the newspaper, but he is standing uncomfortably close and this time he zooms in on my face. I do not look back at him, but I also do not move, as I do not care. He is some ten years older than me, but the years have not pampered me and this difference, which used to be obvious, is no longer visible.

"Have we met before?" he asks.

I shake my head.

He doesn't believe me but he can't remember where he knows me from, and clearly he doesn't much care. He shrugs ever so slightly and gives up. I am no threat. He is taller than me by at least a head, and broader. Now when he stands up straight right next to me I see his fatigues are hanging at a slant. As if something is dragging them down, as if his pelvis bone healed crooked. As if his pocket is full of rocks, or iron. He pays the waitress for the drinks and pinches her behind, absently, out of habit. She doesn't even seem to notice. The sky is still exploding outside, the rain continues to pound oxen-like into the ground, foaming at the storm drains. Clouds heavy as a mound of peed-on pillows smother the light. There is some hopeless justice, I think, in the fact that the darkness has finally spread over the entire city (even the luxury residences up in the Sljeme hills, the glassed-in embassies with pools, the painters' studios uptown), and not just over this out-of-tune neighborhood, cut off from the world by an arc of tram tracks.

Idly, as if in a slow-motion film sequence, the Horse moves

toward the door. I pull the largest bill out of my pocket and lay it on the counter, not waiting for my change. It's time.

Pero the Horse surfaced in my life for the third time while we were smashing glasses, breaking dishes, and toasting at my brother's wedding. In an interlude between the drinking and the sobering up, a local paper made its way into my hands and in it, an item about an armed robbery at the home of Emila and Zlato Š. in Kožina. Two masked robbers tied up the elderly couple, silenced them by taping their mouths shut, and then beat them unconscious. They stole some gold jewelry and a few thousand kuna in cash. They were captured on film by a surveillance camera at a nearby gas station where they stopped after the robbery to fill up. The judge said the savagery and apathy during the commission of the crime were aggravating factors for the perpetrators, with the mitigating factor that the older of the two, Marco Vincetić, confessed to the crime, had no previous convictions, and had fought in the Homeland War.

"It was strange to see Marco Vincetić (36) from Orašje in Bosnia and Herzegovina," wrote the *Slobodna Dalmacija* reporter, "in the courtroom as a defendant. He had spent his life, after all, fighting crime. He was in the Foreign Legion, fought in Corsica, Rwanda, Ghana, and Chad, where he was decorated for valor. During the Homeland War he was deputy chief of the Central Bosnian military police, and, as far as the records show, has no previous convictions."

Pero the Horse was not partial to the written word, but during his rare free time in Corsica he had developed a taste for adventure novels, using the French he had mastered over three years. In them, poor but noble young men with exotic names defied destiny and a superior enemy with their sheer tenacity and fighting spirit (and plenty of gall), finally conquering the riches of the world and the heart of the woman they most desired. The Horse figured out in Corsica that "Marco" or "Victor" would have a far better chance with the French and Italian ladies, and the same, he found, applied to the border police.

With his weak heart, Zlatko nearly died during the armed robbery. Emila spent three months in a psychiatric ward. Mother testified in court about Marco Vincetić's otherwise sterling character, and after the wedding she wrapped the shattered glass and gnawed bones in that issue of *Slobodna Dalmacija.*

Pero the Horse pulls the door open, and as he goes out the filthy torrent gushes into the place, lapping at his boots. He shakes them and steps out onto the wet square of green indoor-outdoor carpeting in front of the café. I catch the door and lurch through, before it closes again. I stand under the awning, a few steps from him. The only car in the parking lot is a big black Audi. A flash of orange headlights and the click of unlocking. It's his. Again he eyes me, but less curious. This time he only asks if I need a ride. I nod. We run through the downpour to the car; I open the door and slip into the passenger seat. The leather upholstery squeals as I sit. He starts the motor, and I point in the direction of Maksimir while fastening my seat belt. The Horse ignores his and the beeping and the red light on the dash. Because of the beeping, the gale-force wind, and the thick stream of rain on the windshield, I hear the question only when he has asked it a third time.

"Got anyone?"

I know he is no poet or all that metaphysical and that Pero the Horse wants to know whether I am fucking anyone, but his question gets me thinking.

After a moment of silence I admit to him that, no, I do not. That I've got absolutely no one left. The Horse grins, turns off the main street, drives away along a narrow, washed-out road, down to the edge of a wooded area. The car bounces, the tires spray and slip. He finally parks in the mud somewhere, while all around us branches are whipping and treetops are swaying. He rests his hand on my shoulder in consolation. My skin is burning from summer and lack of sleep, his palm is soft and cool. It smells of yogurt. He drops his hand to my thigh. He runs his palm over my pants and murmurs compliments. They sound unnatural, almost like curses. He leans over to me, takes me by the head, and sticks his tongue into my mouth.

When Pero Vidović and his fellow fighter Mato broke into the house of a local teacher in Orašje in May 1992, the Horse showed her his revolver, stabbed his knife into the table, and ordered her to take off her clothes. When she refused, she got a few slaps and they did the job themselves. They spent the whole night taking it out on her. They raped her, beat her, forced her to wash herself, and then did it all again. Yanking a whole lock of hair from her scalp, the Horse demanded that she tell him how exciting this was for her.

I lift his T-shirt and unbuckle his belt. I pull his pants down his thighs, past his knees. He takes my head and pushes it toward his crotch. He grabs me by the hair and steers me firmly toward his prick. I run my hands down his naked thighs and finally I feel it—hard. Rigid and cold. Pero the Horse shuts his eyes, his mouth twisted in a grimace of pleasure and scorn, the rain splattering the hood of the car, and the whole living world at the nearby zoo bellowing and howling. The Horse does not see me pull it out of his pants. He does not hear when I cock it. He still notices nothing when I rest the barrel on his right knee. But when I pull the trigger and his kneecap shatters, Pero the Horse snorts and writhes. And screams and screams and screams.

At the camp in Donja Mahala people knew what was what. Pero Vidović the Horse, the camp commander, was very experienced by the age of twenty-five; he had learned from the finest world warriors, he had saved whole companies of lives in Africa and many times they saved his. He learned how to shove a pipe down someone's throat and run the water through him for hours while still keeping him alive. He knew tricks with a cassette-player power cord that would stop you cold; he could tie a person up using hardly more than three feet of cable and then beat him to death with the end. In Donja Mahala, in Mirza's shed, he joined what should not be joined—when he knocked a guy to the ground with a water bottle and it occurred to him, as the man lay there, that he could staple the man's fingers to his ears. While the man's blood poured into his eyes and onto the ground, he pleaded with the Horse to kill him, and the Horse flogged him with his belt and stamped on him with his new boots.

Barefoot, only in his underwear, his knee smashed, Pero the Horse staggers through the mud and howls. I am several steps behind, cocking the revolver and driving him along with it toward the woods. He stumbles, I am walking on water. If you don't sleep, your reflexes fail when you drive and you often slam on the brakes too late, but all your chakras are blooming. And you see everything that was, is, and always will be. When you don't sleep, only then are you really awake. The rain drums on my temples and pours into my eyes, but it doesn't bother me. The water is clear and bright like the sea at Zadar during those few years after the war before the tourists discovered it again. Then we went diving more, and deeper than ever before, with no masks or snorkels, we were fish for those few years of freedom.

Pero the Horse trips and falls and gets up and walks through puddles, over rises and soggy leaves. He falls into the mud and leaves pools of blood behind him which I step around. He comes to the edge of a bog. Because of his leg he can't cross it. His boxers are torn, bloody, and mud-streaked. His face is unnaturally pale, his throat hoarse from screaming. He tries for a foothold for his good leg, but he slips on the edge and sinks into the muck up to his knee. Below are roots and branches, inextricable forest cables. The water is rising, and where the bog is now there will soon be a lake. I look up at the deranged sky and ask myself again, just in case, whether I've got anyone.

I take the stapler out of my pocket.

With my hand in my pocket pressing against the revolver, I walk all night to the hotel. Along the empty road, for kilometers, there are no vehicles. The houses cast light seldom and shakily, as if expiring. The rain does not let up even for a second, a watery curtain after the last act of the play. I enter the hotel quietly, as if anyone cares. I unlock the small room behind the front desk, push the chair over by the safe, place myself squarely in the frame. I shift the revolver from hand to hand. It fits me like a glove. How did that slogan go? *Maybe she's born with it.*

Through the little window the red neon letters blink: *HEL.*

IT ALL HAPPENED SO FAST

BY ROBERT PERISIC

Črnomerec

Translated by Stephen M. Dickey

I tossed my bags into the room. Sat down on the bed, lit a cigarette. Surprisingly, it hadn't changed at all in the last two and a half months.

I loved that room in a way, probably because of the price, though objectively speaking it was a tight little room on the ground floor that had once been a kitchen. A faucet came out of the wall above the bed. Above the faucet there was a wall cabinet. I slept where the sink used to be. I couldn't spend much time there without becoming antsy or claustrophobic.

I went up to the third floor of the building, but no one was there. Not everyone had left, had they?

After thinking and listening for a bit I went off toward Črnomerec. To Blanka and her roommates; there was always something going on there.

As I crossed the tracks by the Pliva pharmaceutical factory, the siren sounded.

When I finally made it to Blanka's, all the blinds were down. I knocked. Tapped on the dusty window. Nothing.

There was nothing to do but go down Ilica Street to the center. Darko was now living near Britanski Square—I would go there. Everyone else was going in the opposite direction—I didn't know why.

On my left was the Yugoslav National Army barracks. It seemed empty. No sentries were visible. Nevertheless I crossed over to the other side of the street.

I walked and cast glances at the barracks: for a moment I caught sight of a muzzle poking out, reflecting the sunlight. I thought about going into a café—there was the Ace Café-Bar in the recessed ground floor of the long building, in the shadows behind columns of concrete that supported balconies above. As I walked over to go inside, I saw that behind each column there was a member of the National Guard hiding with a Kalashnikov.

Aha, I was walking along the front line.

"Get out of here!" one of the guardsmen bellowed.

I kept going. To the left, the barracks; to the right, the guardsmen, behind the columns, a long, level path. I didn't think of running and disturbing the stillness. You could hear birds chirping in the line of trees in the barracks. I kept walking as if I hadn't seen the guardsmen. They're only keeping one another in check, I told myself.

I just walked. I walked and nothing happened. Everything was calm, and I had to maintain that calm, walking *click-clack*. I was a little surprised, mostly by the silence in my head in which I heard my own steps as I walked *click-clack* in my old shoes which wouldn't have been bad for tap dancing.

And maybe they were tap shoes, I thought, I bought them at a flea market—*click-clack*—and what do the people know there?

When I made it past the barracks I felt great relief. As if I'd put the whole war behind me. Then, after another two or three hundred meters, I was stopped by the police.

"Where are *you* going?!"

I wiped the sweat from my brow. "Into town."

"No you're not!"

"But I need to go into town."

I stood there as if I believed he was going to let me pass anyway.

"You can't. Are you deaf?!"

"So where can I go if I can't go there?"

I had to get into town, I had to get ahold of someone, otherwise I would go crazy in my little kitchen. Besides, getting back home wasn't going to be simple.

The policemen were probably protecting some bigwig, because what was on the other side of them couldn't have been worse that what was behind me.

"So where will I go now?"

"Over there there's a shelter. Didn't you hear the sirens?!" the policeman said, angry that I wasn't afraid of him.

I found the shelter and took a look around. A cellar. Iron bunk beds. Bad air. Bad light. Children's voices. Then I had a smoke in the doorway. I recognized someone I knew; I didn't know him well, but his was the first familiar face I'd seen since I got there. So I went up to him as if he were an old friend. He was wearing John Lennon sunglasses, I would see him in bars on Vrhovec Street, where people listened to Can and Amon Düül, kraut-rock. After some small talk, I said: "C'mon, let's go to your place and watch some TV until the emergency is over!"

He didn't want to; he said he lived with his parents. He moved away from me a little.

The emergency sirens lasted a very long time. I ran out of cigarettes and started looking for the guy with the John Lennon sunglasses. He'd disappeared. I went around the shelter trying to bum one. From mothers with children. They were polite.

As soon as the all-clear sounded, I kept going toward Britanski Square.

At Darko's I pressed the doorbell. It was silent.

I kept walking down Ilica Street, and bought some cigarettes along the way. The occasional civilian looked straight ahead. I sought their gazes. Nothing doing.

Uniformed men were watching everywhere, their gazes stretched out into the distance.

I went on, *click-clack*. It occurred to me that my shoes weren't good for war at all.

I finally made it to the center of town. It was like nighttime as far as the number of people was concerned. I made it to the Cinema Club and saw that its windows were boarded up. They had closed too?

"*Wild, wild horses, couldn't drag me away . . .*" The music frightened me when I opened the door. After a while I realized that the boards over the windows were for the blackouts.

There were about fifteen people inside. I looked at them eagerly. Half of them were armed. The other half were druggies. They were sitting as they always did, which gave me a feeling of security. Nothing was new for the junkies; their battle was always the same.

There was a pool game going on. Someone broke the balls with a powerful shot.

But there wasn't anyone for me to talk to.

I ordered an absinthe and smoked at the bar.

One of the druggies came up to me and said: "Need something, buddy?"

"I've got all I need," I responded.

I drank a second absinthe, waited, and smoked. The smoke wafted through the light of the bar.

As the windows were boarded up, there was no way of knowing whether it was day or night, what time it was, or what was going on in the world outside. You were rocked gently, like being below deck on a ship. The Cinema Club was a long ground-floor barracks, but I felt as if we were somewhere deeper below.

I continually wavered between another absinthe and getting up and leaving.

I needed to go, but something kept me from it.

Then there was the serpentine sound from above once again: the air-raid warning. That meant the trolleys and buses would stop running. I decided to wait a bit longer. Two months ago this was the "in" place for the alternative crowd. People should have been arriving right about now. *Theater people, musicians, barroom philosophers—where are you now?*

I went to the door, peered outside, and saw that it was now dark out.

I went back to my seat.

There were five kilometers between me and my little room, *click-clack*. Every so often there were gunshots—sometimes a single one, sometimes a burst. They could be heard inside through the boards, like staccato farting. I swallowed a stress pill; I had some of those.

The junkies were simmering here and there around the tables: each one was sitting with his legs stretched out, not looking at anyone. Their cigarettes burned down slowly between their fingers. A few guardsmen were playing pool under a funnel lamp. One of them went up to the bar to ask for another token, and the bartender disappeared somewhere to get one.

"Do you work here?"

"No."

He drummed his fingers on the bar. He looked at me as if he were wondering what I was doing here if I didn't.

Then the bartender appeared from the back room and gave him the token.

When Darko came in, it was like the coming of the Messiah.

"Where've you been, man?!" I asked.

"Iggy!" he shouted.

He looked me over as if looking at a monument. He said: "Man, I can't believe I ran into someone I know!"

"You too, huh?"

After we patted each other on the shoulder, we sat down at a table. "What's going on?" we asked in unison.

"I signed up for the Croatian Defense Forces," Darko said.

"Really?"

"Today!" he said, opening his eyes wide and nodding.

"Aha," I said, not sure what to say.

"What the hell . . ."

"Well . . . right."

"I had to," he said. "I was watching television and . . ."

"I know . . ."

Ten or so days ago I was on an island on the coast watching television, terrible news, and said, "I'm going to join up!" But then my mother attacked me with her artillery. She's a very difficult person, I can't deal with her.

Darko said: "They told me they'd call me up when they get weapons."

"They don't have any?"

"No!" he said, staring in front of himself.

"Hmm." All things considered, that was pretty worrisome. But maybe not for him at the moment.

"What do you think? Are they going to call me up?" he asked.

"How should I know?" It was like they made a mistake by not calling him up right away.

"What the hell," he sighed. "I signed up."

He seemed to have it a lot harder than I did—I didn't really have any problems. He was drinking pretty quickly. He ordered a spiced brandy and beer.

I patted him on the shoulder. "It's so good to see you again."

Then I added: "I don't mean like in that song by the Fossils, but really."

He shook his head with a smile. "Oh man, I've been here since late July. I was in Germany. I thought about going to the coast, but gave up on that . . . And none of the gang is here! Only people from Zagreb," he said, looking at me as if he were about to hug me, but didn't.

I nodded, and he nodded, and so we looked at one another and kept nodding, and the Rolling Stones came on again. "*I see a red door and I want it painted black . . .*"

He ordered another round for us.

"Did you come to take your exams or what?"

"I promised my mother. If I flunk another year, I'll sign up too."

Suddenly there was a shot, right near my ear, and I saw Darko's eyes grow wide and his jaw drop.

It was as if we were stuck in that moment for some time—that is, it took a little while for us to hear the voices and music again.

Some guy had shot a bullet into the ceiling. He'd been messing around with his Kalashnikov.

"C'mon, watch what you're doing!" someone called out.

"Damn, sorry," said the guy with the gun. He was buzzed. His hair was tied back in a ponytail. His uniform didn't really fit properly.

"Let's get out of here," Darko said, finishing his two drinks.

"But where to?" I asked, keeping my seat. The absinthes and my stress pill had made me pretty lethargic. "Do you think something's still open?"

He looked at me like he didn't know what to do with me and said: "Let's go to my place!"

We staggered off to Britanski Square in the pitch darkness.

* * *

At Darko's apartment the roller blinds had been lowered all the way down, so he turned on an evening lamp on a nightstand next to the couch. He had one of those corner couches—probably leather, or imitation leather, in that awful yellowish color . . . Something I could only dream of having. He started rolling a joint on the glass coffee table. There on the table's edge I noticed a transistor radio and batteries that had been readied for the shelter. Just like they'd said to do on television. Because a transistor radio would allow us to hear official announcements so we would know what was going on and everything would remain calm and under control. For instance: if the shelter were covered over by rubble, they would let us know that they were searching for us. He told me how in the early days he would run into the shelter with his transistor radio.

But now he'd already given up on that, he said. It had become annoying: our people sounded the sirens nonstop, but Zagreb wasn't even being attacked.

First we lit up the joint, and then he put out some pancetta and bread on the table and we started eating. I didn't realize how hungry I was.

He had wine. It was domestic. The grass, the eats, and the wine really relaxed us. So we started talking politics: Milošević, Tuđman, Europe, Americans and Russians, even Germans, the French and the English. It seemed to me that I had a better grasp on things, but I could tell he thought he did. And then he changed the subject and said he'd been seeing a girl recently.

"Why didn't you say so?!" I interjected.

But he went on about how they'd met in the Concordia, and how at first he didn't know that she was a Serb, because they'd hooked up fast, and she spoke like someone from Zagreb. "You know, she's Zagreb through and through," he said. She was a hairdresser, and their sex was out of this world—he said that a little more quietly, almost as if he were admitting that he was in love.

"And her daddy is in the military."

"For real? Is he retired or—"

"Not retired one fucking bit. He's in the JNA barracks over on Ilica Street. The National Guard is blockading them."

"Aha, so that's it!" I said.

"What's it?"

"Nothing," I said. "So, she's out boozing because of that?"

"She really does drink a lot, I don't know whether that's the reason why. We met three weeks ago, and since then . . . Really intense, you know . . ."

"Wait. The guy comes home at night, and then goes back to the barracks in the morning, to his position?"

"No, no. They're barricaded in there now. She doesn't sleep at home either, they received threats. Her mother's already gone, back to Serbia, to some town there where she's from. She didn't want to go. She says this is her home town," he told me, staring at me. He was already pretty drunk.

"She doesn't have it easy."

"Sometimes she sleeps at a girlfriend's place, and sometimes here," he said, gesturing with his head.

"You mean she's here?"

"She's asleep in the bedroom."

Right. I'd forgotten that he had a bedroom too.

Darko's parents worked in Germany. The more fucked-up things got here, the better his apartments were: prices fell, but his parents kept sending the same amount of money. They probably didn't count on a Serbian girl sleeping there, being as they were fairly big Croat patriots.

"You understand?"

"Yes," I said, though I didn't know what he was asking.

"And then today we were watching TV together and had a knock-down-drag-out fight. That's when I left and signed up," he said with a sigh, then took another drink of wine. "Really, I just can't take that kind of thing!"

"What?"

"The Serbs. How they're walking all over us. All that."

"Ah," I said. My head was swimming from all the information.

"Man, there are more of them and they have guns. But so what, fuck them!"

"Easy, she'll hear you."

"Fuck, I'm really crazy. What am I doing—what?!"

"C'mon, cheers!" I said, and raised my glass so he'd calm down, and we clinked our glasses. We were already drunk, but we continued swigging the wine.

Then the bedroom door opened and his girl appeared. She was in a short nightgown; she had good legs. I gaped a little. I could see a spark of pride in his eyes and a faint smile.

She nodded and went past into the bathroom.

"You see that?" Darko asked in a whisper, as if now I would understand his dilemma.

"Uh-huh." I almost added, a little drunkenly, *She's really hot.* But my next thought was, *You can't compliment someone's girl like that.*

She appeared again, and asked him: "You got any beer?"

"No, just wine," he said, and passed her the joint he'd just lit back up. "This is my friend."

She extended her hand. "Nataša."

"Iggy," I said.

"You mean Igor?"

"Fine," I said. "Igor." It was always the same.

She took a couple hits. "So what are you two doing?"

"We're talking," he said.

"We're chatting," I said.

"O-ho-ho," she said, laughing. "Let's *chat!*"

I watched her, probably like an idiot, thinking: *Your old man had me in his sights today.*

"Who's *chatting* anymore, man?!" she said to me, as if to a fool. "There won't be any more chatting!"

"He's a real jokester. He failed the entrance exam for acting school twice; they didn't realize he's the new Woody Allen," Darko said. As usual, he added: "And he's studying traffic engineering."

He always thought that was funny, and I did sometimes too. *What are you studying? Traffic.* Then everyone thinks of cars going back and forth. But worst of all was when he introduced me as a jokester. That carried certain obligations with it.

"I'm just a student," I said to Nataša.

But she laughed again. "*I'm just a student!* Good one! An ordinary student. Terrific!"

"An ordinary student," I repeated like an idiot.

"You're good!" Nataša said. "That's what I'll say from now on: *I'm just a student.*"

"You can't say it like a man," I said.

"How should I say it then?" she asked. "*Oh, I'm, like, a student!* No, that sounds a little too . . . something . . . like someone could just fuck me. I'll stick with *I'm just a student.*"

"Okay, you're just a student."

"Are you two crazy?" Darko asked, smiling.

"Yep, we're just students," Nataša said, and started laughing uncontrollably. I watched her, trying to understand . . . *No,* I thought, *I didn't say anything that was laugh-out-loud funny.* The deal was probably that she wasn't just a student. *She is now a Serb above all,* I thought. And, *That grass hit you quick.*

"We're just taking classes, like lots of people," I said, since the student thing had gotten such a good response.

She was laughing so hard she had to hold her belly. Me too. And Darko. It was infectious.

"I'm no ordinary student," Darko said when the laughing had let up a bit. "I signed up today."

"Where?" she asked, with laughing eyes.

"With the Croatian Defense Forces," he said, looking away and still laughing. But if someone had photographed him he might have looked as if he were crying.

"Ooh, damn!" she said.

His laughter faded. "What about it?"

"Nothin'," she said, crossing her arms below her breasts. I took a little look, as much as was allowed. *How much is allowed?* That was what I was trying to figure out, but . . .

"You don't like it?" he asked.

"Look, it's your business!" she snapped.

It seemed to me as if that day's argument might be repeating itself.

"They don't have weapons!" I said. I was trying to lighten the mood. "Maybe they won't even call him up."

She didn't have a bra on.

They said nothing. They each looked in their own direction.

"And what, even if they do?" I said. "The Croatian Defense Forces isn't a regular army . . . You can sign up, but you don't have to." He was looking at the radio that he'd prepared for the shelter. I scratched my head and went on: "Hey, you showed up, signed up, gave them a chance, and they let you go . . ."

I was trying to tone everything down, but he said: "Are you two fucking with me?"

"Us two?"

"Don't mess with him, you can see he's turned serious. He's a soldier."

"You can fuck off with that," he said. Then he looked up and cried out in the voice of a righteous man: "Oh man, her father is in the JNA barracks, and what's she lecturing me about? Warmongering. Every day."

I didn't know what else to say: they could sort this out on their own.

She sat down in an armchair and poured herself some wine. "My old man's a fool."

After a pause, she added: "And then I found you."

She took a drink and grimaced. Then she drank a little more.

Yes, you just have to get used to the flavor, I wanted to say, but I kept quiet. The radio was playing the latest hit: "*I'm asking for your blessing, Mama / To accompany me into the fine battle . . .*"

She reached out to change the station, but he said: "Leave it alone."

Then came the chorus: "*A Croatian mother bore me / She was proud to bear me . . .*"

These two have some serious problems, I thought.

He was rolling another joint. No matter how drunk he was, he always managed to get himself together enough to roll a joint.

She cut off a little piece of pancetta and ate it without any bread. Then she lit up a cigarette and drank the rest of the wine in her glass. She poured some more and asked me: "You want some?"

"Okay."

"You?"

"I've still got some."

She said: "It's kind of stupid to sign up for the Croatian Defense Forces because of me."

At that moment I thought: *Ah. That thought hadn't entered my mind. This was his way of undoing it all.*

Looking at the joint, as if he were studying how well it had been rolled, he said darkly: "I signed up on my own!"

"Don't get yourself all worked up. Tomorrow I'm leaving."

He looked up at her and said nothing.

I drank some wine, lit a cigarette, looked around, studying the corners in the dark on the other side of the room. If it weren't for that damned blackout I would have left.

Instead I said: "The guy that's singing . . . we went to the same high school."

"Bravo!" she said. "That's like having been in the same homeroom with Ian Curtis . . ."

"You see, they looked like one another . . . pensive like . . . but each developed his own style."

She laughed, but those were facts. Her laughter was tremulous, a little broken up.

He lit up the joint. After he inhaled some for himself, he passed it to me. I took a couple of hits and passed it to her. She took a big hit.

"Where are you going?" he asked, looking off into space.

Oh yeah, I thought, *it's not over yet. I have to be quiet again.*

"I'm leaving," she said.

I wondered what that meant.

"You mean really?" he asked.

It seemed that *really* meant going somewhere far away.

"Yes, I'm leaving. It's over. Problem solved."

She passed him the joint as she got up.

"We're not together. Not that we ever were," she said to him. And after a pause: "There's nothing left."

I think she was maybe waiting for him to say she was wrong. His gaze wandered; he exhaled in a frustrated manner.

Then she did something that surprised me: she went over to him, bent over, grabbed him by the jaw, lifted up his face, and started kissing him. She kissed him aggressively, as if she wanted to suck him in, and he responded similarly from below, like a happy dog on a chain. Then her hand went down and she grabbed his balls—I saw it.

"Let's go into the bedroom," he murmured, as if he didn't want me to hear.

"Let's fuck!" she said, sliding down on the couch with her arms around his neck. "Let's fuck so people will see us."

He stopped. "You're crazy."

She turned to me, with those lips and that hair that fell down on her cheeks, with those eyes and a slightly twisted smile. "We've been fucking for three weeks. Like there's no tomorrow."

"Maybe there isn't," I said.

"We fuck, at least it seems to me, in secret," she said, turning to him. "Ain't that right?"

"Calm down!" he shouted.

"But you can be our witness, proving that we fucked," she said, as if she were talking to me again, although everything was directed at him, and I could remain drunkenly quiet as my temples throbbed.

He exhaled looking the other way, as if she were embarrassing him.

She was peering at him now, waiting for him to say something, to give her a chance, to utter a response. That was clear.

"I'm leaving in the morning, you understand?" she said, getting back on her feet.

He didn't have anything to say. He shook his head, as if some crazy woman were abusing him.

"We're no longer together at all, you hear? I can fuck him too," she said, meaning me. But she didn't look at me.

"Fuck whoever you want," he replied, and his whole body shuddered, almost tipping over.

Then she bent over again, began kissing him like before, but somehow more desperately, as if she no longer loved him but was doing this out of spite, to prove something to him. That was how I saw it, being drunk, and there was something terrible in it, and so I straightened up a little, went up to them, bent over them, and put my arms around both of them. It seemed to me that he started sobbing, and she leaned her cheek against mine, and soon, very soon, she simply put her lips on mine and kissed me. I thought I could taste the bitter taste of tears.

"What are you doing?" he bellowed up at us, and I didn't know whether he was talking to her or me. *They are no longer together*, I thought to justify myself, *and everything is just what it is. It's happening today and there is no tomorrow.*

It seemed he'd pulled down her panties—we were standing and he was sitting. And soon, somehow, it's hard for me to explain it, but soon it seemed to me that she was mounting his cock and then I lost her lips, they were moving in front of me, and I was watching her eyes, so black, so dark, and I was absolutely sure that she loved me. Still, she was fucking him, and so after a bit I sat back down where I'd been sitting . . . and I watched him enter her as she lay on her side . . . I was aroused, but so what? Was I supposed to unzip my damned fly? Put my cock in her mouth like in a porno? He was now fucking her from behind so there was an opportunity to do just that.

Then she took a look at me and it seemed that she didn't recognize me. I waited for her to stretch her hand out to me. But she didn't do it, as they do in a porno, she didn't reach for my cock. So I sat down closer, right in front of her, and we started kissing again. He was fucking her and I was kissing her.

We kept kissing until she came. He came too, inside her, it seemed to me.

I stood up and went to the bathroom. I got in the tub, turned on the hot water, lay down, and came quickly. I must have fallen asleep in the tub and when I got cold I must have gotten out and gone over to the couch, because I woke up there, covered with my jacket and a blanket that had appeared from out of nowhere. I woke up with a dull headache, to the light of the lamp.

I sat for a little bit on the couch until I realized I was naked. The blinds were all the way down, I didn't know whether it was day or night. I got dressed, went to the sink, and drank water out of my hands.

I started toward the front door and then hesitated, with my hand on the doorknob. One question flowed into another. I stood there with my hand still on the doorknob, leaning with my shoulder on the door, as if I were eavesdropping on the world outside. Was it day or night?

Then it hit me: next to me in the vestibule, the greenish phone had started ringing.

Maybe they were calling him.

It was daytime out there.

NIGHT VISION

BY PERO KVESIĆ

Tuškanac

Translated by Stephen M. Dickey

1.

I didn't do anything to get like this, I was simply born this way. Moreover, for the longest time I didn't even know about it myself. I can see in the dark. Put simply, that's what I can do, though it's not completely true. If it's pitch dark, say, in a completely sealed photographer's darkroom before the red light comes on, I can't see anything either. But all it takes is for any kind of light to come in under the door, and I can find my way around.

We grew up on a street on the edge of a big park, and we often played there after the sun went down. When we chased each other through the bushes in the dark I could catch anyone, but no one could ever get me. My favorite game was hide-and-seek. When we grew a little older and would get into fights with kids from other streets after dancing at some party or disco, if the fight was in a dark yard, unlit entryway, or a suburban street without lights, I would swoop down like a great horned owl on guys twice my strength and size, which gave me the courage not to shrink from them even in well-lit places because I'd learned how to handle them. I explained this with the idea that I was used to the darkness and others weren't. Whenever my grandma sent me down into the cellar or up to the attic to get something and offered me a flashlight, I never took it because it would just get in my way. Whenever I was coming back from the park after sundown, I chose the darkest paths under thick trees, because I liked the darkness. I'd always liked nighttime as much as daytime, if not more. Indeed, bright light even bothered me. In the summertime I usually wear sunglasses, and then I forget that I have them on when the sun goes down. It often happened that I would start reading something in the afternoon that was interesting and engrossed me (I remember the books that I was really interested in—*Winnetou*, *Tarzan*, Zane Gray Western novels) to the point that I couldn't tear myself away from the next line to get up and turn on the light, and so time got away from me, and suddenly my mother or grandma would come in the room and ask, "What are you doing in the dark?" Nothing bothered me even when I started taking girls to the darkest recesses of the park. They would clutch my arm and stumble on the path, which I interpreted as coquetry, as an excuse to hold onto them more tightly, say, when they pushed my hands away when we finally sat down on a bench or unconvincingly said, "Don't," before they gave themselves over to me.

It happened many times that me and some friends went into an unlit stairwell and I would get up to the third floor without even groping while the others were still looking for the light switch in the entryway. But I didn't attach any importance to that. It wasn't until I was in the army that I realized I was different. They sent me into Montenegro, deep into the mountains. There I encountered darkness like I hadn't experienced in my life. Many of the soldiers were afraid of the dark, but I felt like a fish in water in it. The military trainers instructed us to observe and move in the darkness.

"Don't look directly at what you are trying to see!"

"If you are watching the horizon, raise your gaze a little higher!"

And when I started consciously following their instructions, I discovered that even I was surprised at how much I could see. I didn't say anything about my ability, but I greedily took in the explanations. There are rods and cones in the eye . . . the former react to black and white, light and dark, the latter to color . . . The cells that are sensitive to color are mostly located in the middle of the cornea, the surface onto which the image is projected; the cells that are sensitive to light are concentrated around the center . . . At night there are no colors, and so those sensitive to color are unused . . . There are people who see well in the darkness and there is a medical term for this ability: scotopic vision. The only use I got out of this was to trade night watches with soldiers who wanted to get out of them for other duties that I didn't like, such as cleaning toilets; after I started doing that, my time in the army became almost nice. At night I would change two or three sentry posts and read a book in peace, and during the day I slept while the other soldiers performed various unpleasant and senseless tasks. Of course, I made sure to take books that had rather large print, but if there was any moonlight the size of the type wasn't any problem at all.

At night, or in the dark, vision nevertheless works differently than in light. A lot of little particulars and fine details vanish; all one can see are bigger things and whole objects, often only as silhouettes, and if it's really pitch dark, not even that. Still, it's rare that it's impossible to see anything at all. On a night with no moon in a forest with thick tree cover—yes . . . but who among us has ever been in such a place? At night, in old bunkers, cellars without electricity, abandoned underground passageways . . . hardly anyone ever ends up there without a very good reason. But I had never missed an opportunity to pass through such places, practicing my skill at moving according to my sense of hearing, touch, and logic. And since hearing is much more important for moving through the dark than it is during the day, I practiced and it became second nature for me to move around silently, even when there wasn't any need to do so. I can pass over ground covered with dry leaves and branches without making a sound, even in army boots, not to mention city pavement in soft rubber shoes, the only kind I buy.

2.

The street where I grew up is in a residential part of town. The houses there are prewar villas (I mean World War II) surrounded by spacious gardens. Those who'd settled in them when the Ustashas were in power either fled or were forced out by the Yugoslav Partisan movement, whereupon these villas became homes for members of the new authorities—ministers, high officers, physicians, and directors—as well as for members of the working class and the oppressed common people. The former mainly received entire apartments, which usually meant whole floors of individual buildings; the latter were settled into a room or two, so that several families would inhabit a single apartment, often together with the former owner, who was now forced to live in a tiny bedroom. Simple math shows that there were relatively few of the former, and significantly more of the latter. But by the time I was born, conditions had already changed quite a bit. After their initial excitement at having any kind of roof over their head, everyone discovered that life under a common roof is also a kind of hell. Some requested and, without anyone's intercession, received new apartments in other parts of town, and moved away. The remaining tenants spread into the rooms that had been previously occupied. Others were aided by the fact that some of their fellow tenants had enough influence and connections to ensure priority placement in what were referred to as "community apartments." (Community apartments had one, two, or three rooms; nationalized apartments had four, five, or six rooms or were built according to the "one house, one apartment" rule.) Such neighborly help by influential friends considerably accelerated the predominance of notable members of society receiving premium apartments over the anonymous members of the working class. In a relatively short time (by around the midsixties), the oppressed commoners had almost vanished from the neighborhood.

My old neighborhood is called Tuškanac, after its main street, which leads up the spine of a hill through woods toward a mountain outside the city. I liked that Tuškanac was in fact mostly woods. I like woods, especially at night where there are no city lights—no lit display windows or billboards or automobile headlights. In Tuškanac there is also a valley, and through the valley there runs a forest road, which is called the Dubravka or Sophia Road.

All the kids from Tuškanac went to an elementary school on Jabukovac Hill. When the time came to attend high school we scattered to various prep schools located, as we said, "in town." To get to class and back I always took the Dubravka (Sophia) Road. During the day I enjoyed the woods, the birds and squirrels; at night I enjoyed the darkness. The crowns of the trees joined high above the road and on nights without a moon it would be so dark that not even I could see anything. I went most of the way by stepping with one foot along a little drainage ditch at the side of the road, and I walked some parts of the road blind, from memory. Nevertheless, that was not only more fun and interesting but also safer.

In two large prewar villas, actually palaces in the middle of Tuškanac, there were homes for orphans, homeless children, kids from troubled families, and other unfortunates. They attended the school on Jabukovac Hill with us, and there were no problems with them when we were all at school together. The problem lay in the fact that among them there were a few dozen pubescent and fairly well-developed girls. On Fridays, Saturdays, and Sundays those girls went into town to the dance halls. After the dancing some boy usually walked each one of them home. The boys didn't like to walk through that sparsely settled and dark area, not to mention going back alone the way they came, and so they usually brought a friend or two with them, and sometimes even three, four, or five. Who knows what those boys expected, one can only guess, or at least what the one who brought his friends along expected, but when the girls finally left them or ran inside their homes, the boys were disappointed and bitter, and often already tipsy. It wasn't pleasant to run into a group of them taking the road back into town. The least you could expect was some name calling, verbal insults, general harassment. In worse cases there was scuffling, pushing, sometimes a punch or two. Three or four times a year one of us was beaten up seriously.

In such cases we had a strategy. The one who'd been beaten up went into the nearest friend's house and got on the phone. The thugs didn't count on there being a telephone nearby. At that time there wasn't a phone in every apartment, and people waited for years for lines to be put in, and in the end it often took a bribe in the amount of an average yearly salary to get a telephone number. However, in Tuškanac every house had a phone. We would call the guys on Goran Kovačić Street and in Rokov Park, tell them how many attackers there were, describe them, say who the worst of them were, and a group would immediately race down the Aleksandar Stairs to Dežmanova and wait for them. All they had to do was keep them there for a bit. As soon as the phone call was finished, several of us from the center of Tuškanac would gather in a flash, and rush down the hill with the one who'd been beaten up in the lead (if he was able to run). We would charge at the boys who'd been detained by our Goran Kovačić Street friends, and without saying anything we'd start hitting them. And the guys from Goran Kovačić Street would start hitting them too. Together we would beat up those wretches so that they would never even think of attracting anyone's attention if they by any chance ever came to our part of town again.

Do you remember Walter Hill's *The Warriors*? A great movie. Not only did I watch it several times, I lived it.

3.

The reason I've shared all of this is to explain why Sophia Road was the safer way home. Namely, it was so dark that even the thugs were afraid to go there. They preferred to go down a lighted street or through an adjacent park that was partially lit by streetlights. If once in a while some group or other dared to go through the black woods, they would cover their fear by making loud noises to scare off any wild animals, thereby alerting anyone in the woods to their location. In such circumstances I would simply move about ten or twenty meters away from the road, sit down by a tree trunk, and wait for them to pass. Nothing ever happened to me in the woods, but on the lighted road they twice ambushed me from some bushes and beat me up.

I grew up in the era before cars were allowed down our small side street, so from morning till night a group of boys and I played soccer in the middle of the street, cowboys and Indians in the park, Yugoslav Partisans and Germans in the yards, and Tarzan in the woods along Dubravka Road. I feel sorry for kids who grew up there later and could no longer play soccer in the middle of the street. When we finished college and all got jobs, we each got our own car and life in the neighborhood changed a lot.

Neighbors no longer gathered on Britanski Square, waiting

together for the bus and then talking during the ride so that everyone heard everyone else's business; they no longer got off at stops in groups that grew smaller as they passed from house to house until all that were left were two or three who would stand for a while in front of the entryways to their gardens. Now every morning, each one got into his own car and went to work; after work he parked his car in front of his house and immediately disappeared into it.

That change became more evident to me after I got married, lived for three years in another part of town, in Zapruđe, and then came back to my parents' house after my divorce. The street was full of parked cars and I had no idea to whom they belonged, and in houses, some close, others farther away, I saw people and had no idea who they were. Nevertheless, I began to hang out with a small group of childhood friends again; we visited one another and I often went out with some of them into town, for fun. Of the original horde of boys there were less than ten of us left. Almost without exception they were the children of state or party leaders, directors, doctors, or military men. One of the few from a different mold was my grandpa, a remnant of a class that had endured a shipwreck of history: before World War II he'd been a wealthy real estate agent, and all that he had left after the nationalization was an apartment that occupied an entire floor of a house in Tuškanac—which he only had for himself because he had managed to evict his fellow tenants by finding them other apartments.

During the separation from my wife, I told her: "Take what you want, but leave me the dog." As far as the dog was concerned, I was resolved not to get into any negotiations. And that's what happened. She took everything and left me the dog. A black one, Blackie. Every evening I took him on a walk through the park and the woods for at least an hour, if not two, running some of the way. I was in great shape. After the walk I usually stopped by a friend's, talked a bit, had one last drink, then went home to bed.

4.

By profession I'm a graphics engineer. I thought about studying painting, but I'm not good with color. So I decided on graphics. Black-and-white, I'm like a fish in water with that. I also have complete control over shades of gray. I'd say that my limitation is maybe that I'm inclined to see other things in life in terms of elementary contrasts.

White: Čedomir. Čedo was born and grew up on my street. He lived three houses down from me. His dad was a major in the JNA—the Yugoslav People's Army—and their apartment took up a whole second floor. His dad was a good man, but a simpleton. I'll never forget Čedo's fourteenth birthday party. That was an important day for him and weeks earlier he'd asked his father to let him invite his friends over. In the end his dad gave in. The agreement was that the birthday party would be in two rooms that were separated from the rest of the apartment, which was where the rest of the family would be. His mom made a bunch of sandwiches. We secretly brought a few bottles of hard liquor. When we got there, Čedo turned out the light, put a record on, and we all grabbed girls and started dancing; when everything couldn't be going any better . . . *Bam*!—the door opened and his dad burst in.

"Why is it so dark in here?!" he asked, switching on the light immediately. Everyone froze. His dad was dragging a chair behind him. He slammed it down in the middle of the room, took a seat, and looked over everything around him. After a couple of minutes he grumbled: "What's wrong? Why aren't you doing anything? Enjoy yourselves!"

That was too much for me so I grabbed one of the girls and

led her off into the other room, where it was still dark. We sat down on the couch, took a swig from a bottle that was hidden behind it, and started kissing. His dad flipped out. When I leaned over I could see him in the light of the other room. He was sitting as if on a hot stove, squirming and craning his neck to see what I was doing, but no matter how much that bothered him he didn't want to abandon his position, from which he was able to keep an eye on everyone else. It ended with us eating the sandwiches and then all going to the park (we took the bottles with us), where we messed around until midnight.

Čedo was basically a nice young man, which made him different than all the others. He got nothing but the best grades in school, and his parents never had any problems with him. He got his degree in electrical engineering on time, finished his military service, got a job in the Rade Končar electronics factory, and soon after got married. He and his wife had two children very quickly. From his job he went straight home and didn't go out till dawn when he had to work the next morning. His wife was pretty and nice; I saw her often when she took the children to the park to play. Čedo seemed like he had all he'd ever wanted, and the only thing his wife had to put up with without grumbling were his frequent trips to transformer stations and similar installations throughout Yugoslavia.

His father had died before he got married, and so he took care of his mother until he buried her too. In fact, the last time we spoke was at the wake in his apartment before her funeral.

Black: Krunoslav. On the ground floor under Čedo there lived another character from our generation, who was the complete opposite. Kruno was the only one with whom no one hung out. His mother was to blame for everything, but in the end it didn't matter who was to blame because all that remained was what was important—that no one hung out with him. In the days when the apartment on the ground floor was still shared by four tenants, Kruno's mother had handled the relations between them by shouting almost every day at someone so loudly that it could be heard up and down the street. And this was how she handled her relations with her husband, who was basically the same as her. Before we started going to school and still played in the middle of the street, his mother watched from the window and if we argued she didn't hesitate to run out of the building, grab whomever she thought was doing something to her son, pull his hair cruelly, and slap him. Soon we ran from Kruno's mother whenever she appeared for any reason, and she forbade him from playing with us, so he ended up sitting in the room in which they lived and stared through the closed window while we chased each other and shouted in the street in front of the house. His mom was a really wicked and jealous person who hated the whole world, thinking she was better than everyone else, which necessarily resulted in her being bitter and hostile. To make matters better (or worse), her husband was a mechanic in some shop and wasn't a caring and homely kind of guy; she didn't work, and so they were really poor. And while everyone around them made progress in some way day after day, they didn't go anywhere.

Kruno barely finished elementary school and was the only one of us who didn't go on to prep school but enrolled in some vocational school for economics, but didn't finish. When he was seventeen he ran away to Germany and was gone for two or three years. People said that he made his living in Germany from male prostitution. I can't confirm that this was true, but it seemed convincing and believable, if nothing else entirely possible because no one who knew him had ever seen him with a girl. He came back at some point and got mixed up in some shady business. On account of him suspicious men would come to our street. Every so often some kind of fracas could be heard in his house.

A few times the police had to get involved, and the cops would come around the neighborhood and ask questions and so on. He was the reason no one could leave nice tools, an unlocked bicycle, or other such things in their yards. They would simply disappear.

One evening, as I came home from walking my dog and passed Kruno's house, I noticed an unfamiliar car parked on the far side in some deep shade, shielded from the streetlights by treetops. Four dark figures sat inside, and kept quiet as I passed. No one with ordinary eyesight would have seen them, but I could tell they were very big. And they couldn't have been waiting for anyone else but Kruno.

Instead of going inside my house, I sat down in the yard on the stoop in front of the entryway, opened a beer, and started leisurely sipping it. After a while, Kruno appeared. I went out into the street, stopped him, and invited him to my place. We sat on the terrace and waited for over an hour until the unknown car gave up on the ambush and drove away. Kruno was moved to tears for not having stumbled into the arms of the men who'd been waiting for him.

After that he disappeared for about a month. I didn't need to check whether he'd come home because an electric drill disappeared from where I'd left it on the same spot where I'd recently sat waiting for him. I went to his place straight away and entered without knocking. His father had been dead for a long time, and his mother had become a withered, hunched old woman. The two of them continued to live in a single room behind the bathroom on the other side of a common hallway while another tenant on the ground floor managed to gain possession of the rest of the rooms and turn them into a very nice apartment. They would have moved out too, if it were possible to agree with the other tenants on anything. The drill was lying in the middle of the table. I walked up and grabbed it. Kruno mumbled: "I borrowed it! I just borrowed it! I was about to bring it back!"

"Right!" I said, and went out without saying goodbye.

That evening I told Nikša what had happened.

"Damn. About a month ago I had to go over to his place like that to get a car jack back!" Ice cubes were melting slowly in our glasses of whiskey as we talked. "Doesn't he get bored stealing things around the neighborhood? We all know he's the only thief in the area!"

Then the topic of conversation switched from the neighborhood to its history.

"This part of town is cursed! Have you ever thought about the houses we live in and who lived in them before? When Austria-Hungary fell apart, all those nobles and Austro-Hungarian generals went off to Vienna or Budapest. When the old Yugoslavia fell apart, the Serbian merchants went off to Belgrade. Many of the mansions belonged to rich Jews. The Ustashas put them in camps and moved into houses and apartments where there were still warm bedsheets, unironed laundry, and closets full of clothes. Then the Partisans came, and the Ustashas fled. If they didn't make it to South America, they probably died at Bleiburg. And all that in less than seventy years! Now we're here, but I don't know whether it'll be for long . . . This part of town is on the windward side of history and might get blown away."

5.

I'm not interested in politics, don't like them, but even a blind man would notice that something was going on, that something bad was simmering. In our neighborhood, in Tuškanac, everything looked normal, but down in the city things were boiling over. Banners suddenly popped up everywhere; every day there was some assembly, and traffic had to be diverted to bypass it.

On one of the TV channels there was always someone giving a speech in lofty tones, so that I would immediately change the channel. The people in the cafés acted like they were in some third-rate movie about a universal conspiracy. Every day the front pages of the newspapers were full of headlines that looked like reprints from fifty years ago . . .

"Damn," I said to Nikša, "none of this has anything to do with me. I'm the offspring of a class that's already been smashed by the waves of history anyway. Come what may, I'm not going to be a part of it."

Still, there are things that sweep everyone up in them, and no one can get away. An air-raid warning. The first time the sirens started wailing over the city to announce the danger of an air attack, no one needed to be told what was going on. So we still live in a country where people immediately recognize an air-raid siren, even if they've only heard about it.

It was a nice, sunny day. I went out of the house and sat down on the stoop out front. As soon as the sirens died down a silence took hold like I'd never heard before in my life. I'd brought out a bottle of beer, and I opened it. It must have been a Saturday or a Sunday or some state holiday because I wasn't at the office. My dog came and sat down beside me and we both listened. Even if Tuškanac was the quietest part of Zagreb, you could always hear the noise of the city in the distance. But that had disappeared too. There were no cars on the road, and the public transportation had stopped running. The best definition I know of silence is that it's when you can hear everything, even from a great distance. I heard the song of some little bird that must have been three hundred meters away. It sounded to me like a nightingale.

Even the wind had stopped. You couldn't hear a leaf. It seemed that the entire city was paralyzed with expectation. I strained my ears, awaiting the sound of the distant approach of aircraft, and wondered whether I would hear them at all or if the first sounds would be of bombs exploding. These modern airplanes, faster than the speed of sound—I don't know what they sound like when they fly over. My mother often told me that during World War II she was most afraid of the roar of bombers. Up to her death, she never recovered from the panic that had seized her when Flying Fortresses had roared overhead. I wondered how much a modern air attack differed from those that my mother had lived through.

I suddenly heard something that I didn't recognize. A little ways off from my house, there's a bend in the street, and something was approaching from that direction. The sound of something like the thud of iron-shod boots, the scraping sound of house slippers, and some kind of clinking . . . From the bend in the street there appeared three figures who looked like they came straight out of the *Mad Max* movies. One was completely bald, the second had a mohawk, and the head of the third was covered by a helmet. They were tall, armed to the teeth, and looked ugly and dangerous. The tallest one was bare down to his waist, dressed in camouflage pants and army boots. He had two machine-gun belts slung crosswise over his bulging bodybuilder's chest, and carried a MG 42 as if it were only an air rifle. The second was dressed in a combination of fatigues and denim clothing, tennis shoes, and some stylish sunglasses. He was carrying a double-barreled shotgun. The third one had thrown a bulletproof vest over his bare chest and had a small pistol; all three of them had Motorola portable radios, bayonets, and revolvers in holsters hanging from their belts. I looked them over curiously as they walked by, at the ready as if they were moving through enemy territory. You know—one looking ahead, and the two behind him looking from side to side with their weapons locked and loaded. As they passed, all three of them turned their heads toward me. I raised my bottle as if toasting them and waited a little for them to move on before I took a drink.

Crazy shit! I thought. *This isn't going to end well!*

About an hour later the sirens signaled the end of the air-raid warning. Nothing had happened. A futile warning. The city breathed a sigh of relief.

The next warning happened at night. A woman from the office was visiting me and instead of rushing down into the cellar, as prescribed by the regulations, we immediately went up to the attic, then climbed up a ladder and through a little window onto the roof. We climbed up to the very top and sat down between two chimneys. Just as I never play the lottery because I'm certain that I will never win anything, now I was sure that there was no chance of the first bomb hitting my house. The night was beautiful. Over the treetops of the park we could see the whole city laid out before us. The streetlights had been turned off and for the first time I saw it in nothing but moonlight and starlight, and the stars had come out in numbers like one sees in the summer on distant Adriatic islands. That heavy silence settled down, punctuated now and then by bursts of fire or single shots.

A story had spread that Serbian snipers were operating in the city, and the gunfire suggested that the story was maybe true. Maybe it was the snipers shooting, or maybe someone was shooting at them. We didn't know. Only years later did I run into a guy who told me that he'd been in an observation post in the vicinity with some soldiers and had noticed when I climbed up on the roof with my lady friend. They had night-vision binoculars and could see us clearly. He said that they could have picked us off clean and that they had a bitter argument about whether they should take us down or not, whether we were some phantom snipers or not, but fortunately—as they saw that we didn't have anything that resembled a weapon on us—the naysayers won out.

After the first air-raid warning the city changed its appearance. In the morning windows appeared covered with packing tape and sandbags had been stacked next to cellar windows and doorways. Many windows kept their blinds lowered or shutters closed throughout the day as well. A great number of people walked around the city dressed in various kinds of pseudo-military uniforms, carrying weapons. Suddenly there were private automobiles without license plates; some were painted with camouflage splotches, some had crudely cut openings in the top along which pintle mounts for machine guns had been welded. It wasn't uncommon to see a luxury car, say a Mercedes, with a hitch that wasn't pulling a trailer but a wheeled, triple-barrel automatic cannon. The air-raid warnings provoked a few minutes of panic during which cars shot through red lights at intersections to get off the roads, pedestrians ran into the nearest buildings, and most people who were out somewhere found themselves in a stampede to get down into cellars which functioned as improvised shelters. After a few minutes the city relaxed, and no one could be seen and nothing could be heard anywhere.

The first time an air-raid warning caught me at the office, I watched in surprise as everyone around me leapt up from their desks, rushed to the exit, and, jumping two or three steps at a time, rushed down into the cellar. Fortunately, the only one left in the empty offices was my female coworker with whom I'd gone up on the rooftop, and that worked out just fine because we didn't have to worry that someone might walk in on us before the all-clear sounded.

6.

I was driving back home from work in my car, and just when I turned onto our street I saw Čedo and his wife coming out of my garden. I knew immediately that I was the only person they could be looking for (they couldn't have gone to talk to the old woman who lived on the ground floor), but I was also surprised because Čedo hadn't stopped by my place since we were teenagers. They noticed my car, and stopped to wait for me. By the time I pulled up to them, grabbed my bag and things from the backseat, got out, and went up to them, Kruno came staggering from the other direction. All four of us found ourselves in front of the entrance to my yard.

I said, "Hello!" and just then noticed that Kruno had a pistol tucked into his belt. "What are you doing with that?" I asked, pointing to the gun.

Kruno opened his blazer and said nonchalantly: "Oh, nothing. It's just a flintlock."

That was more than I could take. In a moment my pulse was pounding, and blood shot into my head.

"So that's what people are carrying now, huh? Every yokel carries a pistol, just as yokels used to carry fountain pens around, to have them protruding from their breast pockets! Just in case you need it, right? If some piece of prosciutto starts giving you problems. Or a slice of salami. You use it to open beer bottles, right? *A flintlock,* you say. A horse pistol! A flintlock is about the same as a horse pistol, it's just that ignorant yokels don't know this. You're off to join a band of highwaymen. Watch out—the way you've got it tucked in there, you might end up with no balls!"

I was inspired and couldn't help myself. Kruno tried babbling something, but just gave me more opportunities to ridicule him. Čedo and his wife froze and didn't utter a peep, but I didn't let up at all. Though he was taller than me by a head, he'd had respect for me since he was seventeen when I'd kicked his ass for picking on Brankica and Vesnica, two girls from the neighborhood. He must have wished he hadn't shown his face.

After a couple of minutes, Čedo tugged his wife by the hand, mumbled something, and they hurried off. But I didn't let Kruno get away. I kept him there until I'd told him everything I thought about carrying guns, and that was quite a bit.

When Kruno left, I still couldn't calm down. I went into the house, let my dog out, and we went over to Nikša's to put an end to my bad mood with some good whiskey.

"Well you don't know, do you?!" Nikša said. "Last night you didn't sleep at home, or the night before. Both nights we had air-raid warnings. When the warnings sounded, Kruno went out in the street and started yelling up at Čedo, *Where are you, Čedo, you Chetnik?!* He cursed his Chetnik mother and father, howling so it echoed up and down the street. *Get back to Serbia!* and stuff like that. I felt like going out and doing whatever it took to shut him up, but how could I in the dark? I've got night blindness."

Instead of calming down, I got more enraged. If I'd known this, Kruno wouldn't have gotten off so easily. I struggled to keep myself from running over to his house, because I knew it wouldn't end well—either I would have strangled him or he would have shot me.

7.

That evening I took the dog out for a walk through the woods. A fairly strong wind was blowing and the treetops rustled with the wind and it almost sounded like a waterfall above my head. Suddenly the sirens wailed. I turned around and started home.

I came out of the woods on a path that leads between two houses to the street and heard Kruno. I didn't see him because there was no moon; only the stars were shining. So I turned toward him based on his voice. At about fifteen meters away I could also finally make him out: a black figure in the shade of the treetops opposite Čedo's house. I didn't have a lot of time to decide what to do.

It was clear to me that I wasn't going to get him to quiet down by talking to him. He howled to shout down the wind, and not even a pig would listen to what he was yelling.

"Where are you, Čedo, you Chetnik?! Fuck you and your saint's day too! Are you off to Knin to chop trees down across the road?! Fuck your dead Serbian mother and her rotten tits!"

I could tell that the content of his rant was borrowed from the current media hoopla, and it got its strength from his despair at having to keep living in a single room with his mother while overhead Čedo was spreading his apartment over a whole floor; at the fact that Čedo had graduated from college and had a decent job and Kruno eked out a miserable existence; at the fact that Čedo had a beautiful wife and sweet children, and Kruno couldn't find anything decent to bang. In his yells I heard the cries of a child who had to sit in a room with his mother while the other kids played outside below his window, the echo of everything good that had slipped away from him and everything bad that had befallen him in place of those unattainable things. Everything was clear to me, including that there wasn't anything to be said about it.

Kruno couldn't hear anything other than his own howling, especially over the swaying branches above his head and all around him. A piece of a fallen branch, about a meter long and as thick as a sausage, lay two or three steps behind him. I walked up to him silently from the side and then moved behind him, bent over without pausing, got ahold of the club, and in a single motion, rising up from the ground and putting all the strength of my body into the blow, I whacked him on the top of his head.

He fell silent in the middle of a word; his knees gave way and he collapsed. I tossed the branch next to him, turned around, and went calmly back home. The wind felt good because it cooled me down.

8.

I went into my dark house (during air-raid warnings no one was allowed to turn on any lights that might be seen through the windows) and started preparing something for my dog to eat, when the doorbell rang. Who could that be at this time of day?

I went down to the ground floor, unlocked the door, and wasn't really surprised to see Čedo. He started talking without saying hello: "Please, can I bring my family over to your place?"

"Of course," I said without asking why. He immediately turned and ran off.

I waited for them in front of the door. After a few minutes, Čedo and his wife appeared, each carrying a sleepy child. We climbed the stairs in silence and went into the main room of the apartment. I lit a little cemetery candle so they could see a little at least and only when we'd sat down did I ask: "What's going on?"

"Whenever there's a warning, some people come into my house in search of weapons. There's nothing for them to find, but every time they throw everything around and mistreat my wife and children . . . Fortunately I wasn't ever at home. I was away on business. I don't know what would happen if they caught me at home."

It didn't make any sense to assume anything or for him to tell me any more details. It was clear to me what the three *Mad Max* characters were looking for on our street.

"A few days ago I wanted to ask you if we could stay at your place whenever there's a warning, but then Kruno came along . . ."

His wife didn't say a word the whole time, but you could see she was completely panicking—she was trembling all over. The children, who'd probably been woken up suddenly, were just as afraid.

"What are you going to do now?"

"I don't know."

We sat and said nothing, each occupied by our own thoughts. I didn't have any helpful advice for him. Of course they could stay with me whenever they wanted. I didn't need to tell him that.

"It's not even safe here . . ." said Čedo finally. "If they come looking for me, and I'm not there, Kruno will know right away where I'm probably hiding. You're the only one of my friends in the area who lives alone, and he's seen me here . . ."

His wife started softly crying and looking around, as if someone might burst in at any moment.

9.

"I have to get to Sesvete!" Čedo suddenly announced, as if he'd been stung by a wasp. "They're waiting for us there. I said I'd come tomorrow and get my family to safety, but this warning caught us by surprise. I didn't expect there to be a warning tonight . . . There were two short ones already during the day—"

"How are you going to get to Sesvete?" I asked, interrupting him. "That's all the way on the other side of town. The taxis aren't running."

"I'm taking my car. We can't stay here."

"Don't be an idiot. Driving is prohibited during an air-raid warning. And how will you drive in the dark anyway?"

"I have to!" he shouted, resolute in his desperation. He got up and called to his wife, "Let's go!"

I couldn't keep them from going, so I went after them. They were carrying their children and only then did I notice that they were dragging a small blue bag that probably had their papers and bare necessities. We went out of the yard and when we made it to where my car was parked I said: "Stop! I'll take you there."

Čedo looked at me in astonishment. "How will you drive us there? The city is under a blackout. Driving is prohibited, and you'll have to make it back too."

"Don't worry," I said. "I have scotopic vision."

"What's that?"

"It means I can see in the dark."

"I've never heard of that," Čedo said.

"Now you have," I told him. "And now you'll see too."

10.

I put them in my car and we drove off. It was really dark and I drove slowly, maybe twenty kilometers an hour, but managed not to turn onto any one-way streets or prohibited lanes. I wasn't afraid of coming upon another vehicle, but instead we encountered pedestrians walking in the middle of the street because there was no traffic. Every so often we passed by defensive positions on street corners, mostly sandbags stacked in circles, over which the barrel of a machine gun protruded. Some streets were blocked with antitank obstacles, and we had to snake our way around them. Now and then we passed by groups of armed men and I had to slow down so none of the jittery ones would take a shot at us.

On one street we were stopped between some antitank hedgehogs by some armed men in unfamiliar-looking uniforms. The barrel of an automatic rifle poked in through the window and pushed against my temple.

"Where are you going?"

Čedo froze next to me. I answered without missing a beat: "Journalists!" and waved the press pass that we had all received in the company, whether we were journalists or not. They couldn't read it in the dark, but I sounded self-confident enough to get the barrel pulled back immediately. Fortunately they hadn't seen the children lying beside their mother in the backseat, covered with blankets. If they had, we would have had some explaining to do, and who knows where we would have ended up.

We were stopped in the same manner two more times, but when we reached Kvaternikov Square the warning was over. The danger of someone stopping us and harassing us about why we were on the road had passed. All that remained was the possibility that someone would stop and harass us for no reason, though it was considerably less likely. In place of a total blackout there was now a partial one. All turn signals, traffic lights, and other lights were masked over with black tape, except for a slit the width of a finger on headlights, which was more than enough. On the empty roads we reached Sesvete in no time. I entered into unfamiliar territory. Čedo led me, saying, "Left," "Right," "Straight ahead," and finally we stopped in front of some house. His wife carried one child, took the other by the hand, and immediately darted off into the house. Čedo and I were overcome with exhaustion. We shook hands without a word, and then embraced, standing there for a few moments clutching one another, and then parted in silence.

That was the last time I saw him. I heard that he stayed in the house in Sesvete for about a month until he received papers allowing him and his family to leave for the Netherlands. They split and, as far as I know, never came back, not even for a vacation.

11.

I no longer remember how I made it home. I didn't go to work the next day; I slept until noon. I was awakened by my dog, who wanted me to let him out into the garden. I went down in my pajamas and as I waited for the dog to do his business, Kruno came walking down the road. His head was wrapped in a gleaming white bandage.

"What happened to you?" I called out.

"Nothing," he said, unable to look at me and hating every word that I pulled out of him. "A branch fell on my head last night. It must have been the wind."

"Don't tell me you went out during the air-raid warning in that wind!" I said, smiling from ear to ear. "This weather is dangerous. Be glad it didn't gobble you up!"

Along with my special ability to see in the dark, I suddenly had a feeling that I'd gained another—to see darkness during the day. The day was sunny and nice, everything was bright all around, but it seemed to me that everything had gone dark, that the darkness was thickening and that it was a darkness that we would not be able to get rid of for a long time. I shivered at the terrible thought of a biblical night in which many good people would disappear. I remembered how my grandfather used to say, "War is a bad thing because it creates many more wicked people than it destroys."

A few months later Kruno received a mobilization call. Panic-stricken that they would send him to the front, he shot himself in the leg with his own revolver. I'm sure he managed to get himself a pension as a wounded volunteer in the Homeland War—since he finally moved out of that room, he must have gotten an apartment somewhere else as a veteran.

12.

The war came to an end. With time new tenants settled in the neighborhood. Now they were mostly foreign diplomats and local gangsters—it was hard to tell who was worse. Yugoslavia broke up into seven states. Those states seem funny to me. Say, Croatia. I always break out laughing when I come to the border right after Samobor. Imagine a state with a border only twenty kilometers from its capital city! Crazy. You say it's forty? Sorry, forty. That's much more serious.

Around five years after the story I've just told, the company that employed me began to work with some printing press in the Slovenian town of Kopar. The Slovenes proved to be a pain in the ass. They only spoke Slovene, and the guy with whom I had to work most often was the worst of all. Svetozar! First, until not too long ago, all Slovenes spoke Croatio-Serbian (or Serbo-Croatian, or whatever that language is called). How could they have forgotten it in just five years?! Second, that Svetozar used particularly crazy Slovene words and it was often almost impossible to understand what he was saying. And his name was Svetozar—typically Serbian! I resolved to only speak Croatian, and he could deal with it as best he knew how; but he even more resolutely spoke back in Slovene. He wouldn't give in. A few times when there were problems at work I switched to English, which I spoke better, and he answered in German, which was easier for him. Hardly anyone at work caused me more problems than he did. There was no chance of him ever meeting me halfway, and he never missed an opportunity to spite me.

That continued until one day when my phone rang at work. I picked up the receiver, and though I recognized the voice, I couldn't believe what I heard on the other end of the phone: "Hey, Mr. Scotopic Vision!"

"What? Who is this?"

"Svetozar from Kopar!"

"What did you call me?"

"Mr. Scotopic Vision! That's who you are!" He started chuckling heartily.

"Maybe I am. How could you have known that?"

"Čedo in the Netherlands is my cousin. We met up last weekend in Vienna. I mentioned you and he told me everything—how you drove him during the air-raid warning, through the blackout . . ."

I was suddenly filled with a stark attack of intuition. "Svetozar, where are you from? Kopar?"

He began to chuckle again, and then turned serious: "From Gospić." Serbs in that Croatian town certainly have seen happier days than those in the fall of 1991.

And from that moment on there weren't any problems. My boss was surprised at how our collaboration with the Kopar printing press improved and continued without incident; they even lowered the prices. It was great. But for me, Svetozar's sudden transformation somehow meant more than the removal of the problems at work. I had that deceptive feeling that there was finally a light at the end of the tunnel.

NUMBERS 1–3

BY NADA GAŠIĆ

Zvonimirova

Translated by Ellen Elias-Bursac

There is only one building in Zagreb more fear-inspiring than the one where I live: a big, long, gray building visible from afar at the intersection of Držićeva and Vukovarska; its visibility is quite a plus compared to the building where I live; my building can be easily ignored. The other building is the more interesting of the two because it is known for an urban legend purporting that the movie *The Trial* was shot there; yes, *The Trial*, based on Kafka's novel, directed, as I recall, by Orson Welles, and it was said that Alain Delon ran through those very corridors. I may be the only person who remembers the scenes shown on TV here while TV was still black-and-white.

This building where I now live is not, at first glance, so very peculiar. It is not the longest, nor the shortest, nor the ugliest, nor the seediest; there is no information about it on the Internet, not even the most basic explanation of where its name, the Fišer building, comes from. Yet really it couldn't be weirder. It has two entranceways and two street numbers: number 1 and number 3. There is no number 2.

Fišerova, my street, has no other building to the east; across from it are the grounds, surrounded by a stone wall, of the Church of the Madonna of Lourdes which can be entered from either Zvonimira or Vrbanićeva streets.

When I moved into this apartment in February, I was not yet fully aware that the building had tricked me. It did this the way a streetwalker would. The building is on a side street, a nice enough edifice by Zagreb standards, and the short one-way street can only be accessed by the residents. It has cute little balconies with a view of the church garden, a decent façade on which there is no graffiti—a true rarity in this city—and a glassed-in entranceway which in no way hints at what lies behind.

After my divorce I was in the clutches of a brief hysteria while I searched for a new apartment to move into, to purchase. I don't know what it was that gripped me, but I know I was not capable of staying on in the place I had shared with my husband for some fifteen years. I searched only briefly for a new apartment and rushed headlong into the first one that seemed like it would do. Yes, this very one. Standing on the sidewalk on Zvonimira I eyed Fišerova, and walked over to the building and into the entranceway of number 3, took the stairs to the second floor, and then to the third, and got a little winded—there is no elevator—and in the end stepped into this apartment which had just then come onto the market. I took an immediate shine to the forty-five square meters: the kitchenette, bathroom with toilet, hallway, and two smallish rooms. I settled the paperwork with the owners, extracted the standard information that the apartment was in good shape, the neighbors were decent, everything was fine with it, and a month later I moved in, pleased to be living in the center of town yet a little apart from the hubbub and the crowds. Only then did I remember that I hadn't inquired about who had lived there before. I never asked whether anyone had died in the apartment, probably because I figured they'd lie: when asked about such things, Zagreb apartment-sellers always say that the people who used to live there are still alive, or died in a hospital, or in some faraway town. No, I did not ask the previous owners anything that would compel them to lie.

At first I was caught up with all the things people do when they move: painting, buying new furniture and parting with old things that don't fit in the new space, sewing curtains, replacing old appliances, frustrated when I overshot my credit limit, trying out new locations for the bed, dragging furniture around the apartment to the point of absurdity . . . I spent very little time in the entranceway and I must have neglected to inspect it carefully. As if I just didn't see what I should have been seeing. I didn't notice that on the courtyard side of Fišerova number 1 to number 3 were what the residents call "galleries." These were, in fact, tiers of concrete balconies running the length of the building on each floor, and together they created a crater of gaping landings, edged by a low cast-iron railing, facing a yawning, dark, concrete pit of a courtyard in which the more privileged parked their cars. This is a fact I really missed in the true sense of the word. Missed, because I did not want to see that the courtyard side had absolutely nothing in common with its outer façade. Or something like that. Had I circled around the building from Zvonimira, and then if I had come out—via Fišerova—onto Vrbanićeva, and from there onto Heinzlova to number 32 where there is a passageway into the shared courtyard, and had I stepped into the courtyard from there, I would have seen that I was standing at the bottom of a cavern, the sides of which went up four floors. I would have smelled the stink of the pit which I now constantly smell, and with it I'd have had a foreboding feeling of misfortune and of some sort of ending that this stench evokes even for people less sensitive than me. I would also have smelled the bakery that briefly masks the pit stench and then releases, even more intensely, the reek of rot and mold.

If I were to seek a simile to describe my building, it would likely be something trite . . . such as: my building is like a sixty-year-old woman pumped up with silicone and Botox who seduces kids in cafés, and whose body has been betraying her for the last ten years just as the last ten years have betrayed this building. The façade allows not a glimmer of the true state of the building's body. The courtyard was, apparently, copied by the architects from the classic prisons you see in American movies: a jailhouse courtyard over which, stacked one above another, run verandas the length of each floor, and from the veranda you can enter your apartment-cell. The kitchen and bathroom windows look out onto the shared balcony. The *gallery*. They look out and everyone looks in. Light from your windows can be seen from every floor and also from the courtyard. And here ends any notion of privacy.

During the first days after I moved in, I spent very little time in the kitchen; there was a lot to do, food was the last thing on my mind, and I had no feeling for the kitchen; and the bathroom, which was supposed to afford a modicum of relaxation, made me nervous. After my first shower I realized I would have to cover the little window facing the outside balcony completely, put up some sort of opaque blinds, something that would prevent the light inside from shining out on the *gallery*, or rather the veranda/balcony and the open maw of the courtyard. Money was running low and I didn't have the time to take care of this immediately; after a while I got used to leaving the light off so that everything in the bathroom was done in total darkness. The same was, more or less, true of the kitchen.

When I look back, the way I remember it is that only a few days after I moved in I started thinking about the balcony access, the windows whose lights shine for all to see, and, with that, the naked fact, the "information"—as we call it today—about whether a resident was home or not, which room they were in, and what they were up to. Perhaps that same day, I can no longer pin down exactly when, I began to listen for the sounds of water sluicing down the pipes from kitchen and bathroom drains and the sudden swoosh of flushing. I do not remember exactly when I starting doing this, but two weeks can't have passed before I drew a low chair over to the kitchen window from which, in the dark, I watched the windows of my neighbors. And then, that very evening when I pulled the chair up to the window, I realized that not a single neighbor's window was lit. I was stabbed by the realization that all the residents at that very same moment were standing by their dark windows and watching the windows of others. I got up from the chair, ran into the room in the other part of the body of this Botoxed, siliconized building, and looked out that window onto a street no one walks along, into the garden around the church and the birches bowing rhythmically to gusts of wind as if they were growing by a mosque and not a Catholic church. My, my, what a blasphemous image for this cleansed city of ours. Not even nature, if one can even speak of nature in such an urban setting, was going to let me off the hook. If there is someone irritated by early spring, it's me. Nowhere does early spring seem quite as ugly as it does in Zagreb; there's nothing green, nothing blooming, there are leftover chunks of ice everywhere and on them little shimmering puddles of oil, the sidewalks filthy with smears of clay where something is always being dug, the pavement corroded by the salt with which the city defends itself from ice during the winter months . . . and the stray cats. The view through the window of that room out onto the birches that were truly bowing in a kind of despair only heightened my extreme discomfort. It didn't occur to me to go into the bathroom or undress for the night. I lay on the new bed that stank of fresh glue. The new-furniture smell is what I blamed for my insomnia. I got up in the morning, managed to see to the essentials in the bathroom, and decided to venture out and buy some food. I got dressed, slung my bag over my shoulder, unlocked the front door, and stopped. I didn't move another inch. Those who know what a pathological attack of panic and anxiety is like know there is nothing that can force a person to leave the place where he or she happens to be. Those who are not familiar with this fear cannot imagine it. The word *fear* will just have to suffice. I tried to lift a foot, step over the threshold—no dice. I pulled back from the doorway. Run and hide, hide in the smallest room, in a shadow, in a hole, in some tight space, tighter than the apartment-cell, in a crack, in soft fur, in a womb . . . This is why almost every person, regardless of age, calls for their mother when they are afraid: not to get help, no, but to summon the refuge of the womb. I understood: the apartment had become my jail cell and there was no way I would leave it on my own. Someone would have to come and get me. If I survived.

That day, or rather the night that followed, I stopped sleeping in the clinical sense, and life continued along the trajectory it had already begun and there was nothing more to be done about it.

Days followed of going hungry while feeling no hunger pangs, forcing myself to chew on an assortment of refrigerator scraps, opening the odd can, faking wakefulness and then fleeing into phony sleep, lifting my head up off the pillow and imagining sounds, listening to genuine feline yowls, rising and standing by the kitchen window through which I tried keeping track of the neighbors' nonexistent lights. Corridors that I could see down became irresistible and I kept perusing them and memorizing even the slightest changes: a cardboard box was set out there a few hours ago and now it's gone—why is it gone? There were boots there—why have they been moved? On the floor below mine someone pushed a cupboard over so it hides the lower kitchen window—why hide it? But what I did not do even once, which would have been the only healthy thing to do in this whole story, was actually walk down the open balcony, this *gallery*; I also never read a single name on a door. The neighbors remained nameless for me and this was the last straw in a process even an inexperienced physician would diagnose as paranoia. Fear of the nameless. Well, yes, if this was paranoia. For the illness, or condition, of paranoia is not based on what really exists, while everything that was happening to me and my apartment was real, real at this moment, to the point of banality. It was, simply, verifiable. Verifiable, as was the elementary fact which those who were secretly watching my door had surely registered—that I tried to leave the apartment several times but got nowhere. Dressed, I would stand for a few minutes in the doorway, lower my gaze, and stare at the threshold as it grew and grew until it blocked my view of the corridor. No, as soon as I pulled back, as soon as I shut the door from the inside, everything returned, more or less, to visual normal and I felt just a little better. I retreated to the room, lay down on the sofa which had not yet become an enemy that smelled like glue, and I would succeed, with extreme effort, in making myself face the fact that thresholds cannot grow, that my condition was a case of jangled nerves, that I was surely suffering from a delayed reaction to the divorce, the move, and that forty-five years was a short time when you were living an orderly life, and a long time when you were starting to live again from scratch.

No, I felt no hunger, but I still knew I should be eating something, forcing it down—the food in the refrigerator was gone. I had a few cans of food, loners always have them. As long as there were still a few left with that nameless little tab on the lid that simplifies opening it up, everything was fine. I'd swallow a few bites and forego the rest. I admit I even did something

I had never done before and which I can in no way explain or justify: whatever was left in the can I would shake out the living room window. I think I recognized my own hunger in some other invisible being and was drawn by a disturbed and more or less hunger-fed pang of solidarity and a diseased awareness that I should be sharing my sustenance with someone else. That *someone else* was not there with me, so my subconscious sought the *someone else* on the street. The hungry are always out there. No, I do not know why, but I do know that this was what happened. Soon all the cans with the easy-open tabs were gone. I still had larger cans of food, but I couldn't open them for they did not have the handy little tab; the can opener had been misplaced somewhere. All sorts of things had been lost in the move. I discovered there were no more caches of rice or instant polenta, and based on this I was able to ascertain that quite a lot of time must have passed since I stopped venturing out. I decided: it's now or never. Go out only to buy that miserable can opener that will save you from starvation. I got dressed, picked up my pace as I neared the door, opened it, and stopped. I stared at the threshold. It did not grow, but it offered me something much more terrifying than a surreal swelling. There was a dead bird lying there. Probably a sparrow. I leaped back and slammed the door. After several minutes of gasping and swearing, I called the police for the first time in my life. After half an hour, or so it seemed to me, the doorbell rang. Overjoyed, I jumped from the armchair and ran to open the door. A policeman was standing there, I greeted him, looked him in the eye, and then gestured toward the threshold which I did not have the strength to look at myself. Then I mumbled: "There, see what my neighbors have stooped to. A dead bird."

He looked down, then up at me, and said, calmly: "Ma'am, where is this dead bird?"

I said nothing. As I remember it, he told me he would have to come in, he had to take a statement, something like that. I know he sat, he asked when I had moved in, he asked about my relations with the neighbors, he said it was possible that the bird *had* been there, but now it wasn't and he wasn't doubting me . . . Yes, of course: as soon as he sat down he asked to see my ID. That's how it's done . . . He left after a few minutes. I sat there confused, disappointed. I knew how this all must look: I had accused an unknown person of something I couldn't prove.

The difficulty leaving the apartment didn't change. Nor did the problem of food. Yes, of course I could have called a friend or an acquaintance and asked for help. But help is sought by people who still govern their actions, and I no longer belonged to that majority. For weeks I called no one, I answered no calls, and for the most essential I responded with a feigned cool and a brief explanation that as soon as I settled in I would give a housewarming party. No one pressed to see me; people soon tire of lame whining from divorcées. Especially from the jilted. They have enough trouble with their own marriages. There was nothing left for me to do then, though I sensed I would not have the oomph to cross the threshold, to keep at it. And I tried. Needless to say. A dead bird. Again a dead bird. I tried twice more, I no longer had the stuff in me for another go. I lay on the sofa, for I had permanently abandoned the bed with its glue smell. Because of the awkward position, my limbs were numb and stiff, but I would not use the bed. Curled up in a ball, I lay on the sofa and with my last ounce of strength I sucked on some stuck-together candies. This was my only nourishment. I was soothed by the thought that I would fall asleep with no pain. Just like that, fall asleep forever. That is what I was thinking.

I don't remember the day, or whether it was even proper daylight, but I do remember that my nearly defunct ear caught the jangle of the doorbell; I remember I wasn't certain whether the sound was real or imaginary. But I got up and, gripping the furniture, made it to the miserable door. I opened it. I know this sounds diseased, but in the doorway was a man who looked so incredibly similar to Alain Delon that I laughed aloud for the first time, or so it seemed, since the divorce. Of course he looked nothing like the Botoxed, wrinkly old-man Alain Delon, but like the one from the old police movies, presumably dating back to the time of the urban legend about the actor running through the terrible open balconies of the building at the intersection of Vukovarska and Držićeva. Or was that actually Anthony Perkins?

"Ma'am, a few days ago you lodged a complaint about a disturbance. My colleague who visited you then has since been reassigned, so now *I* have come to check up on whether anything like that has happened again. Don't let my civilian clothes confuse you, we are not always in uniform," he said, essentially, though I admit that his exact wording was more concise and less courteous.

I let him in, my adrenaline kicking in, the pathological exhaustion from hunger waning. I told him everything, including the dead birds, and said that I had stopped leaving the apartment because of them, though I knew full well that this was a lie, and that I had shut myself up in the apartment before the first dead bird appeared. He listened. Then he took out a piece of paper and a pencil. "Mrs. Levi, are you certain your neighbors are the ones who left the dead birds at your door?"

I responded nervously: "You have it wrong, I am not Levi. I am Anda Palma."

He smiled, glanced at the piece of paper, and said, "No, you are Mira Levi. It says—"

I got up, furious, went to get my ID card, and shoved it at him resentfully. He gave it a passing glance. He didn't smile this time. "Believable first and last name. Anda Palma. Believable document. But you are Mira Levi. We know this for a fact."

I was not frightened, I was not overcome by a panic attack, I was literally engulfed by horror, such a chilling horror that I was barely able to breathe. Still, I snarled at him.

"Who are *you* who *know* this? Why are you out of uniform if you are a policeman? Please show me your badge!"

"Never ask *anyone* for their badge, especially not a cop. You have no idea what a badge looks like, and even if you did, by the time you get around to checking it you'll probably be too late."

Sometimes it happens that a person who looks remarkably like someone else drops the likeness and becomes an ordinary, unfamiliar face. But this face which I had been looking at and whose eyes were looking into mine—this face so much like the young Delon—morphed completely and became the smooth face of the young Anthony Perkins, grinning with a pure innocence. And with a pure innocence he flashed his idiotic ID. I do not know why, but this calmed me down. Somewhat reassured, I managed to say: "You must know who I am. I am Anda Palma."

The grin faded. His face relaxed, then tightened, and showed a row of overly white teeth. Then I clearly saw that he looked nothing like Alain Delon or Anthony Perkins, but like an indifferent German shepherd. This is the look of a healthy murderer.

Strange, only half an hour earlier the thought of death in my sleep seemed a blessing, but now once I had seen the countenance of death, fear set in. An animal fear of animal death. I caved in and my voice shot up: "Get out or I'll start to shout!"

He was no longer grinning at all. Instead he chuckled sincerely. "You'll shout and the neighbors will come running to help, the ones you complained were terrorizing you? A little unlikely, Mrs. Levi, wouldn't you say?"

I did not shout. I whispered: "Where did you get the idea that I am this Levi? This . . . Mira Levi?" I even added, full of hope: "No doubt this is all a simple misunderstanding, maybe there was a neighbor who went through something similar and also lodged a complaint. And you switched the complaints. My documents are genuine, I am Anda Palma."

"Yes, Mrs. Levi, the documents are genuine, but they are not yours. We have made no mistake, you somehow got hold of someone's identity and that is what we are interested in. Nothing more."

"Sir, you are wrong."

"No, we are not."

"Why do you keep referring to yourself in the plural? Perhaps you are only you, you the *individual*, the one who is wrong. Not the plural *we*, but just *you*, the one and only, the one who is wrong. Why hide behind the plural? I am not doing that, I know who I am."

"You probably do know who you are and that's why it won't be hard for you to explain how you got hold of and why you are using documents that belong to someone else. Someone else's identity. Who is Anda Palma?"

I let him go on talking.

"You, Mrs. Levi, lived in this apartment some twenty years ago, then you disappeared. There is no information on you, no files at the police showing you registered at an address. Nor a name change. Nothing. I know, computer error is possible and it happens more often than we'd like. And I am asserting nothing, I am merely asking: whose identity did you take? We know it was more than twenty years ago when you left our city. In this city we don't linger long on those who leave, do we, but we would like to know how a person can disappear and then reappear under a different name. The last information we had about you, Mira Levi, is that you sold this apartment. And after that, nothing. The sale of the apartment was legal, just as the purchase of it was. But it is suspicious that you sold the apartment to people twenty years ago from whom you bought the same apartment back two months ago using a different name. They, of course, recognized you, but said nothing; all that mattered to them was the money. It's tough to sell apartments these days, long gone are the 1990s. Your neighbors recognized you and reported it; we went to speak with the former owners and the story snagged only on the name. Your identity."

"My neighbors . . ."

"Yes, your neighbors recognized you, they say, by the smell of cat urine that always follows you. They recognized you by the smell, though only later did they recognize your face. Women can easily alter what they look like, and some twenty years have passed . . . a long time for a woman's appearance. Yes, they recognized you by your smell and by the way you tossed cat food out into the street just as you always used to. A cat came to thank you with the dead bird. Don't cats do that? And there you have it. The whole mystery of the dead bird. We only care about how and why you took someone else's identity. Let's forget about the cats and the dead birds."

What he was saying was so far-fetched that I clutched at the most ridiculous part of it. "What is that you said about a smell?"

"Mrs. Levi, a person changes over time. But their basic smell, despite all deodorants and perfumes, despite the aging process of the human body, stays the same. A person leaves their smell behind in the apartment where they live. Dogs know that best." Again he sneered like a German shepherd. "No matter what you say, no matter what documents you present, you *are not* the person you claim to be. You are Mira Levi and your neighbors recognized you by your smell." He slapped his thighs with a clap of finality as if he were getting ready to leave, and added: "Perhaps one of the descendants of the cats you used to feed developed a genetic ability to remember your smell and thank you in the name of all its late ancestors."

I got up and went into the kitchen. To stop listening to him. He followed me. I was horrified by his soft steps. The patter of soundless paws. I was being followed by a dog, a German shepherd with a muzzled sneer. I was even startled when it spoke again with a human voice: "Have no fear, Mrs. Levi, have no fear of dead birds or living cats, or living neighbors. Just fear stolen identity. That you must fear, Mrs. Levi."

Fear raised all the hairs up and down my body. He had shaken me . . . This man, this man-dog, was just standing there watching me when I grabbed a large can from the kitchen counter, swung it, and smashed him in the temple. He fell cinematically, as Alain Delon would have fallen. I leaned down and bashed his temple with the can rim until the bone showed through. Then I got up, looked at the dented, bloodied can, and on it, for the first time, I noticed the cat food label. My gaze crossed the bloody kitchen floor and rested on the emptied cans that had kept me alive for a month. Cans labeled as fancy cat food. I heard the hungry cats yowling in the courtyard. I did not look at the crushed face of the man lying there in his cinematic pose. Actually, I don't know who he resembled or whether he resembled anyone at all. A handsome cop? A handsome, quiet killer? I wasn't even sure whether it was Delon who played in *The Trial,* or Perkins. I do not care to check. Truth that comes too late changes nothing. Nothing changes. Nothing.

For I have murdered and nothing can be changed here.

Now I am waiting for them to come and take me away.

Mrs. Anda Palma, if this was she, stretched her stiff neck and glanced once more at her laptop. She did not reread the text she had entered. With her mouse she clicked *forward.* To *all.*

And nothing can be changed here either.

PART III

Downtown Freaks

WRAITHS

BY ZORAN PILIĆ

Downtown East

Translated by Ellen Elias-Bursac

Let's sell this place and buy a house somewhere normal. Give it some thought.

What do you mean, somewhere normal? A village? We'd keep pigs and chickens, plant potatoes? I can't handle that, woman, no way. I'd rather die, right here and now, than live to the age of ninety-five in some village.

It doesn't have to be a village. Just somewhere outside of this rat's nest, these buildings with their grimy façades, away from the maniacs, weirdos, hubbub, away from this chaos and the old people dying alone in their apartments and rotting there for days and weeks or being devoured by household pets, away from the piss-rank entranceways, the cracked walls, the rot, the moronic, pushy neighbors, the children whose shrieks pierce the brain, away from this hell on earth, please . . .

Forget it. I'm telling you, no way. I will never leave here.

Petar, who was born, attended school, grew up, and still lived and worked all within the same few square kilometers, could not imagine what tragic circumstances could move him out of Lower Town—the only place on earth where he felt reality the way you feel the warmth of the sun on your skin. There was a world beyond the borders of what he had always experienced as essential Zagreb, it would be silly to claim otherwise, but that was not his world. So anything east of Heinzelova and west of Republike Austrije Street, north of Ilica and south of the train tracks, was simply not acceptable to Petar. He could nod to the rest of the world, even see parts of it from the perimeter of his territory, but nothing drew him out, and for the last few years, with only a few exceptions, he had stopped leaving the center of town, the beehive in which life and death were constantly abuzz.

In his youth he'd had the courage to visit several places in the outer ring: he went to the coast, Florence, Venice, Budapest, Sarajevo, Belgrade, Vienna, Dubrovnik, Portorož, perhaps a few more places, but none of them impressed him much. Sure, fine, the sea was salty, the people were welcoming and relaxed, they lived in those sometimes even pretty towns carved of white stone, with planted palms, museums with phenomenal works of art, colorful sunrises and sunsets, the women were beautiful and alluring, the sky clear and the blue expanses just like on the postcards, yet his heart would start pounding only when he came back from these brief, pointless trips.

Katja left in silence.

While he stood at the door and waited for the love of his life to pack up her belongings, he pictured flinging himself to his knees and pleading: *Stay, please stay*—he pictured this scene stripped of all dignity, and knew he could never, physically, do such a thing. He would have knocked something over and it would have looked ridiculous.

From the start he knew their relationship would run its course in time. He had never been a babe magnet, he had never harbored illusions about his good looks or charm, after all, and once he'd turned forty things got no better, indeed they'd gone downhill.

After shipwrecks of her own, Katja had come into his life and he did not push her away. He let everything play out as it would.

"Jesus," she had said, appalled, "your place is packed with pornography."

Those are classics, he wanted to say. Instead he shrugged. Before the Internet had nearly wiped out the pornography industry, he had collected almost a hundred films with unforgettable stars of that detested genre which had existed and survived on the periphery of the cinematic arts, shoved aside and unacknowledged, the black sheep of the family. Select titles of films with Teresa Orlowski, Jenna Jameson, Traci Lords, Cicciolina, Vanessa del Rio, Moana Pozzi, Marilyn Chambers, and Linda Lovelace held a place of pride on his shelves side by side with great works of world literature and concert albums by King Curtis, Miles Davis, and Thelonius Monk.

Two forty-somethings in one of their last flings before they inevitably parted ways and drifted off into the swamp of indifference—that was how he saw them. And that is exactly how they were.

For a while he still felt her presence in the apartment. Her fragrance on the pillow, little traces everywhere, but then the place was flooded with the all-too-familiar feeling of angst that spread like rust everywhere, corroding heart and mind.

"Mr. Miller," he began, "I apologize for taking your valuable time . . ."

"Oh, come right in, please. What brings you to me, my good man?" Mr. Miller had hair the color of burnished gold, unusually broad shoulders, and a square, jutting jaw; he gestured generously as if he wanted to dismiss any thought that he would be short of anything as inconsequential as time.

In the twenty years since Petar had been analyzing foreign currency payments at his job, he had exchanged perhaps ten words with his supervisors. The bank during these years had gone through a rough period: first it was sold to the Italians, then they sold it to the Austrians, and finally the Austrians, after a series of mishaps and major scandals with loans which went, as the saying goes, under the wheat fields to highly suspicious clients, they sold it to the Germans. Over the last six years, since Mr. Miller had been in charge of the department for foreign currency activity, he had become acquainted with and had exchanged at least a few words, purely out of courtesy or in passing, with almost all of his employees. He had never, however, met Petar, or at least he had no memory of the man, which was no surprise because, thought Mr. Miller, this is not a face that would be etched in one's memory.

"I'll get right to the point, if you allow me. I have been working here for many years, as I'm sure you know, as a foreign currency payments analyst."

"Yes, of course."

Mr. Miller had inquired of his secretary and learned that Petar did, indeed, work at this job, but what exactly analysts of foreign currency payments did was beyond him. This detail bothered him a bit, particularly because he couldn't come out and ask, yet felt he ought to know what all the people under him did. In an ideal world, yes, but this, God only knows, was not an ideal world.

"I also want to bring to your attention that I have not spent a single day on sick leave to date, which you are free to corroborate."

"No need, please, I believe you and I congratulate you, bravo! This is truly, as they say, an accomplishment worthy of admiration. Not a single day, I take my hat off to you, sir, you must be made of steel. I mean to say—your health serves you well and thank heaven for that!"

"Indeed, twelve years of service, not a day of sick leave, and orderly reports which have never received a single complaint from my supervisor. I approach my work seriously and thoroughly—nothing gets by me. Today I am here with my one and only request, sir: allow me to do this work, with the same fervor, responsibility, and precision, from home—that is what I am asking."

"If I have understood you correctly—you prefer not to come into the office at all but to do your whole job at—"

"In my own apartment, correct. The whole thing is, clearly, technically, absolutely doable. It doesn't matter whether I am here at the office, two blocks away in the silence of my own home, or in any city with an Internet connection on the planet earth."

At a loss, Mr. Miller lightly smoothed his tie as if patting a rabbit or some other small animal. He had expected a request for a promotion or a raise, perhaps a complaint about a colleague, that sort of thing, but this fellow had something entirely different in mind. "Whatever prompted you, if I may ask, to make this unusual request for a change, how can I put it . . . of your work environment, your surroundings?"

"The reasons are of a personal nature. I do not feel comfortable around people, you know, I never have, but recently I've been finding it difficult to leave my safe haven. Even for five minutes. I am uncomfortable going into greater detail. This is the problem of today's society, unfortunately: we are alienating ourselves from one another and retreating into our shells, into a reality we can control. Chaos reigns outside, as you can see for yourself."

"True," Mr. Miller glanced inadvertently out the window, "the outside world is one vast bedlam."

The analyst of foreign currency payments and his boss, each

at his end of the table, gazed for a time, silently, at scenes in the inscrutable outside world.

Freed of the obligation of going to work each day, those strenuous expeditions into the jungle of cruel office life, Petar soared on the wings of euphoria. He felt something not unlike happiness and an electric shock of good will, even elation at times, that would have scared him had not beneath it, under the skin, at the core of his being, his original sorrow been rolling along, his sorrow at the very nature of existence.

"Son," his father had said, knowing his end was near, hence no need to prettify the truth, decorate it with illusions like one would decorate a Christmas tree, "life is full of shit—one disappointment after another. Life will not be merciful, so find shelter somewhere out of the wind, avoid trouble, and watch what you eat."

His father's words, as one might expect, did not fall on fertile ground. For God's sake, he was barely eighteen at the time and still hopeful. Eventually he came to realize: there is no place for outsized expectations, life is truly a travail, a shit storm, and whenever you think, *Here, I've found a place for myself*—just as with his discovery of literature, he had longed to be creative and for a number of years had written and written as if in a trance, reading and writing again, and creating, in the end, an amazing manuscript that was over three thousand pages long—the shit storm invariably followed, and swamped him completely. No one, it turned out, would even look at it, let alone read his monumental work, and, feeling ridiculed and rejected, he realized that even in literature, the tried and true shelter for lost souls, he would find no meaning. Not even a respite.

And besides, he thought, *I am not exercising, I'm not watching what I eat, I'm too old, stunted like a desert shrub, and I'll probably never meet a woman who wants to be with me.*

For days, weeks on end, he did not leave the apartment. He worked at his job on his home computer and sent his analyses daily by e-mail to the main office, his food and other necessities were delivered to his door, he downloaded movies and music from the Internet as did millions of others, and if he wanted to feel the warmth of the sun or a breeze, all he had to do was step out onto the balcony. At some point during the day, usually between ten a.m. and noon, he'd collect the garbage and go down to the building's trash cans. Sometimes, not often and not for long, he'd light a cigarette and stay down there, observing the passersby through the narrow slits of glass in the front door. Women went by on the sidewalk as if in a dream, untouchable, and yet, he thought, probably they, too, from time to time, felt disgruntled, sad, lonely, or simply afraid of disappearing.

By early summer he had gone beyond a hundred days of voluntary confinement. With every day it got harder to imagine the moment when he would venture forth again, stroll around on the sidewalks, get onto a tram with the crowds, or have a cup of coffee at one of the outdoor cafés. Sooner or later, no doubt, he'd venture out into the open. Maybe out of pure curiosity, or, more likely, with some clear goal.

In Lower Town, the most real of all worlds, without much pomp or fuss, two new sex shops opened. If someone were to ask him what we talk about when we talk about sex and Croats, Petar would have answered, *Croats are old school, most of us do it in silence and in the dark, like hard-line conservatives,* but the opening of the new sex shops and the fact that the old ones were still in business did not support such theories.

At first glance, theirs was a standard array such as one can see on the websites for all city sex shops. Just for the fun of it, Petar examined the various toys and paraphernalia. The only thing that drew his attention were the deluxe inflatable dolls. Unlike the ordinary kind, these ones looked alarmingly real. He finally chose the Jessica special deluxe model, clicked on *Add to Shopping Cart*, and paid with his Visa.

A little socializing wouldn't hurt, he thought, justifying to himself why he had indulged his first impulse and without a thought ordered this almost perfect woman. Had he stopped to think, he probably wouldn't have, just as he hadn't done many other things in his life.

Little drops of sweat had merged into a single larger one on the delivery guy's forehead. Who knows how many deliveries he'd made that day.

Petar never felt comfortable around delivery guys. He wondered whether they hated themselves and if that hatred spilled over onto the people to whom they were delivering food, goods, and everything else. He tried to dispel this feeling of awkwardness by giving tips, but each amount seemed somehow pitiful, condescending. Every time, he would remember this one instance with an older delivery guy. He'd taken a pizza from the man and handed him five kuna. The man had stared at the coin in his hand for an eternity, as if Petar had handed him a piece of chicken shit—he'd stared at the five kuna with disgust.

On the other hand, Petar felt equally awkward in the company of people in general, perhaps with all living beings. *I can't know what someone is thinking by the expression on his face. Who knows,* he'd sink deeper into bleak thoughts, *maybe the delivery guy actually enjoys delivering, the postman bringing the mail, and the waiter serving drinks—how the hell can I know what's going on in their heads?*

"There you go, delivery is free of charge," mumbled the guy while handing him the package and, instead of turning to go, lingering for a moment in the hallway.

Petar reached automatically for his pocket, but found only small change. "Just a moment."

He set down the package on the shoe stand and started riffling through his jackets on the coat rack. In one pocket he found two crumpled bills, a ten and a twenty. In a panic he thought ten kuna was too little, twenty was like throwing money around, and giving the guy all thirty was out of the question. What kind of a message would that be sending, he asked himself, if he were to throw around thirty-kuna tips? He imagined this man, who had just delivered an inflatable doll, making fun of him to his colleagues at the sex shop: *What a miserable fool, you should have seen him, boys, I tell you, he gave me those two bills as if they were two wilted leaves of lettuce—the fucking pervert.*

"For your effort . . ." he muttered, and handed the ten kuna to the guy.

"Oh, no, no . . ."

"Please, take it, I insist."

"Okay, but you shouldn't have . . ." The guy finally took the bill and glanced at it briefly. That same glance, again, that could mean anything, and Petar still couldn't shed the feeling that this was a look of total disappointment. "Is everything okay?" the guy asked.

"Yes, everything is fine, thanks. Have a nice day, and . . . yes, cheers."

"Cheers, bye."

Closing the door, he took the package and flung it, in a rage, to the other end of the hall, and then, in passing, kicked it into the kitchen. The package banged against a chair, the arm of the chair tipping over a cup with coffee dregs in it that was sitting, for some reason, on the very edge of the table. He watched the coffee as if entranced, while it dripped down the leg of the chair and pooled on the floor.

Have I gone mad? Did I just have an inflatable doll delivered, give that guy a ten-kuna tip, and then say, Cheers? *Why can't I deal with even the simplest transaction? Who cares what someone thinks of a tip and whether it insults him for some lame reason? No one cares about people they don't know, about their feelings, their principles, so why should I?*

Petar spent hours more in an exhaustive analysis of his past actions, mistakes he had made with others and everything bad that had been done to him; at moments he took pity on himself and then he'd hate himself for it, and for a change he'd pity the rest of the world, such as his parents, his neighbors, Katja, yes, her more than the others, and not because she didn't have her reasons for leaving, but because she had the audacity to enter his life, turn everything upside down inside him, and then leave *him* to deal with the mess! He felt sorry for all those lonely and unhappy people who knocked around their rooms like ghosts, listening to the creaking of the furniture, and always wondering whether *every* life was worth living and why the void that begins at the moment of death would be any worse than the horror that life entails.

Jessica spent the night in the package on the kitchen floor.

She looked crumpled and not at all sexy. After he had inflated her, things improved, but only slightly. He rummaged through the cupboards and drawers and came up with some items of clothing Katja had forgotten in her rush to leave or hadn't wanted to take with her.

We'll dress you up in this skirt and top.

Jessica didn't mind. She lay there stiffly with her arms offered in a factory embrace.

Petar felt something like stage fright; the air, it seemed, filled with the fragrance of the distant southern seas. He fished out a cigarette, went onto the balcony, and after some ten days of abstinence lit up. From somewhere the smell of burning rubber reached him. He scanned the horizon but nowhere did he see a trace of smoke. He felt slightly dizzy from the cigarette. His knees wobbled.

"What the fuck do you want from me?" He stormed into the room and struck the doll. "Tenderness, love, a hug? Forget that . . . forget it, fuck you!"

Jessica said nothing. From the blow to her head she bounced away, tipped over onto her stomach, and stayed lying there. Her skirt had slipped up, exposing her perfect round bottom.

"That wasn't me," he whispered, stroking her red hair. "You must forgive me, Jess, it won't happen again, I promise."

Her dogged silence made him feel worse than all the harsh words or actions such an expensive doll could have used to fight back. Somewhere at the very edge of his consciousness there was always the information, like a flickering lamp: *This is an inanimate thing, you know, it doesn't feel pain, love, scorn, or anything else.* From other centers, however, the opposite information was fast arriving.

"We are equally living and dead, doll, you and me, facing them alone."

Equally real and unreal, dear, like living wraiths at the end of the world.

That night Jessica and Petar made love. Actually, love came later—even he was able to distinguish sex from the various degrees of bonds between two people. He was genuinely disarmed by the way in which Jessica communicated, and she did it, at least at first, telepathically—she'd broadcast her thoughts into space. Part of this he could understand, while the rest turned into incoherent noise melting into the ordinary hum of the city. One time he deflated her, pressed the life out of her, rolled her up like a crepe, and stowed her away in the box.

That was his last act of rebellion against the new form of reality which fell like a heavy curtain cloaking the ossified, fossil world. *The process of change is slow and painful. You want to interrupt it all with violence, but in the end,* he thought, *we are probably headed for something better.*

The next day he was already combing her flaming hair and singing, *"Good morning, star shine, the earth says hello . . ."*

The first fears and insecurities were overcome like childhood diseases. Without considering the consequences, Petar simply gave in to the new idyll. With Jessica he felt somehow whole, as if she—exactly as she was—was perfect, what he had been missing his whole life.

The baseball season was in full swing. She confessed to him that she rooted for the Dodgers and she watched, with intense focus, two games in a row with him, which Katja could never have handled—she'd begin to roll her eyes and pout after two innings, reproaching him that no one in their right mind could understand baseball. He did not have to sketch out for Jessica why it was the perfect sport and why it made most other sports seemed like lowly village games. They laughed over romantic, sometimes silly comedies, listened to old jazz albums, sometimes he talked about himself and she listened with great interest as if his life were an exciting thriller; whatever they did, she never held him back, and Petar, at least a little, began to feel comfortable in his own skin.

"Jess," he declared one day, "I think this is love."

And what else would it be, my dark Petar, than love?

"Does that mean that you love me, you sea bear?"

I love you, you hippo.

"And I love you, you Tasmanian devil you."

* * *

In early August a guest appearance was announced by one of the rare contemporary writers whose books Petar had found a place for in his home library.

"David Albahari is coming from Canada for a short tour of former Yugoslavian countries."

A Canadian writer, is he?

"Jessica, baby, Albahari is a Belgrade writer. It's just that he lives in Canada," he explained.

Well, that's terrif, replied Jessica—literature was not at the top of her list of the most important things in the world.

"He will read from his most recent novel in Zagreb in less than three weeks and it will be right here, near us, in the neighborhood."

Nice.

"Would you like to go? I definitely want to go."

But you never leave the house.

"Jess, of course I leave the house, just not every day like other people."

You go ahead. I'd rather stay home, if you don't mind, my little flying bear.

"I don't mind, my little potato beetle, not in the slightest. You just stay here."

Petar did not mind. He knew he couldn't expect understanding and approval if he was seen with such a young and remarkably attractive woman as Jessica. They'd think he was an old, complex-laden goat who didn't deserve to be with someone half his age and many times more attractive. People are, regrettably, like that—shallow, hypocritical, vengeful, poised for a lynching at a moment's notice.

All day long a south wind plucked, like a seasoned mariachi player, the thin strings of Petar's nerves, pushing him into a state of heavy tension. Two hours before the beginning of the literary gathering, ready to go out, he plunked down on the sofa. His right hand was cold and sweaty, and his left dry and warm—he rubbed them together, linked his fingers, and twiddled his thumbs.

Jessica lay behind him and stared at the ceiling.

He had a bad feeling that something was about to go wrong. But what could possibly happen at a plain old literary gathering? Nothing, he told himself, Albahari would come, the moderator Petar Milat—they shared their first name—would lead the program, the owners of the club—Indira and Anja—and another twenty, possibly twenty-five people would show up, all of them members of various cultural and subcultural groups, the occasional failed writer, drunk actor, a couple of students, a couple of pensioners—all in twos like in Noah's ark.

The assembled audience would, all in all, be one of the most innocuous groups imaginable. Petar knew their type well: They often spoke all at the same time, discussed literature, Asian cinematography, Lacan, Barthes, or Cioran, they were tolerant, they were animal lovers, they spoke at least one foreign language extremely well, they regularly voted in parliamentary and presidential elections—this was their civil duty, they felt—they did not get into brawls in bars, they did not pick their noses and spit on the floor, they were all at Leonard Cohen's last concert, they took yoga classes, they'd flirt with the idea of eating vegetarian, but then they'd change their mind—*Hey, it's complicated*—and aside from their fondness for peculiar haircuts and eccentric clothing, they were as peace-loving and nonthreatening as a school of goldfish in a goldfish pond.

"I'm off now," Petar announced at one point, standing up and smoothing his pants. "Jess, as we agreed, if someone rings the doorbell—don't open the door."

Si señor, she replied, still staring at the ceiling.

The usual city bustle bizarrely delighted Petar these days. Even so, he kept a wary eye on the passersby, their faces, hands, their walk.

All those years he'd seen Lower Town as if it were a broken heart on the broad, lined palm of Zagreb. One late afternoon, finally stripped of all illusions, he discovered the real truth: here, in the very center of the city and the rest of the planet, there was a crime playing out at all levels.

As much as people changed the city, so the city changed them with even less mercy. The mutual destruction dated from the very beginnings and wouldn't stop until civilization was finally crushed. Everything would end in ruins. One day there would no longer be any people on these streets, the musty old five-story buildings would come tumbling down one after another.

From an entranceway, leaning on a cane, emerged an elderly man. He squinted at the sun like a mole. It looked to Petar like he couldn't go any farther, he just stood there leaning on the wall. For the last time, Petar imagined, this guy was taking in the world around him, while other people, blind to death, passed him by silently. Just two or three months before, Petar wouldn't have been able to see him.

Today, when I want it least, he sneered to himself, *today I see it all: people inured to others' pain, silenced, insecure, and lonely, people horrified by life, children and the elderly, men and women, gradually disappearing, vanishing, crumbling into the tiniest particles, which the next rain will rinse off the surface of the earth, along with all the other garbage.*

Just as it would wash him away. *I am,* he thought, *destroyed to the core as much by my own guilt or destiny as by the fact that I grew up and stayed living right on this very spot, and not in some other, less real world.*

Twice he crossed the street and both times waited patiently for the green light. At Zvonimirova he got onto the bus which had been running for weeks in place of certain tram lines because of roadwork, and took it to the Džamija traffic circle. From there, walking on the sidewalk, one step at a time, he reached Martićeva 14 and the reclining statue of fra Grga Martić, behind whose massive bronze back were Albahari, Milat, and a little farther off two young women stood smoking. He noticed the red smudge of their lipstick on the filters of their cigarettes.

Petar still couldn't pinpoint what would go wrong. He simply had this uneasy presentiment that had not subsided, perhaps it had even heightened by a degree or two.

"Hey, Petar," Milat greeted him, pumping his hand, "I haven't seen you in *ages*."

He'd known Milat from when he was still attending literary gatherings and believed there'd be someone who would publish his amazing manuscript of several thousand pages.

"Er, yeah, I haven't been around recently, work, whatever."

Albahari was sitting on a bench and rummaging for something in a bag with a flashy DM logo. Petar nodded to him and Albahari nodded back. Milat was wearing a jacket that looked like it was part of the uniform worn by the leaders of the Communist Party of the People's Republic of China. They ventured into a conversation about László Krasznahorkai. Milat had recently read his latest collection of short stories, and as they had once talked about the famous Hungarian, it was as if they were picking up where they'd left off.

"You wouldn't believe it," said Milat, "the book is 450 pages long and guess how many sentences he uses?"

Petar could not possibly hazard a guess as to the number of sentences Krasznahorkai had employed in his most recent book because it had not been translated into Croatian—Milat had read the German edition—nor had he heard or read anything about it.

"Fifty-three fucking sentences!"

Petar thought it unusual that Milat had inserted the *fucking* into his declaration, but since he had said this with unconcealed relish, maybe the word had simply imposed itself, elbowed its way in, to bring the necessary weight to the whole sentence.

"Incredible," Albahari said, still digging around in the bag with his left hand.

Petar couldn't believe it either and said as much.

"Fif-ty-three . . ." repeated Milat, stressing each syllable.

"Well, that calls for a drink." Albahari had pulled out a bottle of something that could only be homemade *rakija*. "Help yourselves. I can't before a performance." He handed the bottle to Petar.

On the label were the words, *Deadly Brew*, and below that—three grinning skulls.

"A friend of mine gave it to me this morning. Have a swig, go ahead."

Petar smiled in discomfort, handing the bottle off to Milat: "You go ahead, I'll have some in a bit . . ."

Milat studied the bottle and took a swig. "Huh . . . nice burn, absolutely." He blinked, his eyes bugging out.

He might go blind from that noxious homemade hooch, thought Petar. *It wouldn't be surprising.* He had read somewhere that in Russia people often went blind from drinking vodka distilled in unsupervised conditions.

He wasn't partial to *rakija*, but the bottle had come back to him and he finally sipped a little, not wanting to appear to Albahari and Milat like one of those wimps who refuses anything that isn't by the book in its factory packaging.

Albahari sat down and fingered the copies of his new novel and the two of them stood there in silence, handing the bottle back and forth, each taking a swig or two. Then some other people came and joined them. The bottle went from hand to hand as if they were putting on a performance in honor of the guest from faraway Canada.

Taking advantage of the crowd, Petar slipped, unnoticed, into the club. He felt the *rakija* flame in his belly and spread through his whole body. He leaned on the bar and asked for a coffee and mineral water. The air suddenly filled with the fragrance of caramel. He watched the people moving in and out, the music and their voices mingling in meaningless, garbled clamor. He felt like asking all of them if they found nothing odd about the strong smell of caramel. They could smell it as much as he could, but they were pretending this was normal and it brought him to the verge of rage.

He decided he needed to calm down. Gripping the bar he drank down the coffee and mineral water. It didn't help, the flames had engulfed his head and hundreds of thoughts were seething inside. There was no way he could push them away or grab hold of just one; he felt weak and a chill climbed his spine like poison ivy.

Unsteadily, he made his way to the men's room, locked the door behind him, and splashed water on his face for a long time, rubbing his temples and neck. The mirror was right there, straight in front of him, but Petar did not want to peer into that world, convinced he would see things he didn't want to see.

It started more than half an hour later than it was supposed to and though that was nothing unusual—literary gatherings never begin on time—Petar didn't like it. While he was in the bathroom the club had filled with people. Milat was leafing through his notes, and then he leaned toward a young woman perched on an Almodóvar-esque red two-seater to his left, and began explaining something to her in great depth. A very relaxed atmosphere reigned, which seemed obviously fake to Petar—didn't anyone feel the tension, a sour mood, at the very least prickles on their skin, or heat? What a bunch of fucking posers.

"Let's start . . ." he said all of a sudden, not too loudly, but amid the buzz this one phrase echoed like an ugly curse.

All heads turned toward him; they stared at him as if right before their eyes he had picked up a shotgun and blown the brains out of a baby panda.

"Right, now we can begin," Milat clapped his hands.

Albahari was fine with that. Everyone, as if on command, turned from Petar to the guest. Understandably, Petar felt a certain taint of enmity or at least lack of understanding, but being familiar with herd philosophy and actions, he suffered stoically.

Milat opened with a few introductory remarks from which it was immediately clear to everyone that he had fully mastered the matter at hand and was prepared to ask the author all sorts of questions, not only about the novel, but about a host of other things. Petar tried to follow the conversation attentively, he listened and heard the words, but he didn't understand them—as if they were being spoken in some ancient, long-extinct language. The names Thomas Bernhard, Michel de Montaigne, and Jim Jarmusch cropped up, in just that order, but in what context, exactly—this eluded him. He felt a shortage of oxygen in the room. *Breathe in, breathe out, you won't faint*, he repeated to himself. Salvos of laughter spread around him. Albahari was not the sort of writer to handle himself with great solemnity as if interpreting Christ's agonies when he spoke publicly, so he would toss a little something humorous into the conversation, a joke, something lighthearted, not wanting to make a mystery of the literary gathering, writing, or himself. Unfortunately, Petar was still fighting for every molecule of oxygen. Because of the noise, traffic, and everything else, the front door to the club had to be shut. He knew he would have to step outside in the next few minutes to keep from fainting, and yet he really did not want to be the first to leave.

With great effort Petar dropped his head and waited for someone to leave the room, to light up a cigarette or whatever. Second, he could leave; first—no way.

He heard the door open. He turned and saw Katja. She was coming in, taking care so the door wouldn't squeak. Something was different about her, he couldn't tell what exactly. Someone came in behind her and the someone was holding her hand. An older guy, older than Petar and everyone else at the club, gray hair tied back in a pitiful ponytail. He stood by Katja, holding her hand. The fact that he was a whole head shorter than her brightened Petar's mood. He grinned as he watched them. All the tension, the ugly presentiments and anxieties, vanished as if by a miracle; he could breathe, handle himself, he could follow the conversation between Milat and Albahari, but no longer cared to.

Katja shot him a confused smile. *She didn't expect to run into me here*, thought Petar, pleased. *She didn't expect she'd ever see me again, but here I am, ma'am, I am still here*. He smiled at her in passing and left.

The sidewalk rolled on into the distance; other people were also walking along it—there were dogs on long leashes, babies sleeping in strollers, and he strode along with them, the smile never leaving his face. He breathed in the warm summer air and the whole city smelled of burnt sugar.

SLICES OF NIGHT

BY ANDREA ŽIGIĆ-DOLENEC

Borongaj

Translated by Coral Petkovich

If only it doesn't rain today; just let it hold out for today, then it can fall for days on end without stopping, it can flood the whole town, it's at liberty to turn into a torrent and sweep everything away. It can become a boundless lake or a deluge swallowing everything: all the trams and the red roofs, and everything else devised by the human mind, along with the greenery shaped by nature. It can all disappear, but only after this day has passed—so thought Roni when he got up and looked out the window, watching the clouds chase one another, join together into myriad shades of gray.

He would sleep through all alarms and evacuations, hear nothing and see nothing, he would sleep deeply, dead drunk, in the end just dead, but he would die happy. He had a good feeling about it. He knew that what he had been anticipating for weeks and impatiently getting ready for would end the way he wanted, which was the only just and possible way. No doubt about that. He never left even the slightest possibility for the worm of doubt to creep into his thoughts. He did not allow it to sow seeds of weakness and uncertainty, to make him hesitate when making the most important decisions. He thought quickly and always knew what, when, and how he needed to do things; he knew what would happen too, and if he did not, he believed he knew. He believed in inevitability, in fate, and in God; he believed in himself, in his mother with whom he lived in one of the small, quiet streets in Borongaj; he believed in Marek and Gonzo because they had never let him down; and he did not believe in politicians, bankers, journalists, or lawyers. Until now he had never had the opportunity to punch even one of them in the face, but he was sure that he would have that chance now. Because he wanted it, and when Roni wanted something, he made it happen.

For example, he could have become a successful soccer player, if he had wanted to. He had the talent; a ball was between his feet from the time he was small, and he could see the stadium from the window in his room. It was the first thing his eyes caught sight of in the morning and the last thing he saw at night before he closed them. One of his earliest memories was the sounds he heard during a match, when he was still too small to become a spectator because he did not have a father to take him to matches. And that was what he wanted more than anything, more than any of the toys that everyone had and that his mother could not afford to buy him. He imagined the ball rolling on the grass, the players seizing it from one another, how the grandstand would shake when the ball ended up in the net.

Even as a child he was a rough but good player, always the best in the school yard. He joined his first club as an eight-year-old, but they never gave him a chance to show what he knew. With their discipline they had killed all his passion for playing the game and thus lost forever a top player who could have earned millions. So thought Roni. Nothing could kill his love for soccer. He was a regular visitor to the stadium, but more than that, he was a passionate fan, who measured time from match to match, experiencing every defeat and every victory as though it were his own, analyzing every move the players made as though he were their trainer, and cursing the referee scoundrels.

Today Roni awoke close to eight o'clock. He could not remember the last time adrenaline had woken him so early. He twisted and turned in the bed, but from his first waking second, excitement was pumping through his veins. For years now he had not found it necessary to begin his day in the morning; in any case, the day was far too long. He did not have a job, and was not looking for one, so that there was no reason to go out in the daylight—except to the local café for his early-afternoon coffee, after eating his mother's lunch. The night was his time, the time he felt the best, whether he walked in the empty and noiseless streets or spent the hours in some raucous bar using up the money he and the other guys scrounged from passersby.

Sometimes Roni was a little on edge. From time to time he would feel a tension in the palms of his hands which would spread further and take over completely; and when Roni was tense, it was not good. He was angry, he broke things around the house and destroyed the furniture. To feel at peace with himself, he needed a regular supply of fights. That was his medicine, which he happily swallowed together with alcohol. For this reason he liked to go to places where it was easy to find someone he could push accidentally, and then beat up; or someone who would stare at him a second too long, or someone who annoyed him with their loud laughter. Roni had a solution for all of them.

He did not smile much, neither did he talk very much. Why waste words on useless conversation, when everything could be resolved simply and much more quickly? Even when it had to do with women. When he needed them, he found them without conversation, and his taciturnity did not bother them in the short encounters. Longer and more often did not happen, so they had no opportunity to get to know his confused and irritable character, for which only one woman had any understanding: his mother. Roni much preferred male company. He got along well with his buddies; women were always complicating matters. He never could understand what they really wanted.

Now he put his supporters' scarf around his neck and his knife in the right pocket of his pants. He never went out without his switchblade, because a clever man must always think ahead and be ready for whatever could befall him. All sorts of idiots moved around the town and you could never know what might happen. Roni knew he was smarter than them, and had faster reactions too. They would have no chance at all in an encounter with him. He left the house and went toward Branimir Street, where Marek and Gonzo were waiting for him; from there they slowly walked toward Jelačić Square and then by way of Vlaška and Maksimir to the stadium. They stopped at various bars on the way, drank beer and then cognac, then beer again, and conjured victory with much noise, along with those who shared the same passion for bars and soccer.

He liked matches where there was a lot on the line, because of the energy rolling through the streets that filled him with quivering anticipation, that carried him along and threw him in the air, making him feel he was part of something big and important. Those were the days he remembered the best and the longest. He would have liked his life to be an unending chain of such days and nights, a huge derby which was never finished, during which he would again wake up with the same feeling of belonging.

The rhythm, made up of many powerful male voices and the beating of drums, came from the crowd pressing in front of the entrance to the stadium and thundering in Roni's inner self, not only in his head and his breast, but also deep in his stomach where tension roiled. He set off with Marek and Gonzo toward the middle of the crowd, pushing between the congested bodies, touching the sticky skin of those who had equally impatiently come to this place. And since two people cannot be in the same place at the same time, a problem had to occur. Even though he had not intended to start a fight in the crowd, it was unavoidable.

Forcing his way through, he accidentally pushed some character wrapped up in the supporters' flag. The man tripped, but succeeded in remaining upright, stumbling awkwardly into Roni's face and showering upon him his stinking rage. He cursed Roni's mother, and that he should never have done. Roni never forgave anyone for that, not even someone with the big heart of a fan beating in the same rhythm and keeping the same time as his own. His fist flew toward the face decorated with the team colors, but Marek and Gonzo anticipated his blow, catching hold of his arm and preventing the crowd from enjoying the opportunity of cheering before the match. He did not blame them, he relied on their assessment of the situation and concluded that they were behaving as necessary. Although he was sorry he had not satisfied that urge which brought him one of the few true pleasures in his life.

Unexpected and completely unwanted, one of those promising young journalists with a microphone in hand suddenly appeared from nowhere, while a camera filmed from the side. The ruckus had now subsided. Roni felt pins and needles from his shoulders to the tips of his fingers, that same feeling which caused his well-known tension; which was impossible to stop. He looked into the face partly hidden by the microphone and wondered where it would be best to hit the man. Those sports journalists with their mumbo-jumbo commentaries destroyed the experience of the game he respected—and that could not be permitted. That had to be punished, and this was just the right moment to satisfy that long-held desire. He did not hesitate; his fist flew toward the nose, and since no one expected it, no one could prevent it. The young man cried out, and Roni felt relief, which flooded over him like serenity overtakes those who find it in quiet green places along the river, with a fishing rod.

Somebody shouted, "Cops!" but there was no time to escape. Just a few more seconds, and no one could have caught Roni. He knew all the roads and alleyways to put them off his trail. But now they crammed him into the police van and took him to the police station. They shut him in a room with a tall man wearing a suit who sat on a chair staring in front of him. He looked briefly at Roni and continued staring at the floor. Luckily, he said nothing. If he had, Roni would have punched him in the face too. He felt only disgust toward these perfumed wearers of suits and ties. He never would have been able to wear a tie, tied firmly under a white-collared shirt, and speak importantly all those long and empty sentences, as though they were full of wisdom. Wisdom was in simplicity, there was no need to philosophize about that, Roni knew; though perhaps some might think he did not know, that he did not understand those important things of which life is put together. Besides, all that clever talk, nodding of heads, smiling, shoulder tapping, and shaking of sweaty hands annoyed him. All these types should be shut away so that normal people, like Roni, could have a rest from the fakery. It had gone much too far. Now he would have liked to say how much he despised this man and types like him, but he did not feel like talking. *It would be best to just punch him*, thought Roni, imagining the surprise on the man's face at the moment he hit the mark. *He seems somehow preoccupied, he's acting like I'm not here, and that isn't right. He would go crazy if he felt pain.* And Roni knew very well how to inflict pain and where the skin broke the easiest. He liked to see blood coming to the surface like an underground stream. That excited him, but in a calming way, if such a thing can be said.

Why is he even here? Roni asked himself. *Must be some sort of embezzlement, probably big money. His type need brutal punish-*

ment, they don't have the balls to attack and to take something by force. These guys do things nicely and wearing gloves, hypocritically sniggering from the TV screen at poor people. I'll beat the crap out of him in the name of all those he has swindled and stolen from, so that he never thinks about doing such a thing again, Roni decided. And just when he stood up, ready to take justice into his own hands which were made for blows, the door opened and an official came in.

"Mr. Mikić, we apologize for the inconvenience, there's been a mistake. You can go."

Roni had meant to ask the result of the soccer match, but he did not have time. The door shut and he remained alone, and Mikić with his long feet stepped into the corridor.

In front of the building a party vehicle was waiting for Mikić. He recognized Lovrić's shadow by the way he was standing and holding his cigarette, which glowed in the half-lit darkness. Lovrić had come for him in person. That undoubtedly meant something. But what? From the beginning, being led away had seemed like a setup to him. The police had been waiting for him in front of the house when he set off for work in the morning. He had spent almost the whole day in that stinking hole, except for when they were questioning him. Then he had been in a second stinking hole, where they had given no explanation as to why he was there. Actually, they had, but he had not understood, even though he could understand much more complicated things. And now, at the end of this terrible day, which he had spent hitting the walls of his own thoughts, one of the highest party functionaries had come for him.

"We decided today, everyone agreed, no one had anything against you taking over the ministry. That what happened, did not happen. You were never in this place."

Mikić was silent, waiting for the rest. And he had not miscalculated.

"But there's a problem. That young girl you've been seeing . . . it would be good to stop that. The girl is a professional, it doesn't make sense to spoil everything. After all, you have a wife and children. And even if you didn't, you don't need someone like that. Attend to this as soon as possible. I realize, I know she has gotten under your skin. She's hot, and she probably knows her job very well, but . . ."

"Alright, drive me to her."

"Are you sure you need to do this right now? I mean, it's not quite so urgent, you can take care of it tomorrow."

"I don't have time tomorrow, and I don't know when I will have time."

Lovrić continued driving toward Vlaska Street in silence, without asking for the address. He knew it. He stopped a little past the entrance to the lobby, where Mikić disappeared into the darkness, then climbed up the winding staircase to the first floor and rang the bell.

She opened the door in her dressing gown, small, with her hair down and the eyes of a doe. He would have liked to pick her up, take her to bed, and lie next to her. She caught him by the hand and led him into the apartment, and then she hugged him and encircled his mouth with her soft lips. He had never thought of her doing this with others for money. He had never paid her. Of course he had bought her presents and lent her money for the rent when she asked him. Of course he had never asked her to return it because it was nothing. Besides, gentlemen don't do that.

Now he was wondering how to tell her that which he did not want to say or do. But had to.

He would miss this little forbidden place, where he had been his true self, and in which there had been nothing except tenderness and passion, which she had kept for him in that small perfumed body. It was not important now whether she had with equal sincerity or mendacity given these things to others as well, probably including Lovrić. He was angry with himself for his reluctance to tell her it was over, that he would no longer come, and not to call him anymore. After learning tonight about her relationships with other men, that should not have been any problem at all. But it was. He knew he would not forget her scent, nor her taste, nor the timbre of her sighs. It had been so different from everything he had previously known that it was impossible to forget. It had helped him to remain normal, and now it seemed to him that it was the reason he was beginning to go mad. He got up and went to the window, and finally told her. She said she did not accept it, and he told her that meant nothing since he would not be coming any longer. She said she knew this was because of his political career and he asked her who had told her this; and she said no one had to tell her because the media had spread the news.

He went toward the door, and she caught him by the arm and burst into tears. Her small body shook while she implored him not to go in a voice verging on hysteria. She repeated that she would not give him up so easily, and this upset him. He imagined her possible outbursts in public, which must not happen. He had to prevent it at all costs, and the only way to do that was to kill her. That meant in the next few seconds he had to think of a way to do it. If he did kill her, what would he do with the body? If he did get rid of it, who could guarantee it would not be found? If someone found it, that would be the end of everything. Not just the life he had planned for himself in great detail, but everything. He could not believe he had found himself in the middle of a scene out of some silly film. Except that here there would be no repeats, and he had not chosen his own role. It had been given to him long ago. After half a day spent in custody, he knew he could not survive in jail. Therefore he hurried outside, hoping that tomorrow he would think of a better solution.

She went after him, and he took the steps two at time in big strides. She reached him at the bottom of the staircase and tried to embrace him, and he pushed her away without turning around. He knew that she had fallen, but he did not see that she had hit her head on the iron fence and that her doe-like gaze remained staring at one point, somewhere between the doorway and the light switch. Without speaking he got into the car. Lovrić said, "You're quick."

An hour later Frida woke up in her bed. She stayed lying there for a time, letting her eyes get used to the dark. She rose slowly, carefully stretching her legs, her neck, the rest of her spine. Softly she set off through the darkness, from time to time lightly touching the shadows of motionless things. She moved silently, nimbly, and invisibly, not leaving any tracks behind her, not even a shadow. There was no one who could upset her sleep, her daily routine, and her need for solitude. She was alone. For that matter, she had been alone as long as she could remember. Probably it had not always been like that. Actually, certainly it hadn't, but who could know now what had happened. Her memory did not go back that far, and she had embraced loneliness because she had no one else. And she had learned to do everything by herself. That had not always been easy because life sometimes requires someone else, cries out for another pair of eyes and ears, for the warmth of another body. Solitude by itself is not a weight to carry, but the fear loved by solitude is. It is easier when carried by two. However, she had learned to live with it; even to sleep.

She loved to sleep and gave in to it more than to anything else. It was not just a physical need but an escape; security. Although it was often interrupted by noises, which prompted Frida to stare into the dark with wide-open eyes so that she could see moving shadows. She would lie there motionless and tense until overtaken again by sleep. For this reason she slept mostly during the day. At night she went out because night was her protector, her partner and friend. Night creates possibilities and brings rewards. Night does not ask for reasons, causes, or consequences. It is protection for the lonely and the hungry. It sharpens the senses and quickens reactions. It calls and challenges. Like now.

She could not resist the call of the night. It would lead her down empty streets and through dark yards. Sometimes she was satisfied with aimless wandering, but more often she was led to her goal by hunger; hunger as big as a void, as heavy as a mountain, and as persistent as the Arctic winter. It could be deceived by sleep, but it would not let itself be tricked while awake. Now it was still on its way; just a forecast and a cursed reminder that it had not forgotten what it would do to her. Another hour or two and it would completely take over her mind, become master of her body, and if she did not feed it, it would take away all her strength. She knew she could not let that happen. She must do something before she lost control of herself because that would mean less chance of surviving. And for a long time survival had been the meaning of existence on these shores of insecurity.

Frida crept out onto the street. It was wet from the rain, which had stopped falling, but left puddles on the shiny asphalt. She did not like rain, nor snow. She would have liked to turn winter into one long, unbroken sleep, after which she would wake up happy to a sunny, warm day. But that was something she could only dream of.

She was blinded by the lights of the cars. She stopped against a wall, and decided to follow a dark path leading behind a house, between yards, and through the alleyways. She moved slowly, becoming more cautious with every step, sensing danger, which lay in wait for her in the dark abyss. She heard every little noise as though it were a loud uproar, making her cringe and look for shelter. There was caution in her movements and in her senses, and her heart was beating with the pulse in her neck, more and more strongly; she could not calm it. She listened to it echoing in the darkness.

Hunger grew and led her toward some nearby dumpsters. She was hoping she would find in them something with which to feed the animal inside her. She knew the trucks had not yet picked up the trash and in the dumpsters, without much trouble, she should be able to find something edible. Silently, she walked faster, glancing this way and that. The dumpsters were well known to her, some had even become favored. Often she visited them stealthily, not wanting to be seen. This time she did not find what she was hoping for. Either they had changed the timetable for removal, or she had mixed up the days.

Despair and anger were now mixing with the fear brought by hunger. This was stronger than all other fears and pushed her farther and farther, as far as the marketplace. During the day she avoided this area. There were too many people there, too many smells, voices, and altogether too much of everything; and she loved peace and quiet. Now she wandered between the empty tables and crawled underneath them, hoping to find scraps of food. There was nothing. And her strength was running out.

She went toward the fish market. She liked the smell of the fish, but apart from that there was nothing. Shreds of disappointment and anguish dragged behind her, slowing her down. She had no solution, but she was hoping one would present itself, as had happened so many times in the past. There had been other such futile nights, when not even hours of searching had brought peace of mind, and then on the way back, suddenly, she had found the food that she had been seeking so desperately. She favored luck, but never relied on it completely. You can never be certain. Everything, even luck, can leave us at any moment. *And that moment is perhaps right now.* Frida was thinking like this when she noticed a small rat. She bent down and gathered all her strength. Without waiting too long and giving him a chance to notice her, she threw herself on him and sank her teeth into his neck. She clamped down with her jaw long enough to make sure he had stopped breathing, and then she carefully let go. Once again she looked about to see whether anyone was coming or maybe watching her from around the corner. There was no one and she could devote herself to her prey in peace. Even so, she tore greedily at the bloody meat and devoured it, listening to the wild animal inside her purring with satisfaction. When she finished, she relaxed for an instant, but quickly decided to move on, tensed like the string on a guitar, stepping silently, as always. She never stayed longer in one place than was absolutely necessary.

Led by a momentary desire, she crept into the open lobby. Long ago she had learned that desires which turned up suddenly should not be resisted because there was always a reason and purpose for them. At the bottom of the steps she saw an unmoving body and approached it. She saw the fixed stare, the long hair strewn about, covering part of the small face; and the blood which had congealed on the ground. She did not resist; she had to try it. On her tongue she felt the salty taste just as she heard footsteps and glimpsed men's black shoes coming quickly toward her from the street. She hoped they would pass by her without stopping; there was nowhere to escape. She hunched down on the floor, but this time she was out of luck. The tip of a shoe caught her from above, strongly and painfully drilling into her stomach. She cried out, and a deep voice shouted, "Get lost, you disgusting cat!"

HEADLESSNESS

BY DARKO MILOŠIĆ
Mirogoj

Translated by Coral Petkovich

I dropped in at the hospital to see my mother. I found her in the surgery section; she was talking to Dr. Basic.

"Hey, you weren't in Nelly's Café the other day?" she said, mincing her words.

"No, what happened? Something new again?" Dr. Basic replied, blasé.

"Oh my God, something *faaa*bulous! A *terribly* handsome young man presented us with a phen-om-en-al new type of coffee."

"Really?"

"Yes, really something special. It's coffee from Sumatra where they roast it from a special bean which, you won't believe this, is actually pooed by wild cats."

"You're joking?!"

"No, I'm not. And you know how much one cup costs? From 250 to 550 kuna! It's not for poor people, my dear."

"Oh my God, I must try that as soon as . . . What about if we go straight there after the hairdresser's?"

"Can do, old friend. Just give me a shout!"

Before leaving, Basic turned her attention to me. "Goodness, how you have grown, boy! How time flies." She sighed. "Never mind, old friend, I'm off, I'll call you after the hairdresser's and we'll go to Nelly's, okay?"

She waved and left.

"And how much do you need?" my mother asked me.

"Well, at least as much as you're prepared to spend on a cup of coffee made from cat poo," I replied caustically.

"Oh, please, spare me. And what do you need it for?"

"I'm going with Alen to McDonald's, and afterward we thought maybe we would go see a movie."

"Maybe?"

"Yes, maybe."

"And maybe you could be a little more polite, young man, eh? While you're under my roof . . ."

Bloody hell.

"Listen, Alen's waiting for me outside. I'm hungry. I'm asking you nicely to give me some dough, enough to last for tomorrow too." I was trying to be very polite and patient.

"And why can't you find more suitable company than that boy? Truly, when I see him, I get goose pimples. And he was such a good-looking little boy . . ."

"Alen has been my friend since—"

"I know, I know . . . Actually, yes, I feel sorry for him."

In one of the rooms we passed, a patient suffering from lung disease began to cry.

My old lady reached for her purse and handed me some money.

"Thanks, Mama." I tried to sound appreciative. *Go fuck yourself, Mama*, I thought.

Alen was sitting in front of the hospital, killing time by pulling the legs off a daddy longlegs. It's not that he hates spiders; he just plays with them. When only the spider's body remained, he pushed it lightly with his thumb, like a ball. Sometimes he uses a cigarette lighter. He's laid-back, but focused. Creative. He greeted me without looking up. Next to him, a can of Zuja. I reached for it and took a long swig. Alen is cool; I've known him since kindergarten. All my life, man. We knew each other when his father used to be with them, instead of in the loony bin. When we were still small, from time to time his father was allowed home, and he would wander around the neighborhood, up and down on Lascinska Street, Bijenicka, Srebrnjak . . . like some fucked-up zombie. He would call me, put his face close to mine, and ask me if I was fucking anything, and then laugh, a laugh which sounded just like the squeaking of hundreds of mice.

Alen—his father called him "Yellow Shit"—was beaten from a very young age by his brothers and sisters, and his old lady; his old man used to thrash the lot of them. Alen had a small dog he loved very much. Once the dog crapped under the kitchen table. His dad dragged Alen from his room, pushed him under the table, and pressed his palm onto the shit. Then he took a broom from the cupboard and in the corner of the kitchen he beat the little animal. In front of Alen. After he tried once, also in front of Alen, to beat Alen's mother in the same way, they stuck him into Vrapce, where he is now. Alen's old lady in the meantime started to get interested in the church, but not our church, the real one, Catholic and apostolic; but some really weird club, a *wannabe* church, which used to meet in people's apartments. With guitars and tambourines. A "house church," as she called it. And that in itself would not have been a problem, but because he was the youngest, his old lady forced him to go with her to those meetings—she called them "services"—and for hours he had to kneel and "praise Jesus." And this happened two or three times a week, in houses around Hrastik, Dobri Dol, up near Zmajevac . . . at the houses of "brothers and sisters." Alen used to tell me that it all started relatively normally, with coffee and cakes, the warmth a bit forced. But later they would reach such a state that they would randomly open the Bible, read a couple of lines, and fall into ecstasy, literally fall onto the floor, choking with laughter or tears. Alen would be watching, frozen, his stomach cramped like it was when his father raged around the house. Then they would suddenly go quiet and someone would begin to mutter incomprehensibly. One after the other they would begin to mutter—"to speak in tongues"—all of those present, louder and louder, until finally they would be rolling around on the floor again, sobbing convulsively, possessed by "the spirit." They would watch DVDs of American preachers wearing crocodile-leather shoes, in expensive suits, running from one end of a huge podium to the other, shouting that God wants us to be shamelessly rich. *Amen? Aa-men! Hallelujah!*

From time to time they would have a "healing service" to drive out the demon of colds or the demon of depression. All of this only a kilometer or two from the Ruđer Bošković Institute, where my old man works with his colleagues in CERN. Jesus. Alen was ashamed to see how his old lady, cheeks flushed and with sweat stains under her armpits, lifted her arms into the air; once, in a surge of inspiration, she decided to christen him again because she came to the conclusion that the previous baptism was not valid—she maligned the Catholic church whenever she had the opportunity—so that one evening at the "service," at the home of some "brothers" from Rebro, they stripped him down to his underpants and submerged him in a bath full of water, all the while singing psalms and foretelling for him a successful missionary career. Alen, whose experience of constant beatings during his childhood had taught him that the torment would not last as long if he did not resist, simply took a deep breath before they pushed his head under the water. Maybe he would become a minister one day, but right now he was interested in Crowley, he was listening to Marilyn Manson and bands like the

Cradle of Filth, Bal-Sagoth, and the Meads of Asphodel, pulling out the legs of spiders. He was planning to order LaVey's *Satanic Bible* through Amazon. He was still über-cool; in school he did not even bother to choose ethics instead of religious teaching, and in class he now stared at the anxious young teacher in a way that made her noticeably nervous. From time to time he would ask a question, like, what did she think about the Book of Job or about Judas as a positive character. Fuck, in primary school, walking with his mother to the "service," he collected quite a lot of information from the Bible so now he was using it to annoy this poor woman. He covered his nails with black paint; his image, in general, he got from the old Satanists he sometimes spent time with in Maksimir, down near the fifth lake, or in Ribnjak Park. He was a member of the "coven," he had been for a year now. They let me go to one of their meetings once, an "esbat," in a house in Jordanovac.

The boss was some old depressed-looking dude, a bit like Zizek, who wore a T-shirt with his own face on it, and I quickly realized he had *cups* with his face on them, and some cardboard pyramids, and like, some "holy" pics where he, the self-appointed "God," "the Eternal Master," "Lord," stared out at the observer. Older members of the coven mentioned him reverently and nostalgically as one of the pioneers of the goth movement in Zagreb, back in the eighties, when he introduced them as teenagers to black magic, while in Lapidarij and Jabuka they listened to Joy Division and Sisters of Mercy. Alen heard rumors about his alleged involvement in a ritual murder in Sesvete at the end of the seventies . . . Mostly, the meetings started with an invocation of the four crowned Princes of Hell, then the old man begged Beelzebub to inspire their work.

The one time they let me attend a meeting, a young girl was also present, with an attractive little swastika peeping from under her shirt—very serious about wanting to join them. "Alastor," as they called the host, asked her to make bundles of hawthorn twigs and wrap them in aluminum foil, and then bury them at night in certain places around the building where she lived.

Why? He told us solemnly that he wanted to have "his people" in every Zagreb district so that his "positive influence" would expand across the whole town, and even farther. And even farther. The dude was ambitious. There was a plan of the town on the wall with the districts joined by lines which had symbols, unknown to me. I found it all quite silly and that's what I told Alen, but Alen informed me that old Alastor, with the help of crystals, filled him with so much energy that he got all pumped up and did not sleep for several days. What sort of fucking *crystals* was he talking about? I asked him.

"Well, I turn my back to him, and from a distance he fills me with energy from the crystals, so that I just about take off," he explained to me. Alen rarely displayed any enthusiasm so I became interested. He showed me some of those crystals—nice little things, really—which he always carried with him, as Alastor had recommended. Tanzanite stimulates the third eye and the crown chakra, and helps with linking us to beings from another dimension; tiger's eye, "a very powerful stone," is for inviolability and strengthening personal power; black tourmaline, for the transformation of negative energy. ("It's excellent for cleansing the aura and for defense against black magic.") Great, I told him, at least that would protect him against Alastor and his "positive influence."

Still, the whole thing intrigued me, and Alen promised to arrange for me to be present at the next Sabbath up in Mirogoj. I actually think that real Satanists, all perfect gentlemen, walk around in suits and ties, don't sell T-shirts to their followers, and don't cut the throats of chickens in Maksimir; instead, they can readily afford to indulge themselves with a random kid and throw real money around. Alen's "coven" was third class just like his old lady's "church," but hey, Zagreb wasn't the center of world Satanism. Presumably.

When he had finished with the spider, we went down to McDonald's to eat something. I ordered a Crispy Chicken Caesar McWrap, and he ordered a Double Cheeseburger.

My parents are normal. I mean, compared to Alen's. Rationalists and atheists, although my old lady keeps up an appearance of the traditional Catholic woman because she needs it for some reason. Whatever. I was baptized, had my first communion, and was confirmed. It all has to be "observed," right? I see the old man from time to time, he doesn't live with my mom and me anymore. Last year after they got divorced, he left Bijenička to go live in Zaprešić with my grandmother and uncle, and now he travels every day to the Institute. The old man is some sort of harmless muddle-headed character, a typical nerd who is not quite certain what to do with himself, not to mention how hard it is for him to deal with me. He has never hit me, but then neither has he ever really hugged me. Ha. From Alen's perspective, I shouldn't complain, but still, I feel some sort of emptiness inside me. He didn't get along very well with the old lady. She would always begin the argument, he would reluctantly accept it; I almost felt like he did it just to satisfy her. She harassed him with constant rebukes, and if he wasn't there, then she harassed me. Which meant that now she harassed only me. She compared me to him, which I hated. He of course was a genius in his own narrowly professional way, he knew all about bosons, leptons, and string theory; in the Institute he was in his element, he was even some sort of head of a department, but how to come to terms with marriage difficulties or how to be a role model for his son—

of these things he had no idea whatsoever. Clueless. Like it was embarrassing for him to be a father. Well, it was embarrassing for me to be a son too. More than once I asked myself: *How is it possible that those two people at least once—I'm living proof—made love?* I spent the first two years of my life in Zaprešić and then—the old lady got a job in the children's hospital—we came here, across from the Mirogoj Cemetery, so that I had a nice view of the future from my balcony, ever since I was small. We lived right on the border between the town of the dead and the town of the living, and sometimes I felt like those tens of thousands of dead people—as though the old lady was not enough—were hanging around my neck, like the graves were expanding, metastasizing. On Google Earth, Mirogoj looked just like a skin eruption, a big gray mole which was slowly, grave after grave, cross after cross, penetrating into the tissue of the town.

Alen lent me some books which he was all fired up about, the novels *The Angel of the West Window* and *The Golem* by Gustav Meyrink, and told me I had to read them. I guess he wanted to make sure I was ready for the soon-to-be Sabbath. I can't say I didn't like Meyrink, but when I remembered that team of Alen's, that mixture of aspiring Zagreb pagans, druids, wiccans, death metal lovers, wannabe Satanists, and members of various ecological societies, all of them left-oriented vegetarians, with old Alastor at the head, a man who sold tea cups with his own sad ugly face on them, I wasn't at all sure how seriously I should prepare for the awful occult ritual which was soon to be held. But since I was only a guest-spectator, and the performance would unfold in the neighborhood, just across the way, it would be a shame to miss it. After all, there was always the possibility that I'd get to know some attractive little witch, like the one with the swastika tattooed on her breast. Man, for that you *really* needed balls; or whatever the female version is!

Maybe that team of Alen's was off-kilter enough that they should be given a chance? Though the old man used to bore me every night, from the time I was very little, with stories about the beauty of the physical world, in the style of Carl Sagan, with the hope that I would follow in his footsteps. And the old lady let me know indirectly that religion should not be taken seriously. Still, I would continue to give other approaches to reality a chance; for example, an interest in esotericism—if that's what you can call Alen's thing. Hmm, maybe, in a very broad sense. At the end of the line, thanks to the old man, I hadn't even begun school when I heard about black holes and Madeleine L'Engle, but it happened that literature was more attractive to me than physics. My peers mostly ignored books like they were something impossibly outdated, but in primary school I was already reading Hoffmann, Poe, Kafka, and sending Mrs. Micok, my literature teacher, into raptures. Sometimes the old lady in her frustratingly boring way tried to persuade me to enroll in law school, which would be "so nice, right?" Because, you see, "Basic's daughter is already in her second year; and one day you could have your own office and make a lot of money." Not to mention the prestige. Truthfully: I couldn't give a fuck about prestige.

A bell rang. Alastor appeared, covered in a black cape which looked like a sheet. On his head he had rammed some sort of helmet on which were mounted goat's horns. It suited him, the old billy-goat, along with his beard and his bristly eyebrows. He held himself with dignity, as well as he could with his rather large beer belly, and darted sullen glances all around. Everyone became sort of agitated when he appeared, like, *Here is our Great Priest, Lord Alastor! Oooh, bow to him because He—a neighbor from our district—will bring us the latest news from hell.* Hmm, at times like this my father's little scientist awoke in me, and I looked at this sort of phenomenon not with scepticism, but with irony. Whatever, old Alastor just about made Alen cheerful; obviously he needed a father figure. *Okay, so do I, but I doubt Alastor would be willing to adopt the devil's advocate as a son,* I thought with double irony. I was turning around in my head some questions I wanted to ask him. Dad had made me read Sagan's book, *The Demon-Haunted World;* I couldn't help it, I was immunized early against characters like Alastor. Still, the spectacle in front of me was interesting in its own twisted way. Everything was there: black candles (actually, I realized later they were blue, when Alen explained to me that "because of pressure from Christians you can't get black candles anywhere, not even at the candlemaker in Marija Bistrica, but Lucifer's color is blue so that's acceptable too") and a circle drawn with a pentagram inside it. Everything just as it should be, as my old lady would say. We all took our places. Alastor began to slowly turn around, counterclockwise, and then in a hoarse voice rattled off: *"In nomine Dei nostri Satanas, Luciferi excelsi, ave voluptatis carnis!"*

Not bad, I thought. Maybe something would happen here after all. You could almost feel how all those present trembled.

"In nomine Dei nostri Satanas Luciferi excelsi. Satan, Lucifer, Belial, Leviathan. Rege Satanas. Ave Satanas."

I doubted that anyone there knew Latin, but the names he spoke were general knowledge. Still, it sounded effective, especially with the graveside backdrop. We had gathered in the bottom right-hand part of the cemetery, I could almost wave to Mama. The place had been chosen because allegedly it had special "potential energy"—presumably one of the Dragon lines dropped down there from the Sljeme mountain. Alastor swallowed from the silver goblet he was holding in his hand. Drugstore Plavac, without a doubt. He continued to invoke *Lord of the Flies.*

"In the name of Satan, the All-Powerful and Almighty, who made man in his own image and conception, I call on the Dark Forces to transfer their hellish power to me. Open, Gates of Hell, and greet me as your brother and friend!"

The coven members murmured in a sign of approval.

"Free me, oh powerful Satan, from all my delusions, fill me with truth, wisdom, and understanding, strengthen me in my service and faith, so that I will always live in you, in your glory and splendor, oh Torchbearer!"

Again he took a swig from the goblet. Then he pulled out a large knife from somewhere (an "athame," Alen explained to me later. Its main role is to "guide and channel psychic energy, the Essential Fire." *Yeah.*), and began to turn to the left, quite slowly—which was wise, given that I was sure he was not exactly sober—and invoke the "Princes," the just-mentioned Lucifer from the east, Beelzebub from the north, Astaroth from the west, and Azazel from the south.

I didn't notice if any of those called upon appeared, but demons are spirits, are they not, so everyone could imagine they were there. Those present evidently did imagine it; I felt a feverishness overcoming the group. You could hear euphoric invocations from all sides, and old Alastor started chanting some Satanist passages "in Enochian," Alen informed me, the language in which spirits like to communicate. Then everyone went quiet and—similar to that time in Jordanovac, in those intimate meditative moments—they itemized all their life problems related to colleagues at work, partners, finances, and health, to the entities they had supposedly called forth. Hmm, Azazel in Zagreb? A suitable time for someone to invoke a curse on someone else. Several of them were kneeling, some were raising their arms in the air. Alastor stood in the middle of the circle with his cup and knife; everything was progressing in the proper way.

"Glory to Satan!" shouted Alastor, and slowly began to turn to the right. Bells could be heard.

"Glory!" responded those present. *Oh Jesus,* I thought.

The ritual of initiation was supposed to follow. The girl with the swastika on her breast had bought a set of Alastor's cup and T-shirt, and had buried the sticks of hawthorn around her building, and in this way had qualified to be a serious candidate. Alen had explained to me that one could not very easily become a member of the coven. You belonged to the coven body and soul; the ties were tighter than family ties (for him, no doubt about that). The devil is in the detail: in order to join the coven, the candidate *before* that had to ally him or herself personally with Lucifer; then the demon who was the protector of the coven—in this case, Asmodeus—"in some way" indicated whether he agreed that the person in question could join the coven. Alen could not tell me in *exactly* what way, but in any case I think Alastor accepted anyone who parted with the money for the crystals and the other paraphernalia. And obediently performed some sort of nonsense à la that with the hawthorn sticks. The initiate had to convince the members that they were on the same wavelength, that their interests were in accord with those of the whole coven. *We are all one big, happy family*—something like that. Generally speaking, the initiation of a new member was a happy occasion for the coven, because Satanists were happy when there were more of them.

"Come forward, novice!" Alastor tried to exude authority.

The girl, she looked to be about twenty, twenty-two, in a long black dress with a deep neckline—in the light of the candles you could only see a dark speck instead of the tattoo—went into the circle and approached the Fat . . . *oops!* the Great Priest.

"If you have one, call now on your personal demon, let him join us!"

The future "sister" lifted her head and her arms, and in a shaking, melodramatic voice—presumably you couldn't invoke the demon in a normal voice—began the invocation: "Ohh, great and powerful Lilith, my Protector, your obedient servant begs you to augment this sacred act with your presence!"

Lilith, of course. Commonplace. I saw how the female members of the team spontaneously joined in with raised arms. Girl power. This was the fifth wave of feminism. Patriarchy and lower pay for the same work were a thing of the past. Here comes Lilith. Lilith has arrived.

Alastor pulled out a piece of paper from somewhere and held it out to the girl. "Read, novice!"

The young woman took the paper and began to read, irritatingly, pathetically, as called for by the situation. "I, Bozena Skomrak, before the Almighty God Lucifer, before Asmodeus, Protector of this coven, before the mighty Lilith . . . before those assembled here, of my own free will, solemnly swear that I will always keep our secret . . . I solemnly promise that I will work to expand the influence of Satanism in the town of Zagreb and the Republic of Croatia, in every way possible . . . I understand that I am Lucifer's warrior and an earthly member of the army of Hell, and that this coven is my army detachment . . . I promise to use my power and energy, together with the other members of the coven, to destroy selected enemies of Satan . . . I promise to use my power and energy for the good of every member of the coven, knowing they will do the same for me, if it proves necessary . . . All this, I swear on my life, now and forever, and may all the power I possess turn against me, if I betray these sacred promises. Lord Lucifer, all the Demons and Powers of Hell, count me worthy. *Ave Satanas.*"

Alastor went up to her and took her left hand. Everyone calmed down noticeably. The sharp edge of the knife flashed in the dim light as he made a cut across the Mount of Venus on her palm. The girl winced, even though she obviously knew the procedure. She pulled a thin stick from somewhere, and holding the paper with her cut hand, she wet the tip of the stick in the wound and signed underneath the text she had just read. Those present did not actually applaud, though they must all have been gratified by the fact that their society had been enriched by a new member, which would surely bring strength to their unholy cells.

Especially if she knew how to cook, eh? She gave the paper back to Alastor, who put it close to one of the candles, lit it, and held it in his outstretched hand until it had burned.

"*In nomine Dei nostri Satanas, Luciferi Excelsi, amen,*" he concluded.

With that, the official ceremony was over and those present lined up to congratulate the newly introduced "sister" and welcome her. Someone tugged at a bell, and the sound of a flute could be heard. Such considerate people, I thought. We sat around on the graves because now it was time for a short snack. Everyone had brought something, from sandwiches of whole wheat bread with tofu, little plastic containers of miso soup, brown rice, amaranth and algae, unsprayed wizened little apples from some organic farm . . . and hooray: cakes of soya flour covered in sweet barley malt. You could hear the crunching of fresh radishes and the opening of beer cans. If they had been wearing slightly different clothes it would have been easy to imagine those present as picnickers up on the Sljeme.

In the morning my old lady sent me to the fish market in Kvatric to buy sea bream. While I headed that way, I thought about Alen. It was clear to me that he needed company, because in school he was mostly ignored; in the coven he had some sort of team at least, but in the long-term, I counted on his intelligence. Entering the fish market, I noticed a familiar face behind one of the counters. A man in a dirty white apron was holding up a large carp that was struggling, and in his other hand he had a small axe with which a moment later he chopped off its head. Then he threw the lifeless fish onto the scales. I felt like vomiting.

PART IV

On the Loose

SHE-WARRIOR

BY NORA VERDE
Lanište

Translated by Ellen Elias-Bursac

She had already been awake half an hour. In her mind she was rehearsing the plan yet again, finessing the details. Details matter—how many times had an action failed that had seemed so fabulous at first?

She finally pulled herself out of bed and went to the bathroom. She brushed her teeth and studied her face and her hair which was braided in short straggly dreads. In a few days, once the thing this evening was behind her, she'd tidy them up a bit, but no time for that now.

She was alone in the apartment and that pleased her. Her parents had gone to work, her younger brother to school. She loved her solo mornings when she didn't have to retreat to her room to enjoy a little peace.

From the food she found in the refrigerator she assembled a sizable meal. All that mattered was filling up on energy for the day ahead. Pickles, peppers, cheese spread, butter, and bread, she set it all out on a large white plate and looking it over she thought that cooking was an overrated and costly pastime for the human race. She ate sitting before a battered HP laptop smeared in dust, shreds of tobacco, and bread crumbs. She logged into her e-mail account. Waiting for her were unopened e-newsletters and from the subject headings she already knew what was worth opening. She would have to clean it out soon—two, three years ago she had subscribed to all sorts of sites that had seemed interesting enough at the time, but meanwhile they had become silly and pointless. She could not resist clicking on *I-SYNCHRO-U, the network of intuitive communication.* In the e-mail a capitalized English title declared: *USE I-SYNCHRO-U NETWORK AND LEARN WHAT INTUITION HAS TO SAY ABOUT YOUR DILEMMA.* On with the show, she'd already had enough of messing around on the Net now, so she signed off and *sayonara*. Left click, right click, the little green light on the laptop stopped blinking, and from the speakers there came a sound like a cat's plaintive meow. Her HP made that sound when it powered down—her former boyfriend, the programmer, had set it up for her that way.

The time had come to get ready. On her cell she called everybody else: Gagarin, Buks, and Dikinsonka, her three friends from the squat.

She maneuvered her backpack onto her back—into it she had packed what they'd need for this evening's action: scissors, four rolls of wide brown tape, a red marker, a big roll of poster paper, a dark blue rolled-up raincoat, four skeins of black wool, a city map, and a plastic one-liter bottle of water.

Last but not least, out of the closet she pulled her souped-up mountain bike which she had customized with her own hands. She kept it in her room, which made her folks fume, but there was no way anyone was going to get her to store it in the cellar. The bike was one of her body parts, she would not be separated from it if she didn't have to. And it was no big deal carrying it up to the fourth floor and down every day, it was her baby!

She could hardly wait to wheel it out through the front door of the building, sit on it, and ride.

* * *

Her name was Milena, so said her ID and her passport, but fuck, who had ever known an anarchist with a name like some fusty old Partisan. It always sounded to her like the ultimate in female docility, sappy and oh so populist. And besides, she did not "smell like apples" like the girl of the same name in the Novi Fosili song, more like homemade lavender-scented soap and fine-cut Virginia-style tobacco.

Friends called her She-Warrior, or Warrie for short. When she was a little girl she had this thing about the cult classic *The Warriors* from '79 and the kids from the hood dubbed her She-Warrior. She scuffled with boys, started her own neighborhood gangs, and every so often ended up in the ER with a broken bone or a gash. Her folks raged about it, but in the end she finished high school with straight As, and signed up to study sociology and French at the Faculty of Philosophy. She was a junior and could hardly wait to get her diploma and be done with school. She worked part-time at poorly paid gigs through a student temping agency and lived with her folks. Most of the time they let her be, as long as her transcript showed good grades. Soon the time would come when she'd be able to leave the bourgeois lifestyle of her parents and move into a city squat, into Medika; she felt truly at home there.

So here's the thing.

A citizens' group had been putting up posters all over town announcing they'd had it with all the asylum-seekers threatening their purity. The story, as happens, began with some lame-ass petition from these "citizens." They managed to collect 496 signatures in one week and continued putting up posters. The story had been all over the media for two days and then it was nearly forgotten. Until new posters appeared across town with the slogan, *White Power for a Pure Zagreb*, and in the corner was the logo of the Stormfront—a big Celtic cross.

She biked around Lower Town and everywhere she looked, on lampposts, kiosks, tram stops, and walls, she saw the round black-and-white stickers on which the stupid slogan stuck out like a sore thumb.

Everyone at Medika was talking about the posters; a team from the queer group agreed to put together a protest letter which they would send to various institutions and the city government. A small group of them decided they would ride their bikes around the city that night tearing down every poster they found. They would do it after midnight once the crowds on the streets had thinned out. In place of the Nazi trash they'd put up their own posters, handmade, with the message: *Whose mother is spinning black wool now?*

They'd rip the others off the walls, stuff them into their backpacks, and destroy them later. On their poster under the message they'd glue a strand of black wool. She had thought they should put up something from Bakunin but his quotes all seemed wordy and complicated. And besides, these "big Croats" were dumb as a box of rocks and could only handle simple messages.

She got to Medika and saw a Stormfront sticker on the wall right there next to the door. With a quick jerk she ripped it off and, crumpling it in her fist, made a pitiful little wad of it.

"Fucking rascists," she muttered to herself as she walked her bike into the courtyard of the squat. Someone came up from behind and tugged on her dreads. Turning, she saw Dea, a half-pint girl, a designer who had wrangled herself space at the squat last winter.

"What's up, cookie, talking to yourself?"

"Cut it, Dea, I'm tearing down these crappy stickers, the city is plastered with them, and screw the jackass who dared to put this one right in our faces."

"Don't waste your breath, darling, the world is full of creeps, get used to it!"

"See, I don't buy that attitude. Tomorrow these same assholes will come here and mess with everything we did. That attitude stinks too much of the mind-set that sent you packing from Požega. All the registering at town hall, church weddings, holy confirmations, the boxes of chocolates, whiskey for surgeons, and shit like that."

"Well, you sure are She-Warrior," replied Dea, slipping into the gloom of the lower floor.

She-Warrior walked through the dark smelly courtyard and into the building, pulled out a key on a braided lanyard, and unlocked the door. She wheeled in her bike—she wasn't stupid enough to leave it out in the yard. Nobody was there yet, stuffy air enveloped her, she threw open the windows and dropped onto the shabby green couch, upholstered in a threadbare knobby fabric. Who knows where it had come from, a family probably put it in the trash after lounging on it for thirty years or more, and the squat crew spotted it just in time and toted it to Prostor. *Good job,* she thought, and wondered where the rest of the crew was. She had the feeling they were running late.

The door handle finally turned and into the room came Buks. He waddled along with that penguin gait of his, gripping a half-chewed salty roll and a sack full of bottles of no-name beer.

"Hey, you're already here. Comfy?" he asked.

"You bet, stretching from my toes to my crown chakra."

"Heh heh."

"Hear anything from the others?"

"From Gaga, yes, he's supposedly on the way and Dikinsonka's with him," Buks said, plunking down in the armchair across from her. He set the beers on the floor and concentrated on chewing the rubbery roll. "Fuck, this isn't real food, it's like this futuristic stuff, like crap for slaves—what tycoon heirs will be dishing out to grunts for their lunch break in the year 2057. Like in that movie, what was it, the one with all the hype a year ago maybe?"

"*Cloud Atlas*," she replied.

"Jeez, like you know everything," grinned Buks.

"I remember stuff, what can I do? I read the book, that's probably why," she explained.

Buks shrugged and worked off a screw top slow and easy. The CO_2 hissed and the beer foam climbed up the neck of the bottle. "Want some?"

"You know, not today, better not get drunk when I need to stay straight."

"It's all good, the others will," said Buks, sipping a few gulps and setting the bottle on the floor.

They sat there in silence until the door opened and Gaga and Dikinsonka pushed through it. They came in laughing, red in the face with slightly bloodshot eyes, and barely said hello.

She-Warrior scowled. People like them bothered her. She knew exactly what they had done on their way to Medika. They met up at Buks's place for a long smoke and then set off into town. They passed by the Krivi Put bar, then stopped in for a beer. After the first round came the second and now they were, of course, tipsy and high, and on they went to the meeting at Medika.

She was getting tired of this rah-rah anarchism; Žižek the maniac was onto something when he said 99 percent of the people were boring morons. Before she'd lost her activist virginity she had dipped into the pool of love and the unconditional embrace of every living creature she met at Medika. At first, back then, everything was new and wonderful, the days and nights flowed by like one hug after another, and she finally felt accepted. Finally she had shed the status of militant weirdo and met her peers. She didn't give a shit when one of those dolled-up douches from school teased her with comments like, "What's up, change-the-world girl?" or, "So, are you a feminist or what?" She lost the fear that had dogged her for years—that her rebellion was a passing fancy of her youth that would last only until, pressed by her parents, she applied for some job and started working in a company that specialized in killing consciousness and conscience.

Recently she'd begun to tire of her activist crew. She could see they were disorganized, lazy, and often relatively uneducated. Most of them were squatting and doing things out of necessity, not conviction. They cared more about a big party, booze, and smokes than they did about a well-designed protest and action. She was sure that in cities like Berlin and Munich and Amsterdam there were more people who would understand her.

She came back from her thoughts and turned to Gaga and Dikinsonka. "Okay, you two, let's put together the plan," she said calmly.

The two of them settled into an armchair next to her and Gaga pulled a piece of folded graph paper out of his pocket. "Here's where I listed all the places they put up posters," he said confidently, snatching the half-drunk bottle of beer Buks had started.

She picked up the list and read it to herself. "Not bad, Gaga, I have to say, not bad."

"So we have to agree on who goes where and divvy up the stuff," said Gaga. Dikinsonka and Buks nodded.

It was decided that Buks would go to the western parts of town, she would go to New Zagreb, and Gaga and Dikinsonka would deal with downtown, Kvaternikov Square, and Dubrava. When the action was done they'd all meet back up at the squat. Tonight there was going to be a queer party, but they didn't care about that, they cared about the action, and if it was still going on when they got back then they could let loose.

She handed out the poster sheets, tape, markers, and a skein of wool for each. They sat around the big wooden table and went to work, almost like an amateur art class. The atmosphere at Prostor finally had the smell of endeavor, and she liked that.

A half hour earlier people had started drifting into the party. The yard at the squat was getting more crowded, and inside there was cool electronic music playing. Nothing new, Friday at the squat was always chaotic. She was glad they were leaving soon; she wouldn't have been able to take the party at its peak and you could already see that the crush was going to be over the top.

Buks, Gaga, and Dikinsonka were circulating, chatting up the crowd. She kept her eye on them so they wouldn't wander off before the moment came for them to venture out into the night . . . which looked, smelled, and sounded like every other Zagreb spring night.

Streets splashed with streaks of light and dark and from time to time a slow intercity train would whistle. Her bike now slid soundlessly over that black-yellow street linocut. She felt like Wonder Woman on special assignment. The fresh midnight air thrilled her, slicing through it with her body, awash with it, pouring into her nose, mouth, ears, combing her thoughts. It reminded her of a female character in *Loving Sabotage* by Amélie Nothomb. And the seat between her legs lightly stimulated her clit; she must be ovulating, she thought.

She chose to ride on the sidewalk; usually she didn't, but this was Friday night and drivers were mostly drunk. Sava Bridge was half-dark—she traversed it in a few seconds and soon stopped by the underpass beneath the rotary. There, on one of the walls, she spotted the white Storm Front logo and next to it, two posters. *This is it*, she said to herself, then scanned the area, dropped her bike to the ground, and opened her backpack. She stripped the posters in two tugs. It went pretty smoothly, she decided while she taped up the big white sheet of paper with its red message and strand of black wool glued in place.

On she rode. Along the way she checked her cell to see if there were any messages from the rest of the crew. Nothing yet, they were probably just getting started. At Lanište she ran into a larger crowd, the neighborhood was full of bars that were just now closing, but there were Nazi posters scattered around like weeds and she thought about what she should do. Maybe it would be better to come back when she had done the rest of New Zagreb, she thought. So she did. She ripped off and replaced the posters one after another in Savski gaj, Trnsko, Siget, Sopot, Utrine, Zapruđe, Dugave, Sloboština, Travno.

Buks messaged her: *Nearly done, sis, no sweat, kids were after a poster, I said no, worried we'd run out. At the squat by 3:30. ;).* And from Gaga and Dikinsonka: *Center is done, a little hairy, will tell, in Dubrava now, desert, back soon.*

She felt her backpack grow lighter, only two more stops left and that would be it.

She got to Lanište and checked the neighborhood, not a soul on the streets. She spotted a poster on a post by the bank, another by the nursery school. Back she went to the first spot and thought to chill for a minute on a low wall by the entrance to a building, her bottom sore from riding all night. She sat, stretched out her legs, and stared at the neon signs. A drop of rain splashed her face. The adrenaline still held her. For the first time she was doing something that really mattered. After this there would be talk about them in town, the older crew from Attack would take them more seriously now, maybe they would finally ask her to join one of their things. The newspapers and web portals would definitely report about it, everyone would be wondering who they were.

It was time to get back up on her feet. She glimpsed the remaining posters in her backpack and crossed the road toward the concrete pillar she would be redesigning.

As she slipped the backpack from her shoulder, the deaf night stillness was filled with voices, deep and male. Three guys soon walked out of the building entrance right in front of her. They didn't notice her at first, but then . . .

"Lookee, a kitty cat, all alone," said one of the three skinheads who was zipping up his black down jacket with an eagle logo on the sleeve.

"Hot damn, so she is," chimed in the second in a bulging black suit jacket stretched across his massive pecs.

The third guy, the skinniest, had a scraggly goatee and seemed out of it. His eyes darted all over the place and he kept his hands shoved in the pockets of his tracksuit.

She assembled a sour half-smile and looked over at her bike, which was locked to the railing a few steps away in front of the bar. She drew her backpack to her chest. She inched toward the bike and started unlocking the chain. They followed her like hungry strays.

Eagle Logo spoke to her: "Hey, you can't go, I just started diggin' you."

"Sorry, I'm in a hurry," she said, tucking the lock into her backpack.

"Why, where's the fire, girlie? Let's have us a chat," said Eagle Logo, in a creepily cozy tone, and his buddies nodded and mumbled, "Yessiree."

They surrounded her. She realized she was in deep shit. She was still clutching her backpack with both hands, glancing back and forth between them and her bike.

"So you're like a punk, right?" asked Eagle Logo.

"Why do you say that?"

"Shit . . . you look more like a dude, like you have a prick there between your legs, huh!"

She looked at him with a mixture of fear and scorn. She wondered how she should respond. It would be ass-stupid to tuck her tail between her legs and try to run, then she'd really be in for it. She needed to take this slow, easy, gradual. Psych 101. She'd shift her backpack onto her back, sit real chill on the bike, and go . . . Yes, that's what she'd do.

The trio was meanwhile distracted by a farting contest. Eagle Logo was straining to shoot off a salvo and outdo Goatee, but his ass was on strike, he couldn't pull it off. She sat on her bike, turned to heft her backpack onto her back, but it slid down her left arm and dropped to the ground. Their attention swiveled back to her.

"Hey, hold it, no-no, girlie," grumbled Eagle Logo, and leaned down to retrieve her backpack. He grabbed it by the soft, double-sewn handle and swung it in his hand, gauging its weight. "Wow, so light, what have you got in there, like rolled-up feathers, huh? I thought it would be a hundred times heavier . . . shit."

She smiled clumsily. "Women's stuff," she said, and reached toward Eagle Logo.

"Look at her, she wants me to give it back," said Eagle Logo triumphantly.

She realized the moment had come to go as low as she could go. She'd try to soften them, this was no time for revolution, fuck it.

"Boys," she said in a silken voice, "look, I have to get home, it's late, and the rain will be pouring in a minute, I felt a drop just now—"

"I'm interested to know what's in there," interrupted Goatee.

Eagle Logo flashed a predatory grin and unzipped the backpack. He slid his hand in and pulled out a bundle of folded Nazi posters. It was evident that they had been peeled off and stripped from walls. He took more and more of them out until he had nearly emptied the pack. There was quite a heap piled up in front of him on the low wall. "What the fuck?" he blurted spontaneously, while the other two gawked densely at him and the heap of paper on the wall.

"Lookee, there's something else," said Goatee, excited, and reached into the backpack Eagle Logo was still holding. He pulled out the two rolled white posters with the red message and glued-on strand of black wool. He unrolled one of them.

The three guys, astonished, studied the message for several seconds. Eagle Logo moved his lips soundlessly, grimacing precisely the way the long-deceased Croatian president used to do. "Why, goddamn, you're a freak-girl. What the fuck is this?"

She was silent, she did not have a single idea how to get out of there.

"Hear what he asked you, stupid bitch?" said Black Jacket, sneering.

"I heard," she answered calmly.

"So why the silent treatment, cunt?"

"See? Hot damn, she went around town all night tearing down these posters. God fuck her the fucker, what a crock!" shouted Eagle Logo, who clearly was the only one who got it.

With both hands he started crumpling up the posters until he had wadded them into a large paper ball that he tossed a few feet away. He started huffing, then worked his mouth strangely, as if something were caught in his teeth and he was struggling to dislodge it. Suddenly she realized he was pooling phlegm and that in a second he would deliver it to her face.

The glob of Eagle Logo's bubbling phlegm landed on her left cheek, slid down her face, and dribbled onto her jacket and pants. With her sleeve she frantically rubbed her blazing cheek and all her pent-up rage thundered inside her head. Eagle Logo laughed a repulsive laugh that sounded to her like the sputtering of a moped in a low gear. The two others stared at him as if he were a hero.

"No point in wiping it off, you little shithead," he said to her with disgust. "I'll do it again as a warning and to give you something to remember me by."

"Give me my backpack and let me go home," she said, and stepped closer. Goatee and Black Jacket were completely out of her visual field, they no longer mattered.

"Hey, hey, muffin, suddenly so bold," taunted Eagle Logo, dangling the half-open backpack in front of her face.

"I'm asking you nicely," she declared firmly.

"Look, girlie, we can reach an understanding. Don't they say understanding builds a house? I'll give you back your bag if you give me something, okay?"

"Give you what?" she asked, and tilted her head to the side.

"Don't go Little Miss Innocent on me, you know what I mean! Cunt, right?"

"You've got to be kidding."

"Why not! Isn't my cock good enough? I bet those anarchists of yours are all pip-squeaks, obviously you've never in your life seen a real dick," he said, scratching his balls. "And besides, your attitude turns me on, oh yeah."

Black Jacket and Goatee were leering and shoulder-bumping,

clearly hoping they'd be getting some tonight too. Goatee began humming *"Fella, fella, fellatio . . ."*

She clenched her teeth and deftly wrested the backpack from Eagle Logo. She caught him off guard and before he could stop her she was at her bike with her backpack over her shoulder. She pushed down on the pedal, swung the other leg around, and just then felt him lifting her off the seat. She swam in the air, her legs flailing, and the bike banged on the pavement.

"Heeeey!" she got out a shout, but with his left arm around her waist he pulled her in firmly and clapped his right hand over her mouth. He dragged her over to the building, kicked open the door, and trundled down the stairs into the basement. She kicked at his knees, struggled to wrench free of his grip, and then quieted down, trying to think what to do next.

He pushed her into a narrow passageway with wooden latticed storage units on either side. She smelled the sour stink of sweat under his arms mingling with a cheap men's deodorant. He nudged something with his shoulder and a light went on. He carried her a few feet more to the bottom of the passage at the end of the row of storage units. There was a ratty old mattress propped up against the wall. Eagle Logo kicked it over and threw her down onto it. Her body jiggled on the springs.

Suddenly the strains of the guitar solo from the song "Bella Ciao" by KUD Idijoti rang out from somewhere, getting louder from one beat to the next.

"What the fuck . . . ?" said Eagle Logo, spinning around tensely.

It was the cell ringing in her pocket. When he figured out where the sound was coming from he groped for her phone, and flung it with relish onto the dusty floor. She crouched on the mattress and said nothing, she had no clue what to do; there was no sense in screaming hysterically here, she had to think, think fast.

She wondered where the other two were—they were probably waiting for him to finish his business.

With all her strength she threw herself into him, trying to slip through the little bit of free space to his left. But Eagle Logo was ready, grabbed her by the arm, and peeled the backpack off her shoulder. He threw her back down on the mattress, straddled her with his knees, and sat on her stomach. He found the roll of tape in her pack. Terror swept over her, she knew what came next. She could no longer even hear her heart, as if someone had muted all sound. She only saw his grimy fingernail scratching at the tape, seeking the edge.

Then she remembered the scissors which, apparently, he hadn't noticed. The backpack was open in front of her, she saw the see-through yellowish handles on the bottom, snatched the scissors up, and shoved them with all her might into Eagle Logo's gut.

He groaned and clamped his hands over hers, trying to pull the scissors out. She figured she hadn't pushed them in too far; she leaned back, pulled the scissors out, and managed to wriggle free of the sticky grip of his fingers.

He was no longer focused on her. Lying on his side, he clutched at his blood-soaked shirt. She pulled away and slipped out of the passage. Her head was spinning and she shut the door with trembling hands; now she could barely hear his moans. She mustered all the strength she had and burst like a shot through the entrance door. Outside, Black Jacket and Goatee were sitting a few feet away on the low wall. They caught sight of her, hands bloodied, as she sprinted to the left and vanished into the neighborhood. She ran with a mindless speed.

She sprinted by the big cube-shaped clock that stood at the intersection of Savska Road and the Cvjetno neighborhood, its hands at a few minutes to three. The whole way there she never saw a single person. The bloody stain on her black pants didn't seem too bad, it had already dried a little and looked like any old greasy stain.

The moron would live, she hadn't managed to rip him up too much with those dull scissors. The other guys must have called an ambulance—they'd patch him up in the ER and that would be that.

She calmed down, and soon she stopped shaking. She rinsed her bloody hands in a muddy puddle in the park behind the Vjesnik building and decided to walk the rest of the way home.

In the back pocket of her pants she could feel her wallet and her ID. *Good,* she thought, *it's still there.*

Behind her back she heard the screech of a tram pulling into a stop. It was half-empty and for a moment she considered trotting across the street and shortening her trip home, but decided not to. Fuck it, not smart, better to put one foot in front of the other to the main square and then cut across to Zvonimirova.

She felt in her pocket for her cell phone and then remembered where it was. She sighed, realizing they could identify her with the SIM card. They could remove it from the cell and identify her just like that! But maybe the morons got the jitters, maybe they wouldn't report her, maybe they'd concoct some shit of their own at the ER, maybe anything, maybe nothing . . .

She'd come out onto a small square by a kiosk when she heard footsteps approaching along the path through the park. Two men in blue were slowly strolling and talking rather loudly. *What the fuck, now them too?* she thought, and her knees buckled. She had to stay cool, she'd pass by them and keep to herself. She musn't speed up or slow down, just walk along at the same pace. And then she did something stupid. Dead cool she said, "Good evening." It was instinct—good upbringing screws you over when you need it least!

"Good evening, ma'am," answered the older cop, stopping to have a look at her. The other obediently stopped next to him. She did not slow down, she thought it had gone well. But then she heard their steps behind her, they were following her . . . or maybe continuing on their way?

"Ma'am, would you please stop?" she heard the older cop say.

She turned around, assembling the best half-smile she could muster. *No panic, no panic,* scrolled a message across the surface of her mind as if on a digital display. She felt a powerful wave of heat in her solar plexus and her gaze flitted by the stain on her pants; it didn't seem too bad.

Both of them eyed her with curiosity, and the older cop jumped straight to the point. "Where were you headed, miss?" he asked.

He was stout, he had one of those creased, clean-shaven faces of older men on which you can see the results of a heavy diet. Under his police uniform bulged the clear outline of his belly. She registered his shift from *ma'am* to *miss* but had no time for analysis, she just had to keep the small talk going.

"I'm on my way home," she said, in the most natural possible tone. Her hands were sweating but what did the two of them know about her hands and what they had been doing only an hour earlier?

"It is not so smart to be out walking alone this late with no escort," piped up the younger cop, with a crew cut and a trim figure; his uniform fit him better. He was obviously still in the rookie phase of service.

Why am I standing here talking with these two? What was I thinking? "I am not afraid of anyone," she answered, and with both hands she adjusted the straps on the backpack, meanwhile stealthily wiping the sweat off her hands.

Senior grinned, grabbed the suspenders on his trousers, and

pulled them up. "Take it easy now, I have seen plenty of things in this city," he said, shoving his hand into his pocket and rocking back and forth on his feet. "Where are you coming from? Were you partying somewhere?"

At first she said nothing as Senior eyed her clothing and hair. Her nerves were killing her, and suddenly she had to pee. "From work. I'm tired. If you don't mind I would like to go," she said in a conciliatory tone, and sighed.

"You are one of the . . . whatchamacallit . . . those ones who march around waving signs about gay marriage . . . Feminists, right?" he said, and grinned again.

"That's not the same," she answered coldly.

He grimaced and grew serious. "So where do you work?"

"At a fast-food place in Lanište," she replied.

He raised his arm theatrically and checked the watch on his left wrist. Then he looked back at her. Junior's gaze darted off across the road and he shifted his weight from his left leg to his right.

"Three o'clock! Eleven minutes past, in fact! What fast-food place outside the center of town is open until two, three in the morning?" He was already guffawing.

"Why do you care?" she said tersely.

"Oh ho ho, getting a little edgy there, are we? What kind of a tone are you taking with officers, young lady? You might want to change your tune!"

"Fuck, I cannot believe this," she muttered through her teeth.

"What did you say? Huh?"

"I wasn't speaking to you."

"Oh yes you were. You were using foul language, I heard you. Repeat what you said, if you've got the guts, feminist or whatever!"

"That is offensive!"

"I am offending you," he said with a half-smile, and stepped a little closer. "C'mon, your ID!"

"I don't understand," she whined.

"What don't you understand? Am I speaking Chinese?"

She opened her wallet, pulled out her ID card, and handed it over. A black sports car slid by almost soundlessly along empty Savska Road.

"Milena Jakšić, Zvonimirova 26b," he read out loud, and burst out laughing.

She found his fat chapped lips disgusting.

"One of those three-phase households, eh?" he announced with glee, and handed back the ID.

She knew what he meant. It was an old nationalist phrase she had learned from a boy who taunted her in elementary school.

"Father's name?" he asked shrilly.

"Milan."

"There, what did I say, fuck it, don't I always smell out the Serbs?" he hissed, and slapping his legs triumphantly he looked over at Junior. The other cop nodded, perturbed. Clearly the exposure of her family background was not as spectacular a find for him.

"Happy now? Prick hard enough yet?" she snapped. She no longer cared about the consequences. Senior's fat lips stretched as taut as an inflated condom. She longed to puncture them. He grabbed her by the arm, squeezed it hard, and began to tremble.

"What the fuck, you filthy little shit."

"Don't touch me, asshole," she glowered, and was slapped hard.

Her head was knocked to the side. She saw Junior shudder and stare nervously at empty Savska Road. She tried to wriggle free of Senior's grip, but he grabbed her other hand and dragged her a few steps. He was furious and panting like a pig, huffing in her face.

She wanted to explain everything to him, everything that had happened that evening, but her throat stung, she couldn't get a single word out. She slumped to the ground and stayed in a crouch, staring between Senior's legs. He grabbed her by the hair and forced her to stand up.

"Get up, don't start playing lady now!" he growled.

Behind his back the Motorola on Junior's chest began to crackle: *"A case of serious bodily injury, Lanište, perp on the run. Young female, brown hair, jeans, black backpack. Confirm receipt, Kruge Patrol #4."*

It was as if someone had knocked all the air out of her.

"What did they say?" called Senior, who apparently had not heard the message.

Junior stared at her, wordless. His hands shook, they went to his belt, and he started fiddling with something. She couldn't tell what he was doing. Senior spun around and stared at him.

"You have the shakes? What the fuck is wrong with you?" he said, releasing her hands and going over to Junior.

A pistol appeared in Junior's hand.

"*Confirm receipt, Kruge Patrol #4,*" the Motorola barked again.

"What are you doing, are you crazy?"

"She's a . . ." He released the safety on his pistol and aimed it at her.

"Hey, kid, put that away, have you lost your mind?" Senior slowly pushed Junior's hand down.

Junior kept staring at her as if he didn't see his partner.

From her crouch on the ground she shot to her feet, grabbed her backpack, and dashed off into the park.

She heard their halting breathing behind her. Over damp leaves she sprinted through the dark.

WIENER SCHNITZEL

BY IVAN SRŠEN

Rudeš

Translated by Ellen Elias-Bursac

Jagger strode nervously into the Orhideja and ordered a double espresso and a shot of bitters from Mr. Montenegro. It was cold outside and Montenegro had cranked the heat up to the max so they had all made themselves comfortable inside, doffing their jackets and coats so there wasn't a single available hanger left in the place. Jagger briefly cursed their mothers, shed his coat, tossed it over the last free chair in the little café, and went back to the bar.

"What's up?" asked Montenegro.

"Why the fuck ask me, I already ordered," snapped Jagger.

"I know," said Montenegro coolly, setting a demitasse of coffee and a shot glass of the viscous *rakija* on the bar, "but what's up otherwise?"

"Shove it, Montenegro. You blew it at the bookie's and now you want to know if I did too?" Jagger knew everything that passed through the minds of all the regulars at the Orhideja. He loathed their limited vocabulary and their eternal topics of conversation: soccer, politics, and the fresh booty that had strolled down the street the day before out in front of the café. So when Montenegro asked what's up, it could only have to do with one of these three topics and nothing else.

"Prickly, prickly. Okay, the *rakija*'s on the house, but hey, did you hear Darkec broke his arm?"

"I don't give a shit about Darkec and that dumb-ass Astra he cruises around in to show off in front of the bar. Maybe someone broke his arm in a pickup game when he was un-fucking-bearable."

"No, he fell down the stairs at home."

"No shit?" Jagger was interested now. He was hoping Darkec had broken more than that.

"Better believe it. Okay, so he had too much to drink. But never here, the weasel. He parades around town, pays twice as much for beer as I charge here, then he has to go home to keep drinking because those fancy places are too pricey for him . . ."

"The guy can drink where he likes," said Jagger, shifting gears; maybe Montenegro was bugging him even more than Darkec. "But is it coming today?"

"What?"

"What *what?* Fuck your moron mother!" Jagger knew the guy was dodging a straight answer. "Don't pull the jackass thing with me, Montenegro. Is it coming today?"

"It is."

"Good." Montenegro's answer was reassuring. Jagger turned his back to the bar and checked out the café. Everyone there was always huddled around Marijan, an auto mechanic who never seemed to work yet money was always falling out of his pockets. Mate, an out-of-work electrician, Mijo, a plumber with a short fuse who was quick with his fists, and a retired cook with a post-war PTSD diagnosis whose nickname was Karapandža—they all came to the café with twenty kuna in their pockets. After they'd spent it, Marijan held the floor. He paid for their drinks as long as they'd listen to him. He'd send them off to fetch him a sandwich, to check and see whether he'd turned off the gas burner, and once Mijo even delivered flowers to one of Marijan's lovers. Aside from the four of them, Keti, an old drunk, was sitting at another table and talking loudly with Stankec, an old potato vendor from the nearby farmers' market. Stankec had been living for decades in a shed behind a neighboring building and every time he saw him, Jagger wondered how it was possible for the man to still be alive. As far back as Jagger's memory reached, Stankec had been splitting wood around the neighborhood in exchange for *rakija*, beer, and the small change he'd use to buy a quarter loaf of bread and several slices of Tyrol sausage. And yet here he was still, nodding calmly at Keti's escapades and sipping slowly from a beer bottle. This pained Jagger: the man was always cleaning up after others, dumpster-diving for food, he'd drink himself to sleep, yet here he was now nodding with dignity, looking as sober as a judge. A single *rakija*, the one Jagger had just downed, would be enough to send him flying into a rage, fueling his agitation and his big plans.

At the other two tables at the Orhideja sat Suhi, owner of the nearby cardboard factory, and his business partner Kolaković, and next to them was Tomo the ambulance driver and his funny cousin Pjer. Just looking at Pjer made Jagger laugh. The guy was fifty if he was a day and he always looked as if his mother had just dressed him for school in the morning and combed his hair. Why would someone live like that for fifty years, why would someone like Pjer sit all the livelong day with his cousin, a nurse, who was always pulling out porno DVDs that he'd bought from the Romani stands at the marketplace and inspecting them under the light of the café to check whether the discs were damaged? If one of the discs turned out to be scratched he'd send Pjer back to the marketplace to get another. One time Pjer came back with the classic *They Drive By Night* with Humphrey Bogart instead of another porno. Tomo shit bricks. "What the fuck will I do with this? Our *grandmothers* used to get off on this stuff, Pjer!" Montenegro had intervened and bought the DVD off Tomo for five kuna. For the next hour and a half the whole café watched the movie, and Pjer cried several times. Montenegro soon dismantled the DVD player and television after Tomo started bugging him to show porn.

"Like what time is it coming?" Jagger asked.

"I don't know, probably around nine," murmured Montenegro.

Jagger got it. He just had to sit tight until nine. He glanced at his cell. Five p.m. This would not be the first or last time he'd spent four hours at the Orhideja. Better than at home.

Twelve years had passed since Marina had left him. One day she was waiting for him when he came home from the Orhideja, he wasn't even drunk, and she told him that she was sick and tired of having to scrape together the money to pay for gas, to buy bread, that she no longer had any way to shift debt from one credit card to another, that ten years had been enough for him to find a decent job and she was leaving. "I'll fuck you over," was his answer, though he didn't mean it. He'd just wanted to scare her so she'd stay home; it would have been better for both of them that way. They'd have found it easier being down-and-out in tandem, going to bed drunk and hungry, watching the neighbors buy a new car—all of it would have been easier if only she'd admitted defeat, as he had so long ago. They called him Jagger for his big lips and long hair, and the nickname was all he had left of his dreams of a good life. He looked at himself in the mirror behind the bar and studied his graying sideburns.

"For years this country has been marking time, and now the imbeciles want to start taxing unfarmed land!" commented Kolaković loudly, leafing the morning paper.

"Of course that hurts *you,* you inherited land out in Žumberak and you don't know what to do with it!" Marijan always had to have the last word.

"What good is the land to you? Sell it," added Mate. "Instead of slogging around in the mud every winter for the sake of the vineyard and those cows, you could be strolling off like a gentleman to Vinodol Restaurant every weekend for a Wiener schnitzel and a half liter of Riesling."

"You peasants, you really don't know anything," thundered Marijan. Everyone in the café looked in their direction, and Montenegro turned down the radio so Marijan's voice completely filled the place: "You think you can talk to me about a Wiener schnitzel? You, who have never laid eyes on Vienna and have been scarfing up foul sludge from the Jarun marketplace? Why, they could serve you thin slices of bologna and tell you it was a Wiener schnitzel and you'd be licking your lips. Fuck your ignorant mother."

"How can you say to me, a cook, that I'm ignorant—" protested Karapandža softly, but Marijan cut him off.

"Shut up, wretch, anyone who ever ate anything you cooked knows it's pathetic crap! I'd rather be a vegetarian my whole life than eat your food."

"Don't speak that way to Karapandža, during the war he fed half a brigade down by the Kupa River," said Mate, lukewarm in Karapandža's defense.

"Shut up, idiot, that's exactly why the Serbs nearly reached Zagreb!" snapped Marijan.

This exchange had Suhi and Kolaković hooting, and through his laughter and smoker's cough Kolaković barked, "So, Karapandža, ever want to do us in? Have us over for dinner!"

Montenegro always had to maintain at least a semblance of equilibrium at the café, so he tossed in, "Shit, talk all you like, once I saw a big black limo parked out in front of Karapandža's house and this driver in a tux gets out, rings Karapandža's door bell, and then drives him away."

Karapandža stared, flabbergasted, at Montenegro. He clearly had no clue what the bartender was talking about.

Marijan laughed. "Must be he sold his soul to the devil for a hundred kuna and the devil changed his mind and wanted his money back."

Intrigued, Kolaković asked Montenegro, "So where did the black limo take him?"

"Later that night the limo pulls up in front of the café and the guy in the tux comes in for a beer. I don't want to stick my nose into other people's business but the guy himself praises Karapandža. He says, *You have the finest cook in Zagreb just down the street. The ambassador sent me to pick him up, to make dinner for him and his wife.* The guy was the French ambassador's chauffeur."

Suddenly Mijo, who always seconded Marijan, piped up, "Fuck their French mothers, they eat snails and they stole the World Cup from us in '98."

Marijan steered the conversation back: "So, folks, how many of you have ever been to Vienna?"

Then everyone stopped talking. Jagger watched them in the mirror and no way was he volunteering that he'd been to Vienna a few times. Back in the better days, he and Marina had gone to Venice, and Budapest too. In his dad's old Zastava—they had sex in it, joking that they were proving love knows "no borders." They didn't have money for hotels but they were okay spending the night pretzeled up, cramped, in the backseat of the little car, and then they'd sleep another few hours on a sunny field by the side of the road.

An unpleasant feeling of impatience was eating at Jagger. He could still call it all off, let them know they shouldn't come; they must have a backup plan. Would the crew stick to their plan?

Marijan went on: "Not a one of them has been to Vienna, of course, yet here they all are, talking about Wiener schnitzels! Fine, let's have us a look-see then—who knows how to make a proper Wiener schnitzel?"

Keti could hardly wait for the chance to show Marijan up, so, as parliamentary representative, she declared, "Cut a slice of pork loin and pound it thin with a mallet, smear it with mustard, sauté it in deep oil, and serve it up with fries!"

Marijan watched her with a sardonic grin from the seat where he was lounging in the only booth in the café and then, turning to the others, he pounced: "So much for your know-how. Pork in a Wiener schnitzel? My dear Keti, if you were thirty years younger I'd take you to a decent restaurant and show you what a real Wiener schnitzel is like. Remember this, a Wiener schnitzel is made with v-e-a-l! I mean people, what is this? We're talking about elementary culture here!"

For the first time that afternoon Stankec spoke up, in a tone of both aching pity and circus sarcasm: "And what are you, Marijan, our health inspector?"

Mate and Mijo began fidgeting; they worried Marijan might go, leaving them with no drinks for the rest of the evening, because Montenegro had stopped letting them run a tab years ago. Mate said to Marijan: "Stankec is only messing with you."

Marijan rubbed his chin and glanced around. "Stankec, don't fuck with me. Go home, stagger over to your little den, throw yourself onto the ground, and snooze. Tomorrow you'll be awake early anyway, setting up tables at the market."

Stankec squirmed in his seat and began gesticulating and grimacing but seemed short on words. Montenegro had the situation under control—he came from behind the bar with a bottle of grappa in hand, went over to Stankec and Keti's table, and poured more firewater into Stankec's shot glass.

"I . . . c-can't . . . pay for it," stuttered Stankec.

Montenegro patted him on the shoulder, Stankec tossed back the grappa, and Montenegro poured him another.

* * *

Jagger knew there was no going back, it would definitely be coming tonight, and now Stankec and Pjer had to be shooed away, they knew nothing about any of this. Jagger was not the kind to wait for things to sort themselves out; he turned to the tables and glared at Tomo who knew he should be sending Pjer home, but was hesitating. Jagger did not tolerate vacillating wimps so he took two small bills from his wallet and lay them on the bar; he didn't want Montenegro cutting back on his share of the drinks they'd had. He got up, went over to Tomo's table, took Pjer under the arm, hoisted him from the seat, and said, "Pjer, how's about we go for smokes!" Pjer did not resist, nor had anyone ever seen him resist. He scooted by Tomo who was nervously biting his nails and went out into the cold darkness in front of Jagger who held the door open for him.

Pjer was some ten years older than Jagger. Jagger could remember how he and his buddies used to wait, when they were kids, for Pjer on his way back from high school in the evening, and, just for the fun of it, they'd push him into the mud by the road, shake the books out of his backpack, kick him around a little, and run away. Pjer was the neighborhood weakness mascot, a caution to all those who thought they could get by in life easily without fighting or cursing. Pjer didn't say a thing, he walked alongside Jagger toward the little store a block or two away and Jagger thought how he'd have walked alongside him just the same way even if Jagger had said he was going to hang Pjer from the first tree they came across. A queasy shiver ran down him from head to toe: he was no better than Pjer, in fact Pjer was better than him, by a head, by a foot, by a yard! Pjer had never attacked anyone in the dark, he had never stolen gasoline at pumps, he had never broken into kiosks, he had never brawled at soccer matches.

He watched Pjer dogging his every step in the silence, and

thought how much strength a person needs to keep his cool in a setting as tough as Rudeš was, where there'd always be a fist to punch you in the head when you weren't on guard; fifty years of humiliation, threats, ridicule, and still he walked along as carefree as a school kid.

Jagger bought cigarettes at the store because he didn't know what else to buy, though he'd recently stopped smoking. They stepped out into the street again, Jagger spun the soft pack of 160s around in his fingers, finally opened it, and offered it to Pjer: "Hey, have one."

Pjer never refused anything, nor did he ever complain, this was his survival tactic. Who knows how many times they'd made him take a puff; he never seemed to stop and think. He slid a cigarette from the pack, held it in his lips, and waited for Jagger to light it.

"Oh shit, I don't have a lighter!" said Jagger.

He'd thrown out all the lighters he had in the apartment. Since he had an electric stove and hot water heater, he didn't need a lighter or matches to tempt him when he had a nicotine fit. To Jagger's surprise, Pjer pulled out a lighter of his own and lit the cigarette himself. He continued holding down the valve and brought the lighter over to Jagger. For the first time Jagger noticed a spark of vitality in Pjer's eyes; he quickly pulled a cigarette from the pack, fumbling, but Pjer's hand calmly kept the high flame alive with the cheap plastic lighter.

"Look at this! How long have you been smoking, Pjerinko?" asked Jagger, taking his first puff.

"For years," said Pjer. "Think I don't know what's going down tonight?"

"Wait, wait, Tomo told you?" Jagger was wary, it made no sense that Tomo would have said something to Pjer, and it went against what they'd agreed.

"Tomo is a moron, and everybody knows this. You should have never gotten him into this."

"So he told you?"

"No, he didn't, I found out through my guys."

"What *guys?*"

"The garbage guys from Roosevelt Square."

"What fucking garbage guys?"

"The garbage guys, the trash collectors, the street cleaners, I assume you know who the garbage collectors are?"

Jagger laughed inside. He threw his arm around Pjer's shoulders in a protective gesture and set off with him toward the house where Pjer and his mother lived. "You know, Pjerinko, if anyone gives you shit from here on out, including Tomo the moron, just say so and I'll take care of it, don't you worry."

He waited until Pjer had gone into the house and closed the door behind him and then strode speedily back to the Orhideja. As he stepped back into the café he realized that the atmosphere had completely changed. Stankec was gone, and Marijan and Montenegro were sitting at a table wrangling over something in muted tones, gesticulating wildly. Suhi and Kolaković were smoking in silence. Keti stood at the door, on the lookout for anyone unfamiliar approaching the café, while Mate, Mijo, Karapandža, and Tomo were downing cognac that Montenegro had opened for them at the bar. Jagger was sure Montenegro would charge them for it sooner or later.

"It's only thirty thousand now?" Marijan's voice shot up suddenly.

Montenegro spoke calmly, placating him: "They said two days and that's all. And a clean and clear three thousand in your pocket."

"Oh, no, no! Seven and a half for me, and the three of them

get one and a half each," Marijan said, pointing at Mate, Mijo, and Karapandža. "None of this would be happening if it weren't for me."

"Forget it, Marijan, we get our cut or we're out of here right this minute!" said Karapandža, emboldened by the open bottle of cognac. Mate and Mijo nodded their heads in sheepish agreement.

Tomo, who was not under Marijan's jurisdiction, chimed in nevertheless, "Marijan, the boys prefer not to mix business with pleasure."

"Nurse, I'll wring your neck!" Marijan shot back. "Fine, so we'll do it like this then: my three people are divvied up among you three, each of you gets one, and then you have to earn your three thousand properly. I am only here to salvage things if they go haywire. And seeing who I'm working with, they obviously will."

Jagger clutched his head. It was too late to either cancel or panic. They should do what they'd agreed, take the money and get through January, the worst month of the year, as best they could, when no one pays anything, when even the apocalyptic predictions that flourish at the end of the year melt away until Easter.

To cut the tension, Montenegro went over to the bar and took out an old chess set, then came back to the table, shook the pieces out, opened the board, and said to Marijan, "We play for the take."

Marijan acquiesced and began setting up the white pieces. As soon as he opened the party with the queen's pawn, a little crew crowded around the table and watched in silence as the duel progressed. Only Jagger sat at the bar, while Keti stayed on a barstool by the door and called, "Whoever loses is a cunt!"

It was just after seven, there were still another two hours to go. Jagger remembered how he'd waited two hours for Marina at Jelačić Square—she was supposed to come from her new job as a waitress that she'd taken out of desperation. He'd waited without a cent to his name so she could treat him to *ćevapčići;* he was hungry and angry. She didn't show, and after two hours he thought she'd up and left him. He'd always been afraid she might, he knew that once she'd made up her mind there'd be no changing it. He went to a guy for whom he occasionally drove a van with cigarettes smuggled from Bosnia and lied to him, saying Marina was sick and he needed a loan for an urgent medical exam. The smuggler from Herzegovina actually fell for it and gave him what he'd asked for without a word. He drank up the money over the next two hours and came home dead drunk. On the table were cold *ćevaps* with onion, a can of beer, and Marina, tear-stained, who had not, in fact, left him; instead, her new boss at the café where she worked had forced her to do the weekly cleaning which took her another three hours for which, of course, she was not paid. This was back in the days before cell phones, and she'd had no way of letting him know she'd be late. He flung the *ćevaps* at the wall, took the beer, gulped it down, went into the bathroom, puked, and without a word walked out of the apartment, to the Orhideja of course.

Montenegro had chased Marijan's queen into a trap and Marijan balked at continuing. First he whined that Montenegro had caught him unprepared, but he quickly realized that any further excuses would only disgrace him, so he stretched out his index finger to topple his king as a sign of surrender.

Mate suddenly shouted, "Marijan, don't capitulate! Knight to A7, how could you not see it!"

Montenegro sat up in his chair and shrugged. Marijan looked at Mate, then at Montenegro. When Montenegro said nothing, Marijan pulled his finger back from the king and did what Mate had suggested, moving the piece to A7.

Montenegro applauded theatrically and said to Mate, "Now your take is in," and then added, "Come on, boys, who else wants to bet on Marijan?"

Suhi snapped, "Montenegro, you are like the government, all you do is take! You'll do us all in. What is this wine you poured me anyway? You serve us the worst possible rotgut and we are supposed to be docile guests, choke it all down, and then even pay you for it in the end. We'll all be working for you one of these days—wait, who cooked the whole thing up for this evening? Boys, I was in Lipovica, don't fuck around! Do you realize we are screwed if a cop happens to walk in?"

"The cops already know everything," said Montenegro.

"What the fuck?" Kolaković rose to his feet.

"Take it easy," said Montenegro coolly, "you think we could pull this off without cops? Without them there's no deal. Do the math: if we each get just a thousand and a half per person, how much are they getting?"

"Well, why do they even need us then?" asked Mijo.

"The hierarchy of horrors, boys, everybody does his bit. Your bit is for the shit to splatter you when it hits the fan," concluded Marijan.

Jagger was gripped by an inexplicable angst. He wanted to escape, run out of Orhideja, and never come back. Run until he found Marina and told her how many times he'd regretted not pleading for her forgiveness and how deformed he'd become since she left. He felt sure he'd be able to find her, though sometimes he woke up at night depressed at the dreams that were luring him in different directions, always intimating a tragic fate for her. In one she had fallen ill and was living in some distant poorhouse, in another she was working as a stewardess in China, in a third she died in the apartment above his. If he were to leave the Orhideja now, first he'd go home and pack his favorite clothes, then he'd spend the night at his sister's in New Zagreb. Tomorrow he'd take the first bus to Rijeka where Marina's mother lived. She would surely tell him where Marina was, she had always loved him. Although he had only met her a few times, the woman had always praised him. She said things like, "Thank you for looking after Marina." And, "No one has ever taken care of Marina." She herself had seemed the caring motherly type so he wasn't quite sure what she meant by that. But he knew she would definitely help him out, and when he found out where Marina really was he'd get in touch with her, and though she probably wouldn't want to hear him out, he'd tell her how sorry he was. After that he could live, do anything; he realized that his only ambition was Marina's forgiveness. She would surely be able to forgive him, that was her nature, she was a generous soul.

He understood she couldn't love him anymore, he had done nothing to deserve it; indeed, in a way he'd think less of her if she did still love him. She mustn't allow herself such a thing, he destroyed the best years of her life and no one had the right to urge her back to him, least of all himself. And now here he was, a step away from walking out of the Orhideja and never coming back. And why didn't he? Probably because of those nightmares, the nightmares that hinted at distant catastrophe, the downfall of all the dreams they'd shared. Because of the apocalypse that was already playing out, but he did not feel and see it and for now he was holding it at bay.

The chess game was dragging on and on because Marijan was hesitating at each move; the more time passed the more nervous they became. At about ten to nine, while Keti was in the bathroom, the door opened and a man came in wearing a winter jacket and a baseball cap. They all watched him, frozen, and then he took off the cap and said, "A coffee, please, and two glasses of water." Their heads all swiveled simultaneously to Montenegro. When Montenegro answered, "You can have three if you like," they all stood up and went toward the door to the storage room at the back of the Orhideja.

An iron door led from the storage room to the yard behind the building. Montenegro opened it and stepped out with the stranger into the parking lot where tenants parked their cars. In a minute a sizable van pulled up in front of them and a second stranger climbed out of it and opened the back door. People began silently streaming out until they had completely filled the yard. Jagger was certain there had never been this many people in the yard before. They were all wearing heavy winter clothing and their heads were covered in caps or hoods. The driver in the winter jacket separated them into threes, and Montenegro handed off each group of three to the guys from the bar. Suhi took the first three. As agreed, he began walking toward his house with three following him one by one, each at thirty paces behind the next. In the same way Kolaković and his three went off, as did Tomo and the three who left with him, while Mate, Mijo, and Karapandža each left with four, as agreed that evening. Keti went along after them for support, her assignment was to keep watch on the street and let them know if something seemed suspicious. Marijan went out to his car. The two men in winter jackets climbed back into the van and drove out of the yard; after that the only people left were Jagger and Montenegro with six people they had never met.

Montenegro said to Jagger, "You know everything. You go first and I'll lock up the bar and take mine."

Jagger did what he was told and with his hands in his pockets he set off for his house. A strange feeling came over him as he walked the two blocks, at first not turning around, as they had agreed. Eventually he did turn around, hoping the phantom threesome would not be there and this was all just another nightmare. But instead he saw a weird scene: when he turned, the three who were following him froze at their thirty-pace intervals. He felt the silhouettes under the hoods and caps watching and waiting for him to show them where to go. He quickly turned back and strode on so he'd reach his building as soon as possible. When he stepped into the entranceway he did not turn on the light, but held the door open until all three had come in after him at their regular intervals. Now they stepped with his every step, still in silence, and went up to his little apartment.

He did not turn on the light and the three huddled inside the front door. He went to the window and for a minute or two peered out through the curtains to see if anyone was following them. Then in English he invited them into the living room. "Come here!" he said in his hard-edged Slavic accent. The three did what he said, taking off their shoes before tiptoeing into the living room.

All three silhouettes took off their caps and hoods and for the first time the streetlights that shone into Jagger's room lit their faces. They were two men and a woman. The men had mustaches and the woman's hair was covered with a kerchief. He tried to gauge their ages. The men were in their thirties, and the woman . . . he came closer to her, he thought he was imagining it. He stood in front of her. "Marina, is that you?" The woman stepped back, looked briefly over at the two men, and then replied in English, "I don't understand your language. I can speak English. Please, don't hurt us."

The world shook beneath him. He dropped first to his knees, then sat on the floor. The men and woman did as he did, sitting down around him. He watched the woman who looked just like Marina, the same eyes, same facial lines, same timid, unselfconscious smile. He dug his hands into his palms and burst into tears. He felt one of the men's hands pat him on the back. He curled up on the floor and pushed his head under the coffee table and he cried himself to sleep.

In the morning he was woken by the smell of tea. When he opened his eyes he saw the two men sitting on the floor, their backs against the wall, talking softly. They noticed he was watching them so they smiled back gently. The smell came from the kitchen that was divided from the living room only by a bar partition. The woman was preparing tea she had found among Jagger's scant provisions. He got up, tidied his hair in the mirror, sat on the couch, and said, in coarse English: "This very fucked-up town. You stay at home, everything good. We have a deal, I drive you tomorrow to the border. You cross to Slovenia, you free. You listen to me, everything okay."

One of the men said something to him in a language that sounded like Arabic. The woman from the kitchen brought a tray with four cups filled with hot tea and first offered one to Jagger. "He wants to express his gratitude," she said. Jagger took the cup and nodded. He took out his cell phone and called Montenegro.

"Have they all reported in?"

"Holy shit, Tomo slobbered on the two women at his place and almost had a fistfight with the guy who is probably the husband of one of them."

"Please don't tell me he blew it."

"He didn't blow it but he called me at three in the morning, terrified that if he fell asleep the guy'd slit his throat."

"Better if they had, but look, what don't they eat, I forgot to ask."

"Just pork, anything else is fine. Don't forget, a van is coming tomorrow evening and you are driving."

Montenegro hung up, and Jagger immediately called a

nearby pizza place and ordered four margheritas. "Food coming soon," he said. The men sipped the tea, the woman looked at him gratefully. "I call you *Marina*," he said to her. She did not respond.

When the pizzas arrived, Jagger took them out of the cardboard boxes and served them with cheap Spanish olives from his refrigerator.

The men exchanged glances with the woman and for some reason they did not want to start eating. Jagger understood, so he quickly sat down with them and said, "I am not hungry, cheers! Bon appetit!" The woman nodded and all three of them began eating eagerly, though they were clearly making an effort to behave as politely as possible.

Jagger watched the woman while she bit off pieces of the pizza: even her cheekbones and muscles moved the way Marina's had. When she finished the first slice, he took her by the hand and peered into her eyes. The two men looked at him, startled, but they did not stop eating. He mustered the strength to say: "Marina, please forgive me."

One of the men must have thought Jagger was declaring love for their travel companion and burst into brief laughter, but the other jabbed him in the ribs and the first began coughing after a mouthful of pizza went down the wrong way.

The woman got up, wiped her hands on Marina's old apron which she had unwittingly put on, and hugged Jagger. Then she said, "You are a very good man, sir, but I have a husband and three children back home. I am a seamstress, and I have to earn some money in Vienna to send home. Please understand."

Jagger nodded and choked back the tears that filled him with relief. "I understand, I understand . . ."

"Hey, Jagger," Montenegro woke him with an early phone call

the next morning, "it's a real miracle that everyone is still here. Tonight at midnight, my place, you drive, like we said." Then he hung up.

The two men had made themselves at home and were smoking cigarettes, sitting on the floor. They offered him some of their rolled tobacco. He took a short cigarette with no filter and realized he no longer was tormented by the desire to stop smoking. He could hear the shower running in the bathroom and he lit up with pleasure. He smoked while listening to Marina dry her hair with the blow-dryer.

A little before midnight Jagger put on his coat and the three people in his apartment dressed in the same heavy clothes they had been wearing when they arrived two nights before. In halted English, Jagger said to the woman, "Marina, please tell guys the last one out close door behind him." She nodded and translated Jagger's instructions.

"Okay," said the man who decided he'd be last to leave, and then he smiled.

In the same way they had left Montenegro's yard they went back to it now, and some twenty people were already standing there in silence. A few minutes later a van arrived and a man in a winter jacket and baseball cap stepped out. When the last group, Tomo's three, arrived, they all climbed into the van. Jagger sat at the wheel, switched on the powerful diesel motor, and steered handily out of the yard. He drove unremarkably, taking the curves with caution; he knew the travelers were sitting on the floor in the back.

After ninety minutes of driving, the last half hour of which was down forest roads, Jagger stopped, climbed out, and opened the back door of the van. Some thirty people got out in silence, following previous instructions, and formed a line. Since Marina spoke English, Jagger gestured for her to stand at the head of the line and told her, "Follow this road half a mile, maybe twenty minutes walking, then you in Slovenia. Go more, maybe one hour, then they will pick you up." It was an old dirt road through the woods, overgrown and unmaintained. He saw Marina's summer shoes and remembered she wore size 41. He took off his hiking boots, size 42, and offered them to her. She quickly removed her shoes and pulled on Jagger's. Then she hugged and kissed him on both cheeks. She set out ahead without looking back and the others followed. Jagger climbed into the van barefoot at the wheel and drove it slowly back to Zagreb.

At the entrance to the city, on the old two-lane road that runs from Samobor to the center of town, he saw an unusual sight and stopped the van. By the Podsused bus terminal where there was no traffic now at three a.m., some fifty garbage collectors had gathered on green tricycles with trash cans built onto the front. The roadblock looked like a sort of protest, though there were no police in sight; there was no one except the garbagemen in their green uniforms. Jagger lowered his window and called to them, "Hey, let me pass!"

From the crowd one of the garbagemen pulled away and drove over to Jagger's van. Under the green cloth cap and shabby uniform, Jagger recognized Pjer.

"Pjer, what the fuck is this?"

"No worries, Jagger, my men have seen to it that all the city police points were blocked while you drove to the border."

"But why are you messing with this?"

"You're tired, Jagger. Go on, drive home, tomorrow is another day!" Pjer slapped the van's hood twice, turned on his bike, and, standing on the pedals, raced back to the crowd.

"Boys, victory lap!" he heard Pjer call to the other garbagemen.

* * *

The next day, as soon as he woke, Jagger hurried over to the Orhideja.

"Espresso and a shot of bitters," he said to Montenegro as he sat down at the bar.

Everyone except Pjer was there, sipping their drinks, reading the paper, and bickering as if nothing special had happened in the last few days.

Montenegro whispered to Jagger, "The cash has already been divvied up, I'll give you your cut tonight after we close."

Marijan sneered at Jagger, "Nice job, Mick! A little drive and three thousand in your pocket, not bad, eh? But one thing's for sure: the wretches you drove are definitely not going out for Wiener schnitzels in Vienna. Like the rest of you—they are a bunch of useless newcomers."

Jagger got up, lunged at Marijan, knocked him off his chair, and kicked him repeatedly until the man stopped moving.

HAPPINESS ON A LEASH

BY NEVEN UŠUMOVIĆ

Trešnjevka

Translated by Will Firth

I stood in the hall in the dark. The din outside—an explosion of bad folk music—was unbearable.

I nervously nudged my dog with the tip of my shoe and shouted to him, "Mishko, Mishko!" as if he hadn't been stone deaf for three years. I was seething with rage. "We're gonna beat the shit out of those fucking Ustashas! Come on, Mishko!"

Mishko stood by my leg like a good dog, but neither he nor I dared to take the decisive step toward the door. We had already done our early-morning walk that day, and it was hard for old fellows like us to go out of the house a second time. But now we heard real explosions, as if someone was throwing hand grenades.

"Mishko, you're lucky you're deaf."

But that didn't help much, and he stuck his tail between his legs. Everything was shaking, and that was enough to make both of us edgy.

"Come on now!" I whispered to myself, and finally unlocked the door.

We plucked up a little more courage as we stood in the corridor separating our apartment from the bar.

I knew very well what was going on: today was April 10, the national day of the former Independent State of Croatia, and a field day for Croatian fascists. What's more, it was a Friday and the ideal day for whooping it up. The Tango Bar—the simple pub we shared a modest little house with in the working-class district of Trešnjevka—had been a meeting place of Ustasha-minded nimrods since the early nineties.

I opened the door of the corridor and went outside. Mishko squeezed through my legs and ran ahead. He stopped at the kindergarten fence and lifted his leg. The bar had an open terrace facing the kindergarten, so our apartment echoed the yells and screams of children in the daytime, while at night, at the end of the week, we had to put up with the rage and ruckus of teenagers and drunken singers. I didn't see Mishko do any "business" by the fence; he was standing on one leg and shaking with fear.

Smoke was rising from the children's playground and an acrid stench filled the air like on a battlefield. Now Mishko was glued to my leg again. I really should have gotten myself a pistol, I thought to myself for the umpteenth time.

I looked through the large, opaque window of the bar to see who was working that evening; it was Tilda, the young waitress I fancied. It was her, as well as the reverberating silence outside, that made me go into the bar, although Mishko resisted.

Tilda was alone inside, sweeping up broken glasses and beer bottles.

"What's going on here?" I asked.

"Everything's okay, neighbor," she said, as if everything really was okay.

"What's that smoke outside?" I asked, grabbing her by the arm. "There were terrible sounds, and even Mishko here got scared."

She flinched, as if I was about to hit her. "I'm sorry, Anton, it's not my fault. Today's the Ustashas' day, you know. They got plastered and threw grenades into the playground." She swallowed. "Some of them were chucking grenades, others bottles of beer."

"Talk about sick in the head." I let her go. "Was that fashion model Raša leading the gang again?"

"Yes," Tilda said in a hushed voice, as if the guy was still sitting there drinking at a table.

Raša . . . I had seen him at the bar several times, perfectly costumed in Ustasha black. Once he was even pulling an ugly, drunken accordionist along behind him on a leash. They sang ribald ballads and folk songs: "*Don't cry for me, O mother dear, I love the black Ustasha gear* . . ." Raša the model cut a fine figure to go with his unseemly conduct. Delicate, long fingers; a smooth and radiant face. His only imperfection was the thumb of his right hand, which jutted out like a foreign body, burnt to the bone.

I left Mishko with Tilda and went to get a flashlight. I was away for less than a minute, I guess, but when I came back Tilda was crouching beside Mishko, patting him, and crying like a little girl who'd lost her mother. Although I'd never dreamed of having the opportunity to hug her in a fatherly way, I now sat down next to her on the floor, where some broken glass was still gleaming, and pulled her to my chest. Mishko nuzzled her in the armpit with his pointy little nose, and we stayed like that until the living sculpture we made with our bodies literally became too steamy!

We got up and spent the next hour picking up shards of broken bottles in the dark of the kindergarten courtyard, for the children's sake. It must have looked as if we'd lost something, but none of the neighbors stuck out their heads to ask.

I've been reluctant to leave my apartment ever since the Croatians got their own state. I moved to Zagreb from Ljubljana forty years ago for work; as a Slovenian, I had no trouble getting permanent residency and Croatian citizenship, and I didn't feel like going back to Slovenia; my pension allowed me to lead a quiet life.

Early each morning, Mishko and I would go out for a walk. We'd head up the stream to the Remiza neighborhood near the tram depot and back again, doing all we had to do in the lines of trees and shops along the way, and then shut ourselves in the apartment again. I spent years putting together my memoirs; everything around me changed or was destroyed so rapidly that writing was the only thing that kept me from losing my mind.

But after those grenade attacks I didn't even feel like doing that anymore.

Over the next few days, Mishko and I watched the children from the kindergarten bringing up sand in little wooden wheelbarrows and, bit by bit, filling in the craters and holes made by the drunk heroes.

But at home in the apartment Mishko whined. He didn't want to drink and he wasn't hungry, so that wasn't the problem. I stroked him and kept asking him what hurt; Mishko was older than me (if you converted his age to human years) and I was afraid he was going to die soon.

I felt helpless. For want of a better idea, the next Friday I decided to do some serious spring cleaning. I reread my scribbling—memories of people who had mostly passed away. Several pages were dedicated to Mishko's mother, Gloria. What a lovely dog she had been! Zagreb was a complete city back then, in the midseventies, when Gloria ruled the streets of our suburb, Trešnjevka, roamed the embankments and railroad tracks all the way to Kustošija, the next suburb, and caught huge, gorged rats. The neighbors fed her as much as I did. The whole of Trešnjevka was hers!

I tore out those pages about Gloria and laid them under Mishko's rug.

The next day, in the still of Saturday morning, I went out with a boxful of my notebooks—my "albums," as I called them with self-deprecation—and looked for a spot in the playground that couldn't be seen from the street. The kids had done a good job in the last few days: there was sand everywhere and I felt like I was walking on a beach. Everything had been smoothed over, and only the biggest craters could be vaguely glimpsed.

Mishko stayed in front of the fence, as if he knew he'd only bother me now. I finally found my hole and placed the papers in it. They didn't burn for long. If I was a smoker I wouldn't even have managed to finish my cigarette. When the fire died down, I mixed the ash into the sand and left the playground to take a walk with Mishko.

The road, the posts, and the roofs were all damp, but the sky was a clear light blue; the world was waiting for the rise of the great sun. We headed for Selska Road. The old Trešnjevka workers' hovels on our left-hand side, dirty and decrepit, were slowly but surely collapsing. It wouldn't take long: the wave of "urban renewal" was steadily sweeping over Trešnjevka too, and four- and five-story buildings were shooting up everywhere, each in its own color, with empty apartments behind huge windows.

Mishko dashed off farther along the street, through the garden of one of the little old houses where weeds now competed with the daffodils and violets. I waited for him with an uneasy feeling, as if I'd sent him on a robbery. Within a minute he was back at my side, disappointed—he'd found nothing that interested him there.

We came to the intersection and crossed the road right away, taking no notice of the traffic lights as we rushed to our park. The sun's rays were touching the tops of the tall, slim chestnut trees and reflecting off the highest panel of the monument. Mishko immediately disappeared into the bushes that bordered the park.

Although the benches were gleaming with the damp morning dew, a woman was sitting drowsily on one of them.

The monument stood out like an enormous totem pole. I loved that memorial to the fallen fighters of the national liberation struggle in World War II. Bronze and expressive, it pictured fearless, self-sacrificing heroes in prison, agitation, battle, and dance. The liberation of the people was displayed in four separate reliefs, like a story from bottom to top, with one version on the front and another on the back. The bottom relief showed the sufferings of a prisoner behind bars, above it was a mother fleeing with her little girls, and the reverse showed a young Communist activist; the flame of struggle burned at the third level, with a woman charging the aggressors' rifles on the one side, and a man doing the same on the other; but the radiant light of progress, industrialization, and urbanization shone at the top of the monument, and on the reverse everyone had joined hands and was dancing in a ring.

Although the benches were still damp, I sat down on one of them and watched the rays of light caress the molded images of our suffering civilians and fighters, old but still full of avant-garde crispness, sharpness, and intensity.

The monument was too much for the war-fraught nineties. A Partisan in one of the reliefs, who was giving the three-finger salute in the ecstasy of agitation, had now lost his thumb. That didn't happen in the war of national liberation, but in the last one, the Croatian war of independence, since the three fingers were the sign of the Serbian enemy in the 1990s. Some zealot acting in the rear (I personally suspect Žarko, the lathe operator, who worked nearby) had sawed off his thumb, a good four meters above the ground. The consolation was that Žarko's workshop wasn't doing very well, so he didn't have the tools to bring down the whole monument.

The sun's rays pierced the chestnut trees' branches, and now the light stabbed me straight in the eyes. I had to find another bench, so I moved a little closer to the old lady. Only now did I notice her cigarette, which she held unlit between naked fingers sticking out of ragged winter gloves. She was singing something in German in a drunken sort of way, but beautifully and melodically. I ignored her until, after some time, she spoke to me.

"Do you know who I am?"

"Yes," I mused, in the mood for a bit of repartee, "a streetwalker past her prime."

"Oh, far off the mark," she replied with only a cluck of disapproval, as if I hadn't said anything particularly rude. "Do you see that little girl on the monument skipping around between all those sad-looking women in head scarves? That's me, the ballerina!"

"Er, yes," I said, not wanting to get into an argument. The little girl really stood out, as if she had been cast there before us, cheerful and looking forward to the five-year plans of the future, wearing a short, airy skirt like a spring daisy.

"Would you like to walk me home? I live just here on Meršićeva Street. I'm Jelena Lengel," she said, as if the name should mean something to me.

"Nice to meet you. I'm Anton, just Anton."

Rays of sunlight now rained down on us from all sides, reflecting off every puddle and dewdrop running down the monument's metal frame. Jelena began to sway after just a few steps.

I pulled her along behind me, and then put my arm around her even though she complained. We crossed the road and started walking along Meršićeva Street in the shade of the massive, dilapidated three-story buildings. I've always found that row of residential houses off-putting and rarely had the courage to go near them; everything there was dark and daunting, like an old barracks.

But there I was now going up the stairs in one of those buildings with my new "lady friend." On the third floor we entered her apartment through its broken door and staggered to the bed by the window.

Pungent perfume hung heavy in the air. I sat down on a chair, and she started to undress as if she was alone in the room.

The window faced west, so the small room was now without sunlight. Her bra fell, and with it her sagging breasts. Illuminated only by the pale gleam from the window, they seemed to be covered with blue blotches. And just like that, she collapsed half-naked onto the bed.

I managed to cover her with some blankets. I tried to close the shutters but they didn't work. When I turned round, my gaze fell on a photograph on the wardrobe: it was of Raša and Jelena, and they looked happy, like a son with his mother, or even worse—husband and wife. But it could hardly have been a wedding photo because Raša was wearing his Ustasha cap and Jelena had a hat like a little old Zagreb lady. The only curious thing was that, instead of pearls, she had a dog collar around her neck.

That made me feel sick and I was about to leave, but I noticed Jelena was staring at me.

"Ah, you've seen Raša, the Ustasha. That's a scene from the film where we met. They found us here in the neighborhood and we both had small parts. Ever since then I've been wearing the dresses they gave me as a present. But I lost the hat or drank it away, I don't remember." She laughed until she started coughing. "In the film I was the wife of some lawyer who went off to join the Partisans, and as punishment Raša made me tag along behind him like a dog. I had to sing German songs for him."

"So Raša stayed an Ustasha and you stayed a dog."

"Don't say that." She began to sob. "He used to come and see me afterward too, with a leash. It was lovely, and he never beat me. But I was too old for him. It couldn't last."

"No," I remarked, not knowing what to say after all that. I looked at the photo again for a while. A cinematic wedding indeed.

The old dog finally fell asleep, and I pulled the blankets up over her breasts.

On Sunday, Mishko and I discovered that Blato Restaurant on Selska Road was open. It had never opened on a Sunday before. The waitress said it was because this was a special weekend. I didn't want to ask what made it so "special." At noon, I left Mishko at home to gnaw on his beef bone and went back to Blato, where I treated myself to two servings of *brodetto* with polenta and washed it all down with half a liter of Plavac from Korčula.

Then I went to the park again. When I gazed at the monument now it looked like a fish set upright, albeit in four sections, without head or tail. The fish is a symbol for Christians, but does it have significance for Communists too?

I couldn't resist the temptation, so I crossed the street again and started walking along Meršićeva. Without thinking, I made for Jelena's building and was on my way up the stairs when I heard people making noise down in the courtyard. It sounded like they were chanting, "*Death to fascism—freedom to the people!*" That was enough to make me go back down to street level in search of those like-minded fellows and find a way through to the large inner area.

I was a little frightened and, as if I'd brought it upon myself, a black Labrador sprung at me from out of a bush. But it didn't bark; it only sniffed at me and then bolted off wherever it was going; it had probably been drawn by Mishko's scent on my pants and shoes. I went in between a long line of old wooden huts overgrown with greenery and flowers. Hopelessly rusted satellite dishes alternated with gleaming white ones on the low roofs. People lived here, that was plain to see: bright-colored rags and gym shoes were out drying on makeshift fences, children's toys lay in the grass next to chairs . . . The woodsheds were in an even worse condition and looked like they would collapse at any moment if they weren't being held up by the high metal fence of a handball court. The wooden slats, plastic sheeting, and pieces of corrugated iron on their roofs were succumbing to gravity.

The shouts were coming from one of these rows of woodsheds. At the open door of one of them, a dozen or so young guys were standing around drinking beer out of cans and smoking. I said hello as I came up, but they just looked at me blankly. Music was blaring and I recognized the refrain: "*Fuck the government, fuck politics!*" The crew took that without any emotion and just nodded in time to the beat.

Soon I had a beer in my hand too. A nice feeling. I found somewhere to sit. Another part of the group was sitting on the stairs of the common toilet block. Everything was falling to pieces, but the toilet cubicles were still in use, judging by the smell.

A figure with long, plaited hair caught my eye. He was wearing a tattered green army jacket. He had probably noticed me staring at him—the beer was starting to take effect—and he spoke to me: "Howdy, neighbor!"

"Howdy!"

"Death to fascism!" he yelled in greeting before taking a swig from his can.

"Freedom to the people!" I shot back.

He broke into a laugh. "Hold on, are you really a neighbor?"

"Yes, from Tango!" I teased him.

Then everything seemed to stand still.

"Are you some kind of provocateur?" he probed, and two guys stood up over at the stairs.

"Spying, huh?" one of them snarled.

"No, kids. I've got something to tell you. The Ustasha from Tango blew up our local playground."

"No shit?" two of them cried together. Someone turned off the music.

"Well, it *is* shit. What can I say? Pointless destruction."

"Oh no!" the long-haired guy went, and then he thundered from the stairs so everyone could hear him: "Comrades! A playground in our neighborhood got demolished while we stood here drinking. The Ustashas don't care about kindergartens, or children. This has gone way too far. I propose we settle the score with Tango tonight!"

"Fuck Tango, fuck Tango!" rang out all around.

"Everyone take a stick or pole from the woodshed—we're taking action! See you all at seven at the monument!"

And, like a little army, everyone dispersed in the blink of an eye. A little old man came up to me, extended his hand, and said with a smile: "Bravo."

At seven, I led the others silently through Trešnjevka. It was Sunday evening without a living soul out, and all the blinds were lowered. We muttered obscenities to each other to keep our spirits up.

When we arrived at Tango, I went in last "for tactical reasons," after the dozen others armed with sticks—I was the only one who'd keep on living there, after all.

When I entered, the waitress threw herself at me as if she had seen the Savior. It was Tilda, high as a kite as usual. The pounding music from the speakers went straight to the brain.

I don't know how many times I'd argued with her about it. "But it's techno," she'd say, as if that was sufficient explanation and it couldn't be any other way. She mostly arranged to have shifts where she could work alone; then she'd invite her girlfriends, the rhythm would be sped up, forcing me to come out of the apartment, and I'd find them shaking and quaking at the bar, absently, like automatons.

"Anton?" she looked around, bewildered. "Was there a match? Did we get trounced?"

"There are no matches on Sundays, Tilda. Only church mice play soccer on Sundays," I gibed.

"Where's the fash?" yelled Marjan, the leader of my antifascists. And then, in a softer voice: "So are you alone here, Tilda?"

"Y-yes," she stammered. "They were here yesterday and threw grenades around. Anton here knows. But that was the first time in a while—they prefer pubs downtown, and that's where they meet now."

"I should have known," Marjan groaned.

"Come on, crew, never mind," I said melancholically, but then again I was relieved. I'm not exactly street-fighter material these days. "Regardless, I really appreciate it—I'm glad to have guys like you in the neighborhood."

We sat down at the tables. Tilda came up and took everyone's orders with a humility I hadn't seen in her for a long time. She even put on some different music, I think it was hip-hop.

I stood at the bar, following her movements and the rhythm. Most of all I liked her tattoo, with its dark blue tendrils snaking up her neck to her right ear.

I was onto my sixth beer, the crew from Meršićeva Street had dispersed, and I was pestering Tilda, when my friend Jelena Lengel turned up at the door. She was dressed in exactly the same clothes as when we met back in the park.

And she was already quite blotto.

"Where's my pretty boy?" She looked me angrily in the face and hit me with a stifling cloud of her aromatic chemicals.

"You mean costumed Raša?"

"I mean my fine-fingered darling!"

"The lover of kindergartens?"

"What are you talking about, idiot? Get off my back!" she shouted.

I pulled her toward me and said into her ear: "He went and got himself another 'love on a leash,' you know. Someone who not only sings like you but also plays the accordion. And male, so he can hump him in the ass."

"You animal! That's bullshit!" she screamed.

But I was just starting to have fun. "We burned him up, the Ustasha bastard, and we used the ashes to fill the crater he made in the playground."

"Bullshit, bullshit!"

"Come and see then." I took her by the hand and led her to where I had burned my papers. "Look!" I scooped up two handfuls of ash and threw them into the air. The burnt smell spread as the ash wafted down.

"You scumbags! You killers!" She fell to her knees and dug her hands into the sand.

I was satisfied with my little game; I finally had something go my way.

She crawled on the ground, choking on her tears.

I pushed her away with my foot. I skirted the house, avoiding the bar, and went into my apartment. As I closed the door I felt triumphant, as if I had finally won the battle.

But I went outside again just twenty minutes later and lifted her up. She was shivering and had sand in her hair, on her cheeks, and under her fingernails.

I took her to the apartment. We went into the bathroom and filled the bath with hot water. Mishko darted around us, happy to have company.

She went along with every move I made, without the slightest resistance. I looked at her haggard blue breasts as she sank into the suds.

She laid there in the bath and stared at the ceiling, as if unconscious.

I got undressed and climbed into the bath at the opposite end.

She looked at me as if seeing me for the first time.

"All the hairs on your chest are white," she said, and dabbed froth on my shoulders. "Epaulettes," she added, "decorations." She kept putting handfuls of froth all over me. "You'll liberate me—you're my Partisan."

"Yes, I'll liberate you," I agreed, and washed the grains of sand from her face. "And you'll be beautiful again and dance like a ballerina."

"I will." Her eyes shone. "And you'll liberate me again."

"That's right. And then I'll liberate you again."

ABOUT THE CONTRIBUTORS

Stephen M. Dickey (translator) is an associate professor in the Slavic Department at the University of Kansas. He has translated Bosnian, Croatian, and Serbian fiction, including Meša Selimović's *Death and the Dervish*, Borislav Pekić's *How to Quiet a Vampire*, Miljenko Jergović's *Ruta Tannenbaum*, and the poetry of Damir Šodan. Most recently, he translated Miljenko Jergović's *The Walnut Mansion* for Yale University Press.

Miljenko Sajfar

Ellen Elias-Bursac (translator) has been translating work by Bosnian, Croatian, and Serbian authors since the 1980s, including writing by David Albahari, Neda Miranda Blažević-Krietzman, Daša Drndić, Antun Šoljan, and Dubravka Ugrešić. ALTA's National Translation Award was given to her translation of Albahari's novel *Götz and Meyer* in 2006. She is a recipient of an NEA translation grant, and was a fellow at the Banff International Literary Translation Centre in 2011.

Will Firth (translator) was born in 1965 in Newcastle, Australia. He studied German and Slavic languages in Canberra, Zagreb, and Moscow. Since 1991 he has been living in Berlin, Germany, where he works as a freelance translator. He translates from Russian, Macedonian, and all variants of Serbo-Croat. For more information, visit www.willfirth.de.

Ognjen Alujević

Nada Gašić was born in 1950 in Maribor, and has lived in Zagreb since 1952. She translated *The Fateful Adventures of the Good Soldier Švejk* from Czech. She writes novels that are on the borderline between crime fiction, noir, and social writing. *Mirna ulica, drvored* (*Quiet Street, Trees*) and *Voda, paučina* (*Water, Web*) have received several prizes and have been translated into Ukrainian and Macedonian. She is currently working on the novel *Četiri plamena, led* (*Four Flames, Ice*).

Bartul Gašperov

Ružica Gašperov was born in Split and currently lives there. Her stories have been published in magazines, anthologies, and on the web in Croatia and abroad. She was short-listed for the VBZ Award in 2011 for novel of the year. The Bjelovar Theater staged her play *Adio pameti* (*Goodbye Reason*) which was published on the website Drama.hr.

Tatjana Jambrišak (translator) was born in Zagreb in 1965. She is an award-winning literary translator and writer. Her translations include authors such as Cormac McCarthy, Elizabeth Strout, Alan Moore, Art Spiegelman, and Neil Gaiman, as well as Croatian comics and literature published abroad in English. She is an author of ten volumes of poetry, short fiction, and travelogues.

Pero Kvesić was born in Zagreb in 1950. For half of his working life he worked as a journalist, for a quarter of his working life he was unemployed, and for another quarter his status as a writer was officially recognized. More than twenty adult and children's books of his have been published. In recent years he has mostly been writing for blogs.

Fabijan Černeka

Darko Macan was born in Zagreb in 1966. He is best known for writing comics he scripted ranging from Star Wars and Captain America to the Eisner-nominated Grendel Tales. His Croatian creations include the comic strip *Borovnica* and the young adult horror series Neruševac. He has recently completed the series of graphic novels Nous, les mort for Delcourt.

Antonijela Bogutovac

Darko Milošić was born in Zagreb in 1967. He earned a degree in literature at the Faculty of Philosophy. He is a translator from English, and the author of two books: *Fifty-Five Easy Pieces* and *New Easy Pieces.*

Benjamin Dobutovic

Josip Novakovich emigrated from Croatia to the United States at the age of twenty, and recently to Canada at the age of fifty-three. He has published a novel, *April Fool's Day*, a novella, *Three Deaths,* three story collections, three narrative essay collections, and two books of practical criticism, including *Fiction Writers Workshop*. He has received a Whiting Award and in 2013 he was a finalist for the Man Booker International Prize.

Robert Perisic was born in Split in 1969. He has written six books that have been published in translation in a number of European countries and the United States; he has received awards in Croatia and abroad. His novel *Our Man in Iraq* has been well received in the United States and was included on a list of notable translations and books of the year in 2013. He recently published a new novel, *No Signal Area,* and currently works in Zagreb as a freelance writer.

Coral Petkovich (translator) was born in Subiaco, Western Australia. She lived in Croatia with her family from 1966–1989. She has translated poetry, short stories, and two published books—*Seven Terrors* by Selvedin Avdic and *Ivica Osim* by Marko Tomas. She is also the author of two books, *Ivan, from Adriatic to Pacific* and *May's Story,* and several short stories.

Matina Kenji

Zoran Pilić was born in Zagreb. He writes on paraliterary themes for the website booksa.hr. His short stories and excerpts of his novels have been translated into English, German, and Spanish. He is the author of the short story collections *Doggiestyle* and *Nema slonova u Meksiku* (*There Are No Elephants in Mexico*); the novels *Krimskrams* and *Đavli od papira* (*Paper Demons*); and the poetry collection *Dendermonde*.

Jelena Topčić

Mima Simić is a writer, translator, and first guitar in the family band Drvena Marija (Wooden Maria). She is the author of the cult story collection *Pustolovine Glorije Scott* (*Adventures of Gloria Scott*) and a collection of essays on film, *Otporna na Hollywood* (*Resistant to Hollywood*), which earned her the honor of best film critic. Her short stories have appeared in magazines and anthologies in Croatia and abroad, and currently she is working on assembling them into a collection.

Osanhemen Imarbiagbe

Ivan Sršen was born in Zagreb in 1979. He has edited publications on music, politics, history, economics, and literature and has written two books of prose: *Skela—bajke iz automata za kavu* (*The Raft—Fairy Tales from the Coffee Machine*), the novel *Harmatan*, and he has coauthored a nonfiction work, *Povijest zagrebačkih knjižnica* (*A History of Zagreb Libraries*). Since 2007 he has been co-owner and editor at the publishing company Sandorf.

Martina Kenji

NEVEN UŠUMOVIĆ was born in Zagreb in 1972, and grew up in Subotica, Serbia. He now splits his time between Kopar, Slovenia and Umag, Croatia. His published works include *7 mladih* (*The Seven Young Men*), *Makovo zrno* (*The Poppy Seed*), *Rajske ptice* (*Birds of Paradise*), and a short story collection, *U stočnom vagonu* (*In the Cattle Car*). A story of his was included in the anthology *Best European Fiction 2010*, edited by Aleksandar Hemon.

Dada Žitko

NORA VERDE was born in Dubrovnik in 1974. Since 1998 she has been working as a journalist and editor in the daily and weekly press and in the nonprofit media in the sectors of culture, music, television, human rights, and independent media. She is the author of the books *Posudi mi smajl* (*Lend Me Your Smile*) and *Do isteka zaliha* (*Until the Supplies Run Out*), and is currently working on a story collection.

IVAN VIDIĆ was born in 1966 in Zagreb. He attended elementary and high school in Zagreb and earned his degree at the Academy of Dramatic Arts in Zagreb. After fighting in the war from 1991–92, he began working professionally in literature. He is a freelance artist, and writes plays, prose, and screenplays. He has written nearly twenty plays and books of prose, including *Gangabanga*, *Violator*, *Ona govori* (*She Is Talking*), and *Južna država* (*Southern State*).

ANDREA ŽIGIĆ-DOLENEC was born in Varaždin in 1966. In 2003 she was given the Forum 21 Award from the Croatian Journalists Society for her radio journalism. She writes poetry and short stories which have been published in books and newspapers. The first of them appeared in *Ispod stola* (*Under the Table*), which was published by VBZ and Transparency International Hrvatska.

HEALTH AND WEIGHT MANAGEMENT

Teachings from the East

Caroline Rainsford

Emerald Guides
www.straightforwardco.co.uk

ISBN 978-1-913776-07-7

Printed by 4edge www.4edge.co.uk

Cover design by BW studio Derby